Qarakh woke to the se͏ naked beneath a bearsk bedmate shifted position next to him, and he felt the smooth curve of a feminine behind press against his side. He thought he—they—were inside a *ger*, but the fire was little more than smoldering embers and didn't provide enough light to see by, so he wasn't certain.

Qarakh wasn't fully awake yet, but he knew something was wrong. He remembered riding toward Alexander's camp with Deverra... remembered stopping when the eastern horizon began to grow light. They'd tied their horses to the low-hanging branches of a sapling and then walked to a majestic oak that Deverra had chosen. Using her Telyavic powers, the priestess had merged with the tree, and therein she would sleep untouched by the sun's rays. Since one patch of earth was much the same as another to Qarakh, he elected to inter himself in the ground at the base of the oak. He remembered sinking in the soil and succumbing to the darkness of slumber, and then...

And then he'd dreamed of fleeing the Anda hunting party, and of his first meeting with Deverra. So was this another dream? It couldn't be anything but, and yet... it felt so real. He reached over and slid his hand along the smooth skin of a woman's hip and smiled. It felt more than real—it felt good.

CLAN NOVEL

GANGREL

BY TIM WAGGONER

WHITE WOLF

Dark ages GANGREL ™

Tim Waggoner

AD 1231
Tenth of the Dark Ages Clan Novels

What Has Come Before

It is the year 1231, and decades of warfare and intrigue continue among the living and the dead. The Teutonic Knights and Sword-Brothers have embarked on campaigns to conquer and convert pagan Prussia and Livonia, spreading the crusading zeal into new lands. Bloodshed has, as always, followed in its wake.

Away from the eyes of the living, in the shadowy world of the undead, matters are even worse. Alexander, the ancient vampire who had ruled Paris for many centuries, was deposed some eight years ago. Seeking allies to recapture his throne, Alexander traveled to the Saxon city of Magdeburg where he imposed himself on the prince, Lord Jürgen the Sword-Bearer. The two vampires now wrestle for control of the court and a claim on the heart of the vampire Rosamund of Islington, sent into exile with Alexander.

Jürgen, who heads the vampiric Order of the Black Cross, has many interests among the Teutonic Knights and Livonian Sword-Brothers and supports their crusades. Livonian efforts, however, have recently faced a setback. Apparently a Tartar vampire named Qarakh has formed a war band among the pagans and has defeated many Sword-Brothers in battle.

Alexander has stepped forward to lead Black Cross Knights against Qarakh, and Jürgen has been unable to refuse the request. Meanwhile, Rosamund has kept secret the fact that Qarakh has the aid of a group of sorcerers called the Telyavs.

So Alexander, powerful and mad with ambition, marches into Livonia. All that stands before him is the chieftain Qarakh....

Prologue

Steel rang on steel, swords wielded by arms so inhumanly strong that sparks flared to life with each impact. The brief flashes lit the faces of the two combatants as they fought. Not that they needed the sparks' illumination to see. Darkness was light to their kind.

As if by mutual agreement, the two broke apart and circled each other warily, moving with liquid, feline grace. Their footfalls made no sound on the damp grass, and despite their exertions neither was breathing hard. They weren't breathing at all.

The adversaries stood upon an open plain beneath a full moon, deep in the lands of the Livs east of the Baltic coast. A furious battle raged around them as mailed knights fought wilder warriors in leathers and furs, many of whom possessed animalistic features: tufted ears, jutting fangs and feral-yellow eyes. The knights fought on horseback, while many of the others battled on foot. Swords clashed, arrows flew, claws maimed. The battlefield was littered with bodies, many of the corpses savaged beyond recognition, and the fetor of spilled blood and Final Death hung heavy in the air.

The larger of the two combatants was a swarthy and muscular man with wild black hair, a short beard and a long, thin mustache, the tips of which hung well past his chin. He wore leather armor, a bearskin cloak and wielded a curved saber. His most striking feature, though, was his flat, expressionless eyes. They were the eyes of an animal, the eyes of the dead.

His opponent appeared to be a youth of no more than sixteen summers and was clad in the mail vest and tabard of Christian knighthood. Emblazoned on the chest was his coat of arms--a shield with a pattern of black spots bisected by a broad vertical stripe upon which rested a gold laurel wreath. He was handsome and slim, with curly dark hair and a regal bearing that belied his seeming youth.

The leather-clad warrior knew better than to judge his enemy by mere physical appearance. The "youth" was two millennia older than he, and the ancient blood that flowed through his veins granted him immense power. He wielded a broadsword one-handed, moving the tip in slow, small circles as if the blade were light as a dagger. But the ancient also had other weapons besides those made of steel. As they circled one another, the leather-clad warrior sensed his opponent reaching out with his mind, sending out waves of fear and awe, searching for a chink, however small, in the warrior's resolve.

The youth smiled, but his eyes remained cold and deadly. "Your mind is as strong as your body, Tartar."

The warrior didn't bother to acknowledge his opponent's words, or to correct his usage of a bastard term for the faraway steppe tribe he had been born into. Talk was nothing but a waste of time and energy in battle. All that mattered was who would prove stronger this night—the Ventrue prince called Alexander or the Gangrel chieftain known as Qarakh the Untamed.

Qarakh grinned, displaying a mouthful of sharp teeth. He raised his curved saber, bellowed a war cry and charged.

Chapter One

Two Weeks Earlier

The sky was clear, and stars hung in the darkness above, cold and glittering like chips of ice. Though it was spring in Livonia, the night air held enough of a chill to turn his mount's breath to mist. The temperature meant nothing to Qarakh. He'd endured much worse during his mortal life on the steppes of Mongolia. And since his rebirth as a creature of the night, the only time he had ever truly been warm was when he had a bellyful of fresh blood. His horse, however, wasn't quite so hardy. Even a steppe pony would've had trouble keeping the pace Qarakh had set for the last week, and with this less hardy breed the effort was finally beginning to show. The mare's coat was covered in froth, and her gait had been erratic for the last mile or so. She was a ghoul—fed on his own blood since she'd been a foal—and therefore stronger and faster than a normal steed. For all that, she was still a mortal creature. But unless her master commanded otherwise, she'd continue on until her heart burst.

He slowed the mare to a walk by merely willing her to do so. There was no need for Qarakh to tug on the reins—the blood she'd drunk meant his desire was her desire, simple as that. Sparing her was no product of sentiment; the mare was no more than a tool to him, akin to his saber or bow. And he hadn't spared her out of need. He could travel just as easily, and more swiftly, in wolf form. But he was returning to his *ulus*—his tribe—after months away, and it was more dignified for a khan to return on horseback from a long absence.

The landscape in Livonia was primarily flat and forested,

and there was little to differentiate one place from another—at least by sight. But Qarakh navigated by other means: the position of the stars, the sound and feel of his mount's hooves on the ground, the scent of the trees. All told him that it would take a little over two hours to reach his tribe's main territory, its *ordu*, at this pace. He would still arrive well before sunrise, and his horse would be alive, its death postponed for a night when its blood was more needed. On the Mongolian steppe that had birthed him, Qarakh had learned not to waste anything. That lesson held true even here, in this distant land to which he had been exiled. Where he had made a new home.

Since his Embrace twenty-four years ago, Rikard had—like all Cainites—shunned the deadly light of day. But now, sitting here in the branches of an oak tree, arrow nocked and ready, with nothing to do but sit and listen to the sounds of nocturnal animals scurrying about as they foraged for food or searched for mates, he found himself actually looking forward to the pink of predawn. For then he could retire to his tent, crawl beneath a blanket and sleep while one of the mortals was forced to endure the mind-numbing monotony of watch duty.

This wasn't exactly the glamorous existence that his sire had promised Rikard before his Embrace. The picture she had painted was that of an eternal bacchanal filled with unimaginable power and endless dark pleasures. So how was he spending his unlife these nights? Sitting in a tree like some damned owl.

I should be nuzzling the smooth, alabaster neck of some young virgin instead, he thought. *Running the tip of my tongue over her artery as it flutters ever so gently…*

His canine teeth began to ache at the roots, and his stomach cramped. His sire had told him all about the Beast—the raging fury and hunger that was the curse of all Cainites. But what she hadn't told him was that the Beast could manifest itself in numerous ways. In his case, as pain—from mild discomfort, like now, to agony so intense that he would do anything, anything at all, to make it stop.

Thank you so very much for the dark gift you bestowed upon me, Abiageal. The thought was directed at his not so dear but very much departed sire. He hoped she could detect his sarcasm from whatever level of hell she'd been consigned to after her Final Death at the hands of overzealous churchmen.

He'd come to Livonia because he'd heard rumors of a Cainite kingdom here, a place where the undying could live openly and without fear. And while all that was true enough in its own way, what the rumors had failed to mention was how dreadfully boring it was. The leader of the kingdom, a savage called Qarakh, insisted on being addressed as "khan" instead of "prince," as was more common with Cainite rulers. He also insisted that all the members of his "tribe" be skilled warriors in order to protect the region from "those who would take our land from us." Those would be the Livonian Sword-Brothers—second-rate Templars intent on Christianizing the place—and the few German vampires who seemed to lurk among them. But they'd been beaten back last year, well before Rikard arrived. No, his time with the tribe had been spent training. The Cainites in Qarakh's tribe, as well as the ghouls, trained nightly in the martial arts, learning how to use a bow, wield a sword and ride a horse. Tedious though such training was, it had proven effective. While Rikard didn't consider himself a soldier yet, he had become competent with a weapon, though he still needed work on his horsemanship. At least he didn't fall off the damned animals anymore.

He never should have sworn allegiance to Qarakh. He had convinced himself that the Tartar's kingdom would one day become the Cainite paradise that Abiageal hadn't been able to deliver, but in the months since he had come to Livonia, all he'd done was train and, for the last week, sit watch in the trees.

"I should just leave," he whispered to himself, giving voice to his thoughts to help relieve the boredom. "It's not as if the Tartar would miss me, even if he were here."

"Yes I would."

A lance of cold terror pierced Rikard's unbeating heart. The words came only inches from his left ear, which meant their speaker was crouching next to him, but he hadn't heard anyone climb the tree. He knew he should turn to face the newcomer, but he was too scared to move.

"Once a man or woman swears fealty to me and is accepted into my tribe, they become as my own childer, whether they are of my blood or not. And 'Tartar' is the Christians' word for my kind. I am Mongolian."

The words were spoken in Livonian—a language Qarakh insisted all members of his tribe learn—but there was no mistaking that accent. The khan had returned home.

"Like any good father, I would miss my children, should they stray from the tribe. Miss them so much, in fact, that I would hunt them across all the lands of the earth until I had found them again."

Rikard felt the cold, sharp edge of a dagger suddenly pressed against his throat.

"And do you know what I would do once we were reunited?"

Rikard was so frightened he lost his grip on his bow, and both it and the arrow he had ready tumbled down the ground. Beads of blood-sweat erupted on his forehead, and he would've swallowed nervously if it hadn't been for the dagger.

"I would clasp them in my arms and say, 'The tribe misses you. I miss you. Come home.'"

Rikard felt the first faint spark of hope that he was going to survive. He didn't fail to notice, however, that Qarakh kept the knife to his throat.

"But you didn't leave, did you?" The khan's voice was utterly devoid of emotion now. No anger, no disappointment. Nothing. "You merely failed to remain alert at your post. You didn't hear the approach of my horse, and you didn't hear me climb up next to you, though I purposely made enough noise to alarm every sentry from here to the Great Wall. If I were an invader, I could slit your throat before you could make a sound, and then continue on to the camp undetected. Do you understand?"

Rikard couldn't speak. His throat felt full of sand. The best he could manage was an almost imperceptible nod.

"Good. Then you will do better next time."

A wave of relief washed over Rikard. Qarakh was only trying to teach him a lesson! A hard lesson, but one that Rikard knew he deserved. In the future, he would be more careful to—

Fire-sharp pain blossomed in Rikard's throat, and warm

blood gushed onto the front of his tunic.

"If you are strong enough, your wound will heal and you will make your way back to camp before dawn. If not..."

Rikard felt a hand press between his shoulder blades and shove, and then he was falling through darkness toward the forest floor. He didn't feel the impact when he landed.

Qarakh leaped into the air and came down less than a foot from Rikard's head, his leather boots hitting the ground silently. He intended to walk back to where he'd left his horse tethered to a low-hanging branch, mount up and continue on to the camp, but he hesitated. The scent of Rikard's blood hung thick and sweet in the air. Mortal blood was for nourishment, but Cainite vitae—no matter how diluted—contained *power*. It was the smell of that power which called to Qarakh now.

A harsh, animalistic voice spoke in his mind. *On the steppe, one learns not to waste anything; survival depends on it.*

Qarakh gazed down at Rikard. The Cainite lay on his back, eyes wide and staring, blood still bubbling from his slit throat as he tried to speak.

"This is not the steppe," Qarakh whispered.

And you are not a man. You are an animal. You hunger and there is food before you. Take it.

"This man swore allegiance to me as his khan."

He is no man. He is a weakling. His kind exists only to serve the strong. Right now, he would serve you best as sustenance.

Qarakh shook his head. "Perhaps that is how he would serve *you* best. He would serve me and my people far better if he survives to learn from his mistake and makes the tribe stronger." The Mongol warrior knelt down, wiped his dagger on a clean spot on Rikard's sleeve, then straightened and returned the knife to its belt sheathe. He then walked off toward his horse, ignoring the frustrated howls of the Beast inside him.

The boundaries of Qarakh's tribal lands were marked by a quartet of small altars, one for each point on the compass, representing what Mongols called the Four Directions: Front,

Back, Left and Right. Qarakh rode up to the southern (front)
one and, as was his custom, cut several hairs from his horse's
mane with his dagger. He then dismounted and approached the
altar on foot. It was a construction of sticks and poles built on
top of a stone mound. Qarakh had made all four of them himself, after the style of the Mongolian tribes he had left on the
steppe. Tattered blue prayer flags were tied to the poles, and
they stirred in the gentle breeze. Offerings were piled onto the
stones: coins, fox tails, eagle feathers and, of course, patches of
dried blood. Qarakh walked three times around the altar, then
tied the horsehairs to one of the poles. Now it was time to leave
his offering. He lifted his right wrist to his mouth, bared his
fangs, and bit into his own flesh.

Qarakh extended his arm over the stones and squeezed his
hand into a fist. Thick drops of blood splattered onto the previous patches of blood. When the old blood had been completely
covered, Qarakh drew his hand back and lowered it to his side.

"Welcome home, my khan."

If she had been a stranger, the interloper would've been
slain before finishing her sentence. But Qarakh recognized her
voice, and so turned calmly to face her. "Deverra."

He noted that her gaze was fixed on his ragged wrist, and
her nostrils flared as she inhaled the scent of his blood. He was
unconcerned. He doubted Deverra would be so foolish as to
give into her Beast and attack him. Still, she was a sorceress and
possessed mystic abilities beyond those of ordinary Cainites,
and thus bore watching. But then, as far was Qarakh was concerned, everyone bore watching.

He didn't ask how she knew he was coming and that he
would stop at the altar first. She was a shaman; knowing such
things was her lot.

She nodded toward the altar. "Building up *hiimori*, I see."

Hiimori meant "wind horse," the power that came from such
sacrifices. He gave her a simple nod.

The shaman was not a Mongol. Tall and thin, she dressed
in a dark blue robe, its hood down to better display her long
flowing red hair. Her features were delicate and fine, and her
complexion pale, as was normal for the unliving. Her eyes were

a touch too large for her face, but the effect merely added to the overall air of otherworldliness that she and the other sorcerers cultivated. More striking was the color of her eyes: They were a bright emerald green, so bright that, in the right light, they almost sparkled.

"You were gone longer than usual this time," Deverra said. "Some of the mortals in our flock were beginning to worry that you had run into mischief during your wanderings."

Her tone was even, but Qarakh detected a hint of disapproval.

"I trust you reassured them otherwise."

Deverra smiled, revealing the pointed tips of her canines. "Naturally, though some required the special kiss of a priestess to draw out their ill humors."

Qarakh wasn't certain how to take this. She sounded almost amused, but he knew from long association that she took her roles as tribal shaman and high priestess of the cult of the Livonian god Telyavel very seriously. She had tended to the needs of the god's mortal worshippers and taken their blood as her due for many years before he'd come to Livonia, before they had made common cause to create a new tribe. Still, he found her tendency toward ambiguity puzzling and often frustrating. Over the few years he'd known her, he'd learned the best way to deal with her unclear comments was to ignore them, which he did now.

"You have my thanks for coming here to welcome me back, but it was not necessary. I would think you'd have more productive ways to occupy your time."

Deverra smiled and stepped closer to the warrior. She reached out and gently touched his now-healed wrist. "Is it so hard to believe that I simply might have missed you?"

Another Cainite might have recoiled from Deverra's touch. She and the rest of her brood of priests were blood sorcerers, and such folk could be very dangerous indeed. Even Qarakh had heard rumors of the sorcerous Tremere who stole the blood of other Cainites in their dark witchery. But Qarakh judged people by the deeds they performed, not by their lineage, and to his mind, the Telyav were nothing like the Tremere.

Deverra rubbed her fingers over his wrist in slow, small

circles, then brought her hand to her nose and sniffed. She frowned. "Your vitae is weaker than usual. It has been too long since you fed." She said this last as if she were a mother chiding a naughty son, despite the fact that Qarakh was her khan—but then she was also high priestess of the Telyavs.

Take her, whispered his Beast. *She fed well tonight on one of her acolytes. Think of it! Living blood filtered through the veins of a Telyav priestess... a heady brew indeed!*

The Beast's guttural laughter echoed in Qarakh's mind, and the Mongol was surprised to discover that his mouth was watering. He found the loss of control most disturbing, and he took a step back from Deverra.

"I will feed upon returning to the camp." His voice was thick with barely repressed need and sounded too much like that of the Beast to his ears.

If Deverra noticed, she gave no sign. "There is another reason I came here once I sensed you were to return this night." Her tone became grim. "There have been certain signs of late. The land speaks to me—the wind that rustles the leaves, the squeal of a mouse caught in the claws of an owl, the silhouettes of trees outlined in silver moonlight, they all say the same thing: He is coming."

Qarakh scowled. "Who?"

Deverra looked at the Mongol for a moment before answering, and the warrior was surprised to see fear in her eyes.

"A prince with the face of a boy."

Chapter Two

By the time Qarakh and Deverra reached the cluster of round felt tents—what the Mongols called *gers*—that made up the campsite, the eastern sky was tinted by the coming dawn. Qarakh invited the priestess to seek shelter from the sun in his tent, as was the Mongolian custom. But Deverra declined, giving her thanks (which was not only unnecessary but almost insulting to Qarakh) and walked away from the camp, across the clearing where it was currently set up, and toward a stand of pine trees. Qarakh watched her go, wondering where she spent the daylight hours. To his knowledge, she had never remained in the camp after sunrise. He wondered if it was out of some Telyavic necessity, or merely to maintain her priestess's aura of mystery. Probably a little of both.

He tethered his mare to the single wooden pole in front of his *ger*. The other tents in the camp all had similar poles with horses tied to them as well. Qarakh didn't remove his mount's tack. That was work for a ghoul. He'd dismounted and walked with Deverra as they spoke, leading the horse behind them, and the mare was much better for it. Still, she needed a rubdown, water and food. Qarakh bent down and entered his *ger* through the single low door facing south. The doors in all the tents in the camp faced south, as was only proper.

Even though Qarakh was khan of this tribe, his tent was like all the others in the camp, inside and out. Woven red rugs covered the floor, and the bed for his ghouls was against the left wall. A man and a woman wearing simple Livonian peasant garb lay there, cuddled together beneath a fur blanket. Normally a tin stove stood in the center of a *ger*, but since Cainites hated fire, only the handful of tents used solely by mortals had them.

Qarakh removed his sword, bow and quiver, and placed them on the ground to the right of the door. He then walked over to the sleeping ghouls and kicked the male's rump to rouse him.

The mortal woke with a start and sat up. He blinked grog-gily for a moment, but when his eyes finally focused, his mouth broke into a wide grin. "My khan! You're home!"

"Tend to my horse," Qarakh said.

Still grinning, the male—a youth barely into his manhood—said, "At once, my khan." He threw back the blanket, rose and started toward the door of the *ger*.

Before he could crawl through, Qarakh said, "Hold."

The youth stopped and looked up expectantly.

"When you finish with the mare, tell the other ghouls to inform their masters that I wish to hold council after sunset."

"Yes, khan." The youth hurried off to do his master's bidding.

The female roused then and opened her eyes. "You've come back to us." Her tone was that of a woman welcoming home a lover.

The Beast that laired inside Qarakh growled softly at the implied familiarity. The woman was merely mortal, after all, a ghoul and a servant. But she was also Livonian, and the mor-tals of these lands still held fast to their ancient beliefs, and they viewed Cainites not as demons, but rather as supernatural beings akin to gods, as Deverra had taught them. Qarakh wasn't always comfortable with this perception, but he had found it useful in establishing the tribe.

So he did not chastise the woman. Instead, he sat down next to her.

She sat up, and he smelled the odor of sweat and semen on her. She and the male had lain together not long before he'd entered the *ger*.

Good. The exertion would add spice to her blood.

"Your face is more pale than usual, my khan, and I can see the hunger burning in your eyes. You must feed." She rolled up the right sleeve of her tunic and without hesitation offered her bare wrist to him. Qarakh preferred not to drink from the necks of those mortals who gave themselves to him willingly, lest he risk damaging their living soul, which all Mongols knew resided there.

Qarakh could smell the blood surging hot and sweet through her veins, and he could deny his hunger no longer. He grabbed her wrist, brought it to his mouth, and plunged his teeth into the flesh. The woman gasped—half in pleasure, half in pain—and Qarakh began to drink. As he swallowed mouthful after mouthful of life itself, the woman ran the fingers of her free hand through the wild tangle of his hair. He found the intimacy of her touch distasteful, but even though the Beast's growling became louder, he decided to allow it. The Livs often wished to touch the "gods" as they fed, and desiring contact with the divine was a natural impulse for mortals.

After a few moments, he began to draw less and less blood until finally he pulled his teeth from her crimson-smeared wrist. If he allowed himself, he would drain her dry, and as satisfying as that might be, it would be wasteful. Alive, she could continue to produce blood for decades to come. Dead, she would be worthless.

No! howled the Beast inside him. *I—We still hunger!*

Hunger was a frequent, if not particularly welcome, companion to those who lived on the steppe, and though Qarakh's mortal days were years behind him, he well remembered what it was like to have a belly that was never quite full. The hunger for blood was much stronger, of course, but if he had been able to face the specter of starvation on an almost daily basis as a man, he should—

"Have you gone to see your friend yet, my khan?" The woman's words were slurred, as if she had drunk too much wine. She lay back on the bed, eyes half-closed, a contented smile on her lips. The wounds on her wrist were already healing.

Qarakh looked at her, his canine teeth suddenly longer, his eyes grown wolf-feral. "What did you say?"

His tone was colder than a winter wind skirling across frozen tundra, and the woman drew the fur cover up to her chin, as if it might somehow protect her from her master. "I—I meant no offense, great khan. I merely asked if you had paid a visit to your friend yet. His name is Aajav, isn't it? The men of the tribe all say that you always go to see him upon returning home. I thought—"

Qarakh's hand shot out faster than a striking snake and clawed fingers wrapped around the woman's neck, cutting off her words—and her air.

"Aajav is not my *friend*." He spat the word. "He is much more. He is my brother and my blood." He squeezed tighter, and the woman—eyes bulging from sockets, face turning a deep dark red—reached up and tried to tear his hand away from her throat, but the Mongol's grip was like iron. "I wouldn't expect you to understand. You are a woman, and a Livonian one at that." His vision had gone red, and there was a roaring in his ears, as if he were underwater. In his mind, he heard the Beast panting its lust.

Yes, yes, yes, yes, YES!

"The bond between Aajav and I is a most sacred thing, and not for the likes of you to speak of. Do you understand?" The mortal didn't respond, so he gave her a shake. "Answer!" Still she did not reply, and Qarakh squeezed tighter. She was his ghoul, and by Tengri, she would obey him!

"Answer!"

A sound cut through the roaring in his ears then: a harsh crack like a tree limb being snapped in two.

The next sound he heard was the Beast's mad laughter... then silence.

He looked at the woman and frowned, confused, as if only just seeing her for the first time. Her head lolled to one side like a rag doll's, and her bulging eyes were wide and unseeing, the whites streaked red. Her skin of her face was almost black now, and her tongue, swollen and purple, protruded from her mouth like a fat slug.

Qarakh released his grip and the woman fell onto the bed, limp and lifeless.

What are you waiting for? Drink!

Qarakh did nothing.

What do you care if she's dead? She was nothing more than cattle to you, as are all mortals. You didn't even know her name. Now drink, before her blood spoils and goes to waste!

Qarakh started forward, fangs bared, but then he stopped. "Her name was Pavla," he said. He expected the Beast to respond, but his inner voice was silent for a change. He felt a sudden heaviness in his limbs, and he knew it was more than drowsiness from having just fed. The sun had risen.

He crawled to the middle of the *ger* and moved aside one of the red mats to expose a bare patch of earth.

He should've known better. The Beast could only be denied for so long before it had to feed. And it needed more than mere blood. It needed pain and death and carnage. Most of all, it needed to prove its dominance over its host body, to humiliate the Cainite so foolish as to believe that he could ever be its master. He knew that some called him Qarakh the Untamed, but the only truly untamed thing about him was the Beast that was his eternal companion through the endless nights.

He scooted onto the patch of earth and concentrated. As he sank into the ground where he would slumber during the daylight hours, he vowed that he would never forget the hard lesson the Beast had taught him this night—just as he had vowed many times before.

Deverra stood before a large pine tree at the edge of the tribe's immediate territory. She drew a sharp nail across her palm and vitae welled forth, mixing with the tree sap already in her hand. The Telyav priestess stirred the mixture with a finger, then brought it to her mouth and lapped it up. She didn't need to look at the lightening sky to sense the coming dawn. She felt it as a heat in her veins, as if her blood were on the verge of boiling. She swallowed the blood-sap, closed her eyes and calmly recited an invocation. Then, just as the first light of dawn broke over the horizon, she stepped toward the tree trunk and melted into the wood.

Safely encased within the pine, Deverra would sleep until sunset. But though she felt languor washing over her, the peace of slumber proved elusive. She continued to think about Qarakh and the conversation they'd had on their way back to the camp. The Mongol chieftain intended to hold *kuriltai,* a war council, after sundown.

It was the "war" part of the council that worried her. She had full confidence in Qarakh himself. Despite his relative youth, he was a mighty Cainite and as strong a leader as she had known. He'd also gathered an inner circle of seasoned warriors from across the northern fringes of Christianity and beyond, but the rest of his tribe was a rag-tag collection of Cainites, ghouls and thralls. They trained in the arts of war and were not without skill, but it had been a hard fight last year against the Livonian and German crusaders and the vampires in their midst. If this boy-faced prince was whom she feared it was... well, they would be no match for him.

A high priestess with so little faith, she chided herself. Qarakh had only arrived in Livonia a few years ago, but she had been born here and had spent the majority of her long unlife here. She had forged a bond with the spirit of this land, with Telyavel, the guardian of the dead and maker of things. As long as the flame of that bond burned, as long as she and the others in her extended coven were willing to make the necessary sacrifices, then there remained hope. Deverra had helped the young Mongol found his tribe here with that bond to the spirit and people of the land at its core, and she would not surrender to despair now.

The boy prince was coming. The only question was how they would face him.

At last, sun-sleep finally came for her, and her consciousness slipped into the darkness that was Cainite slumber. She had two last thoughts before oblivion claimed her for the day. First, she would not inform the other Telyavs about Alexander—not before consulting the man she had sworn allegiance to as her khan. And second, she wondered what Qarakh's vitae would taste like.

Sweet, she decided. *And burning hot...*

Then she thought no more.

Qarakh slumbered and remembered. A night years ago, when a rough whisper cut through his sleep.

"Qarakh..."

He ignored the voice, rolled onto his side, and pulled the bearskin blanket over his head. Outside, the wind howled like a hungry demon across the steppe, and though he was warmly dressed and covered with fur, Qarakh shivered at the sound.

"My brother…"

He tried to say, "Go away," but it came out as an incoherent mumble. He wished Aajav would go back to sleep. It had been a long day of hunting with little to show for it: a single scrawny marmot and a few field mice. He was bone weary and the small amount of meat he'd managed to catch had done little to fill the emptiness in his belly. He wanted nothing more than to sleep and wake up in the morning when hopefully the steppe would prove more generous.

He felt a hand on his shoulder then, and it began to shake him gently.

"You have a visitor, Qarakh. Will you be so rude as to not greet him?"

He came instantly awake then, and sat up in a single smooth motion, dagger in hand. He tried to see who had entered his *ger*, but the interior of the tent was too dark for him to make out more than a rough outline of the man.

"If you come seeking shelter from the night wind, you are welcome," Qarakh said. "If you come seeking more than that, you are not."

The visitor chuckled. "The cold means nothing to me, brother. Not anymore."

Fully awake now, Qarakh recognized the voice. "Aajav! It is good to hear your words again!" He tucked the dagger back into his belt. "Come, get beneath the blanket and I will start the fire." Qarakh started to get up, but a hand—stronger than he remembered—gripped his shoulder to stop him.

"There is no need. As I said, the cold doesn't bother me."

Even through the cloth of his tunic, Qarakh felt the chill emanating from his blood brother's hand. "But you feel like ice! Please allow me to—"

"Enough. I said there is no need." His grip on Qarakh's shoulder tightened to the point of being painful.

Something else struck Qarakh as odd, though he couldn't

quite... and then he realized what it was: the smell, or rather the lack of it. Mongols smeared sheep fat on their exposed skin as protection against the cold wind. But Qarakh detected no hint of the scent wafting from Aajav.

"Very well," Qarakh said. He had no wish to argue with a guest seeking shelter in his *ger* late at night. Besides, Aajav was nothing if not stubborn.

"Good." Aajav removed his hand and settled into a cross-legged position next to Qarakh's bed.

Qarakh stared into the darkness and tried to discern his blood brother's features. Though his eyes had adjusted somewhat, he still could make out only a shadowy figure where Aajav sat. But this didn't matter. He knew Aajav's face better than he knew his own: head and chin smooth-shaven, a broad and easy smile, and the unflinching gaze of a warrior born.

Qarakh also assumed a sitting position, but though he was cold and would've liked to pull the bearskin blanket around his shoulders, he did not. If the temperature did not bother Aajav, then it did not bother him.

Aajav chuckled softly, as if he knew why Qarakh did not cover himself and found it amusing. But if so, Qarakh took no offense. His brother had always had something of a strange sense of humor, and Qarakh was accustomed to not always understanding why he thought certain things were funny.

"It has been many months since we have sat together like this," Qarakh said.

In the dark, Aajav nodded. "Nearly a year. Much has happened to me in that time."

"You must have many good stories to tell. But before that, we should exchange gifts." It was customary to give and receive presents when someone paid a visit. Often these were mere tokens, the most common being blue scarves that were used in religious ceremonies. Qarakh believed he had one such scarf left... somewhere. He patted his tunic, searching for wherever he had tucked the scarf.

Aajav laid a hand on his wrist, and Qarakh flinched at the touch of his brother's cold flesh.

"I have a specific gift in mind," Aajav said. "One to

strengthen the bond between us. A sharing of blood."

Aajav's request was odd, but Qarakh loved him. "As you will."

"Good. But first I have a most wondrous story to tell you, my brother." He grinned, and even in the dark of the *ger*, Qarakh could see Aajav's sharp white teeth. "Most wondrous indeed."

Chapter Three

Qarakh woke to darkness and a feeling of being closed in on all sides. Panic welled up within him. He tried to thrash his arms and legs, but he could not move them. He struggled to draw in a breath, but his lungs felt as if they were full of something thick and heavy.

Aajav had been talking to him just a moment ago... telling him about his encounter with a strange man named Oderic, and the dark gift this man had given him, a gift which he in turn wished to pass on to his beloved brother....

Then Qarakh remembered. That night in the *ger* with Aajav—when he'd first become Aajav's ghoul, when he'd taken his first step away from mortality and toward becoming a vampire—was decades gone now. It had been a dream-memory, nothing more. Then again, perhaps the dream had been an omen of sorts, a message from the spirits that he should go speak to his brother and seek his council. Qarakh decided to do so immediately after the *kuriltai*.

He willed himself to rise from the earth in which he had slept, and a moment later he stood in the center of his *ger* once again, the ground beneath his feet freshly turned. Lying on the bed was the still form of the female ghoul, the one whose neck he had broken last night when the Beast had gotten the better of him. Her loss was regrettable. A Mongol hunter never killed except for food and fur, and then he killed in the most humane way possible. A Mongol warrior killed only to protect his tribe or when conducting a raid. But Qarakh wasn't only a Mongol; he was also an unliving thing, what the folk here called a Cainite or a vampire. He drank the blood of men to feed the great Beast in his heart—and the Beast needed sating from time to time. Mongols believed the ideal person attempted to live *yostoi*, in balance with the world, but when one also had a Beast's soul, *yostoi* was most difficult to achieve.

He prayed to Tengri that having her neck broken hadn't damaged Pavla's soul too severely, otherwise she could not be reincarnated.

Qarakh looked down at Pavla's body. "Goodbye, woman. You served your khan well. I hope you find many rewards in your next life." He then strode toward the *ger's* door, eager to get the council underway. But when he stepped outside, careful as always not to allow his feet to touch the threshold, he was met by a chorus of cheers.

The camp was filled with mortals: men, women and children, all wearing the dress of Livonian peasants. Some of them he recognized as ghouls and thralls, but most were unknown to him. He estimated the newcomers at three dozen or more. Standing apart from the crowd were the other Cainites in the camp—evidently he had slept longer than he'd intended and was the last to rise this night.

Deverra stood with the other Cainites, and now she stepped forward. "These mortals live in the nearby village of Gutka. They heard that the great khan had returned to their land, and they have come to pay homage."

Qarakh knew he should have expected this. The camp was always set up close to a human village so the Cainites in his tribe would have easy access to sustenance, and since the Livs believed the vampires were demigods, they were more than eager to sacrifice their blood for good fortune, a bountiful harvest and strong, healthy children. In order to keep from draining any one village dry, the tribe moved every few months and made camp on the outskirts of another human settlement. The arrangement—not unlike that of a Mongolian sheepherder in some ways—worked quite well, but occasionally it meant that Qarakh was forced to play host to his "worshippers."

As a priestess of Telyavel, the Protector of the Dead, Deverra served as the liaison between the mortals and the spirit world, so it was only right that he address his words to her. "Priestess, your people are welcome among us." His tone was formal, and he spoke loud enough for all to hear. "We accept their tribute and bid that they remain among us for a time and receive our blessing."

This brought a few scattered cheers from mortals who were quickly shushed by those standing close to them. The ritual wasn't finished yet.

Deverra folded her hands over her chest and bowed. "On behalf of the people of Gutka, I thank you, oh great khan. May Telyavel hold our ancestors close and lend them his ear when they seek his favor on our behalf." She straightened and Qarakh was surprised when she winked at him.

Qarakh turned toward the humans and spread his arms wide.

"Let the communion begin!"

In the center of the camp, a celebratory fire had been lit, though it was not very big, and the Cainites kept well away from it, averting their eyes from the bright flames. The villagers sat around the fire, eating bread and cheese and drinking wine, all of which they had brought themselves. They offered none to the Cainites or their ghouls; the people knew what fare they subsisted on. An old man played a sprightly tune on a violin while several pretty young women danced, no doubt trying to attract the attentions of the male Cainites.

Qarakh sat on a felled tree trunk, Deverra at his right side. The Livs viewed her as the female complement to his male energy, almost a consort of sorts, and so the two always remained together when in the presence of mortals that revered them. Sitting on a second log and facing Qarakh and Deverra were three other Cainites, all members of the Mongol's inner circle.

In the middle, wrapped in an old blanket, sat an ancient vampire known simply as Grandfather who served as the tribe's lore-keeper. His face was wizened, as if he had been Embraced toward the end of his mortal lifespan, and his eyes were slitted like a cat's or a serpent's. His arms and hands, neither of which was visible at the moment, were covered with coarse gray fur.

When he spoke, his deep voice belied his apparent feebleness, and though he normally remained still, when he chose to move, he could do so with a panther's deadly speed.

To Grandfather's left sat a large brooding man with long black hair that spilled past his shoulders. A ponytail hung back from the center of his head, and two twin braids dangled past his bearded chin. His eyes were cold blue, and a scar ran across the right, a legacy of his mortal life. Despite the fact that his mouth was closed in a grim line, the tips of his two razor-sharp canines protruded over his lip, and his ears were tufted like an animal's. Though concealed at the moment, his torso was covered with fur—another mark of the Beast. Before his Embrace centuries ago, Arnulf had been a Goth soldier, and now he wore simple leather armor, deerskin pants, black boots and a black cape. He carried a broadax that Qarakh had rarely seen him without.

Like Qarakh, and much of the other blood-drinkers in the tribe, Grandfather and Arnulf traced their line to the Gangrel clan. One of the great lines of the undead, the Gangrel were known for their animalistic gifts and their stalwart hearts. The hidebound Cainites of the cities and settled lands looked down on Gangrel as wild and barbaric, but Qarakh knew they simply hid their fear. Unlike the khan and most others, Grandfather and Arnulf were both elders even among the unliving, having spent centuries under the night sky. Still they had both sworn oaths to their khan and that superceded age.

On Grandfather's right sat Alessandro de Garcia, sometimes referred to as the Hound of Iberia. Not a Gangrel at all, Alessandro was a handsome man with short black hair and a small thatch of beard beneath his lower lip. He wore a simple black shirt and pants, a red sash around his waist, and a pair of highly polished black boots. An Iberian whose blood ran to the Brujah line, he appeared to be in his midthirties and had been a soldier and mercenary during his mortal life. He remained a skilled fighter, but was also a philosopher who sought a more complete understanding of the Beast. He served as Qarakh's second-in-command, running the camp and the tribe's training sessions whenever the khan was away.

Only one of his inner circle was missing. "Where is Wilhelmina?" Qarakh asked.

"She left a week ago to patrol the western territory," Alessandro said, speaking Livonian with a slight Iberian accent. "There have been rumors of trespassing Cainites preying on the mortals there, and she went to determine if they were true. We have had no word from her since."

Qarakh grunted. A week was not long to be away, and Wilhelmina was a Viking warrior-maid as well as a savage huntress. She could take care of herself. And it was possible the interlopers were tied to this boy prince. Anything she might learn about them would prove valuable to the tribe.

Qarakh was about to begin the *kuriltai* in earnest when his male ghoul—whose name was Sasha—came over, leading two other servants with him. All of them held clay goblets filled with blood.

"My khan, please forgive the intrusion, but I thought you might hunger." He lowered his head and held out a goblet toward his master.

Qarakh looked over his shoulder at the celebrating villagers. The lower-ranking Cainites in the camp—about a dozen in all— were moving among the humans, drinking first from this one, then from that. Some were bleeding the mortals into drinking vessels, while others partook straight from the vein. The mortals closed their eyes and drew in sudden hisses of breath, lost in the throes of ecstasy. Qarakh approved—the Beast must be fed, after all. He only hoped his people would be careful not to bleed too many of the villagers dry, for the continued health the herd.

He was surprised to see that one of the more enthusiastic Cainites—a man on the verge of completely draining a small female child—was Rikard, the incompetent sentry whose throat he had cut last night. So the man had survived to make it back to the camp after all. Perhaps he was made of sterner stuff than Qarakh had given him credit for. Rikard's complexion was ivory white from loss of blood, and his throat was an ugly mass of scar tissue. The tribe had strict rules about slaying children, but the man had earned a reward for making it back to camp. Qarakh knew the sweetness of a child's blood and let Rikard be.

The khan's mouth was watering as he turned back to Sasha. "You may serve us."

Sasha and the two others gave Qarakh and the elders mugs full of blood. They bowed one last time, then turned to go, but Qarakh said, "Hold for a moment, Sasha." The mortal did so, motioning for the other two humans to continue on.

He turned to face his master once more. "Yes, my khan?"

"Last night…" Now that he had started, Qarakh wasn't sure how to phrase what he had to say.

"I saw Pavla when I brought your saddle and tack inside the *ger*," Sasha said, voice and face expressionless. "You had already retired for the day by then. I would've taken her body from the tent, but I wasn't certain you were finished with it. With your permission, I'll remove the corpse after the feast."

"Of course." Qarakh felt a vestigial twinge of an emotion he hadn't experienced much even during his mortal life: guilt. Sasha had lain with Pavla last night, as he had many nights before, but now all she was to him was *the corpse*, trash to be removed from his master's *ger* and disposed of. And he had become this thing—this ghoul—because Qarakh had made him so.

Sasha bowed one last time before departing.

"It's never good for a Cainite to become too attached to his own ghouls," Grandfather said, as if sensing Qarakh's thoughts. "If a butcher begins to love cattle, how can he wield a cleaver?"

Arnulf took a gulp from his mug, then lowered it, leaving his black beard and mustache smeared with crimson. "You should kill the mortal as soon as you get the chance, so that you might extinguish whatever feelings you have for him." He drained the rest of his blood in a single draught, then wiped his mouth with the back of his hand. "Never had much use for ghouls anyway. They make you weak."

Qarakh had been about to take a drink, but now he lowered his mug and gave the Goth warrior a hard look. "What do you mean by *weak*?" His voice held a dangerous edge.

Deverra laid a hand on the Mongol's arm. "Pay it no mind, Qarakh. We have far more important matters to discuss this night."

But it was the Telyav's words that Qarakh chose to ignore.

He shrugged off her hand then stood. "Answer me, Arnulf."

The Goth's eyes seemed to take on the same shade of red as the blood smeared on his mouth. He made a fist, and his mug shattered into clay shards that fell to the grass. "Take care, Mongol." He spoke through gritted teeth, voice low in his throat.

Grandfather smiled, clearly amused. "So priestess, do you have a spell for calming two belligerent Gangrel?"

"This isn't funny," Deverra said.

"No, but it may well prove instructive," Alessandro put in. "Arnulf is eldest and thus nominally the more powerful of the two, but Qarakh is a more cunning warrior. It's difficult to decide who would be the victor in a battle between them."

Qarakh wasn't happy to hear his lore-keeper and his second-in-command calmly discussing the battle that was about to be joined as if he and Arnulf were nothing more than common tavern brawlers to wager on. He would've have said something to them, but he knew better than to take even a fraction of his attention off Arnulf.

Neither Alessandro nor Grandfather realized just how young Qarakh was. They thought their khan had stalked the night for two centuries, not a handful of years.

Deverra stood and put herself between the two Gangrel. She turned first to Qarakh. "If you two fools wish to tear each other apart, so be it. But keep in mind that you'll only be doing our enemy's work for him." Before the Mongol could respond, she turned to Arnulf. "Did you not swear an oath of allegiance to Qarakh as your khan?"

The Goth's only reply was a bestial growl.

"Did you?" she insisted.

Arnulf's muscles tightened as if he were about to spring, but then he relaxed. "Yes." He fairly spat the word.

Deverra looked back to Qarakh, an eyebrow raised as if to say, *Well? It's your turn.*

Ignore the bitch! Tear the bastard's heart out and feast on it!

Qarakh said down on the log once more. "Your council is wise, Arnulf. I shall slay the ghoul before the sun rises."

The Goth scoffed but was mollified. Deverra gave them both a last look before retaking her place on the log next to Qarakh.

"You are ever the tribe's scolding mother, Telyav," Grandfather said. "A tribe of querulous little boys." He let out a snuffling laugh that sounded more animal than man.

Irritated at Deverra's interference—however necessary it might have been—and the lore-keeper's laughter, Qarakh drained his mug in a single gulp and then turned to Alessandro. "Why did you assign that fool Rikard to sentry duty last night? An entire army could have marched past directly below him and he would never have known it."

"He's a city-dweller," Arnulf said with a sneer, as if that explained everything.

"Rikard wasn't the only sentry on duty last night," Alessandro said. "There were three others."

"I was aware of them, and all three were alert to a man. They are not the issue. Rikard is."

"I posted him to sentry duty as a test. Since joining the tribe, Rikard has been somewhat... ambivalent about performing his duties. I wished to gauge the level of his dedication by having him serve sentry duty for a few nights. If he failed to perform his task well..." There was no need to complete the thought. The tribe must be strong. Weak members were culled from the ranks, one way or another.

"I am somewhat surprised that he not only survived the 'instruction' you gave him last night," Alessandro continued, "but that he returned to camp at all."

"Perhaps he now wishes to prove himself to his khan," Arnulf suggested.

"Perhaps," Grandfather acknowledged. "Then again, perhaps he wishes more."

Qarakh scowled at the lore-keeper. "Such as?"

Grandfather's only reply was a shrug. Qarakh hated it when the old one did that.

"I shall keep close watch on him," Alessandro promised.

"See that you do," Qarakh said. "Now, to the matter at hand: Deverra has had a vision."

"Not a vision, precisely," the priestess said. "More like a warning from the land itself. A new enemy is coming, a prince with the face of a boy."

Qarakh caught a slight start in Grandfather, but it was Arnulf who spoke first.

"Let the whelp come," Arnulf said. "This tribe needs a good battle."

"Perhaps," Qarakh said, but turned to the lore-keeper. "You have something to add, Grandfather?"

The old Gangrel let almost a minute go by before speaking. "When I roamed the woods west of the Alps, I heard word of such a prince with the face of a boy. His name was Alexander and he was terrible indeed. But he was said to lair in Paris and never to venture from his city. We are far from Paris indeed."

Qarakh did not know of this Paris, but if he himself could have come from far-off Mongolia he doubted very much this Alexander couldn't make the trip here if he wished. But why would he wish it? The city-bred vampires were sedentary, lairing behind their walls and feeding off the fat merchants and harlots.

"Alexander no longer rules Paris," Deverra said, in a tone like a death knell. "He was exiled some years ago and sent east."

"Toward us," Alessandro said.

"It would seem," she said.

Grandfather frowned. "If so, this is distressing indeed. The Alexander I knew of was a powerful ancient, Embraced in Athens seven centuries before the birth of the Christian god. If he has been driven from Paris, he will seek dominion over others. It is in his blood."

"Could he be allied with the knights we faced last year?" Alessandro asked. "They were Germans, I thought, but still…"

Arnulf snorted. "I've heard stories of French and German high-bloods fighting together in the Carpathian wars. Still, they were driven out then and they will be driven out now."

"Not easily, if he is nearly two millennia old," Qarakh said. "And even if this Alexander's reputation is exaggerated, he will not come alone. He will bring a fighting force with him. Perhaps large, perhaps small, but they will be deadly to a man."

"How do you know this?" Arnulf challenged.

"Because we defeated the smaller force last year." Qarakh smiled, displaying his fangs. "And because that is what I would do."

Alessandro looked thoughtful. "This would explain the reports of trespassers that we have received of late. Perhaps they are Alexander's scouts."

"Spies, you mean," Arnulf growled.

"Whichever the case, we shall know more of that upon Wilhelmina's return," Qarakh said. *If she returns*, whispered his Beast.

"The question is why Alexander is marching on Livonia," Grandfather said.

"He no longer rules in Paris, and wishes to establish his own empire here," Deverra said.

Qarakh shook his head. "He is used to ruling a city. I doubt he's developed a sudden fondness for the wild. More likely he is planning some manner of campaign to help repair his damaged reputation."

Arnulf nodded. "So he might increase his military strength and ultimately return to Paris and take revenge upon his usurpers."

Qarakh grinned in agreement. "Again, that is what I would do."

"But we are still targets, whether or not he wants our lands," Deverra said. "If he has made common cause with the Germans, then he will support their crusade. They seek to bring the Cross to Livonia. We are pagan heathens to them."

"You sound like Wilhelmina," Alessandro said.

"The Christians rooted out her gods and they would so the same to ours," the priestess said.

"Your gods," Arnulf said. "Not mine."

The priestess looked at him for a moment before closing her mouth and averting her gaze.

"Enough," Qarakh said. "There is only one way to know Alexander's intent for certain. I must parley with the former Prince of Paris."

"My khan," Alessandro said, "let me go in your place. I am expendable. You are not."

Not for the first time, Qarakh thought the Brujah a good man, and he was glad to have him as his second-in-command. "Your bravery does you credit, Alessandro, but were I to send anyone in my stead, this prince would be sure to take that as a sign of weakness. Besides, I would see this Alexander for myself, the better to gauge his strengths and weaknesses."

"If he has any," Deverra added.

"All men—breathing or not—have at least one weakness," Grandfather said. "The trick is to learn what it is and discover a way to exploit it."

Arnulf stood and in a single fluid motion drew his ax from the stump in which he'd planted it. "Everything falls before a keen-edged blade and a strong arm! That is all we need!"

"Hush now," Deverra said. "You're scaring the mortals."

True enough, a number of villagers were looking in their direction with expressions of alarm. Standing and swinging his ax, hair wild, razorlike teeth bared, Arnulf looked like a demon from the deepest pits of hell.

The Goth warrior laughed. "What do I care for mortals? Let them be afraid!"

"If you scare them, they will leave," Alessandro said. "And they will take their blood with them."

Arnulf considered this for a moment before lowering his ax and once again taking his seat. He looked down at the broken shards of his mug lying in the grass, then lifted his head and cupped his hands to his mouth. *"More!"* he bellowed, and a half-dozen ghouls snapped to attention and scurried to fill mugs from open veins.

Qarakh smiled. In many ways, Arnulf was the Beast made solid: He lived solely to hunt, kill, feed and sleep. Qarakh envied the Goth's simplicity and wished that his own existence could be so uncomplicated. But he was khan, and he couldn't afford to live like an animal, much as he might want to. Not if his tribe was to thrive and prosper.

They waited until the ghouls had served them once more before resuming their council.

Qarakh turned to Alessandro. "I will leave tomorrow night in search of Alexander and his men. Most likely they will approach from the southwest, so that is where I shall look first. In the meantime, send out our swiftest runners to spread the word: I want all of our wanderers to return to the camp lands as fast as they can. And I want all Cainites in the tribe—including the four of you—to send forth appeals to whatever childer they might have. Though they are not members of our tribe, ask if they will stand and fight with their sires should Alexander and his forces attack. More, tell them to bring whatever ghouls and thralls they possess. If we are Alexander's true target, we will need all the people we can get as quickly as we can get them."

"Yes, my khan," Alessandro said.

Qarakh nodded, then turned to Deverra. "Send word to your coven and fellow priests. We will need them as well."

Deverra merely nodded, saying nothing.

"And do you have a task for me, great khan?" Grandfather asked, without the slightest hint of mockery in his voice, though he was older than Qarakh by hundreds, perhaps even thousands, of years.

"Search your memory for all that you know of Alexander, and find out more any way that you can. If I am to fight this boy-faced monster, I need to know him as well as I know myself. Better, even."

Grandfather nodded. "As you will."

"As for myself, I shall—"

"Master?"

Qarakh whirled, a snarl on his lips. It was Sasha.

The ghoul held up his hands in a placating gesture and took a step back. "I—I hate to interrupt, but there is among the villagers a man and woman who were recently married and are now expecting their first child. They seek your blessing, yours and Mistress Deverra's."

Qarakh was beginning to wish he'd killed Sasha instead of Pavla last night.

Deverra stood and held out her hand to the Mongol. "Come, my *consort*. We have a holy duty to perform." She grinned.

The blessing consisted of Qarakh and Deverra drinking from the bride at the same time—one on either side of the woman's neck. Not only did Qarakh dislike drinking from the neck as a rule, the intimacy of performing the ritual with the Telyav was... disquieting.

He took her hand—only because he knew the villagers

would expect it—and stood. "You are enjoying this entirely too much."

She grinned even wider. "Come, let us—"

Before she could finish, one of the lower-ranking Cainites standing watch at the edge of the camp shouted, "A rider approaches from the west!"

Qarakh swore. If the thrice-damned mortals hadn't been making so much noise, he would have heard the rider himself long before now. He turned to the Goth. "Arnulf?"

The warrior stood and inhaled deeply through his nostrils, eyes closed that he might better concentrate. When he exhaled, he opened his eyes and said, "Wilhelmina."

Qarakh started to relax, but then Grandfather said, "And she's brought us a present."

Chapter Four

Wilhelmina rode into camp on the back of an ebon gelding, a chestnut mare trotting alongside. The Norsewoman held the reins of the second horse, and sitting in the saddle, hands bound by strips of leather and tied to the pommel, was a male Cainite.

She brought the horses to a halt and dismounted with a graceful leap from the saddle, her feet making no sound as they touched the ground. She was taller than most men and thin as a willow twig, but her slim form belied her true strength—a perception she had used to her advantage many times in battle. She wore an iron helmet of Viking design, with a mask to protect her eyes and nose, and metal flaps to shield her neck. The only armor she wore was a padded leather jerkin, and she carried a sword belted around her waist. Though she was a woman, she wore trousers and boots like a man. To Cainites, the distinction between the sexes wasn't always as clear-cut as it was for mortals, and it meant little to Qarakh. He didn't care what warriors had between their legs; all that concerned him was whether they could fight. And Wilhelmina was savage as a Mongolian tiger in battle.

She removed her helmet and tucked it under her arm. "My khan, I bring you a gift." Her voice was devoid of emotion and cold as a blast of northern wind. Her blonde hair fell to her shoulders, and the lines of her narrow face were sharp as a knife blade. Her blue eyes were so bright they seemed to glow with frozen flame.

Qarakh walked over to Wilhelmina and her captive. Deverra, Alessandro, Grandfather and Arnulf followed behind. That the prisoner was a Cainite was obvious to any of the Damned who had eyes to see and a nose to smell. He was a handsome youth likely Embraced in his mid-twenties, with light brown hair and a neatly trimmed beard. He wore a mail vest beneath a tabard with a coat of arms emblazoned on it—a red shield with a white section at the top, on which two black ravens sat with folded wings. Qarakh didn't know what the arms stood for, and he didn't care; European heraldry meant nothing to him. The man was a knight of some sort, though probably not a Sword-Brother like those they'd fought last year.

"You do your tribe credit, Wilhelmina," Qarakh said, "and you honor me with your gift. What is his crime?" The Mongol knew that the man had done something serious for Wilhelmina to capture him alive. The Viking maid usually didn't take prisoners—especially knights. Christian raiders had some years ago murdered the other members of Wilhelmina's war band by burning down their house. Upon learning of her band's destruction, she'd vowed to hunt down those responsible and slay them all—which she did, mortal and Cainite alike.

But she didn't stop there. She continued killing Christian knights and clergy, blaming their church for her people's deaths. She'd come to pagan Livonia and joined Qarakh's tribe because she believed they would stand against the Christian scourge, perhaps even grow to wipe it from the face of the earth. Qarakh wasn't certain how realistic a goal that was but had no intention of disabusing her of the notion. Even a Cainite needed her dreams, dark as they might be.

Wilhelmina looked at her captive as if he were a particularly loathsome species of worm. "Poaching, my khan."

Hackles rose and patches of fur sprung up on the backs of the Mongol's hands.

Slay him! shrieked the Beast. *Tear his throat out!*

Qarakh felt the change coming over him, and he fought to resist it. Soon, he promised the Beast. For an instant, he thought he would fail to hold back the transformation, but then the fur subsided into the flesh of his hands, and he had control once again—for the moment.

"What is your name?" he asked the prisoner.

The man affected a haughty air and answered in a language Qarakh did not understand.

"He speaks French," Grandfather said in the Livonian the tribe had adopted. "He is Sir Marques de Saignon, vassal of Alexander of Paris. He demands you release him at once." The lore-keeper did not stifle his mocking tone.

Qarakh smiled just slightly and turned to Wilhelmina.

"Two nights past, I encountered this one, two other Cainites and six ghouls near the western village of Burian," she said. "All were on horseback, and all wore mail and carried swords."

Qarakh looked at the Viking's horse and saw that the prisoner's weapon was lashed to her saddle. He returned his gaze to Wilhelmina as she continued.

"I was patrolling the western marches of our territory, investigating reports of trespassers in the area. As I rode past a small farmhouse, I saw a number of horses outside, several untethered. I knew then that they were ghouls ordered by their masters to remain put until they returned. I dismounted, drew my sword and stepped inside. There I saw the knights gorging themselves on mortal blood while the human ghouls stood to the side, looking on with hungry eyes. The farmer, his wife and their five children were all dead, their corpses dry and brittle as old wood."

Qarakh looked to the prisoner. Marques appeared suddenly pale, even for a Cainite. Ruby beads of blood-sweat had broken out on his forehead.

Wilhelmina went on. "I immediately attacked, and since I had the advantage of surprise, I was able to slay one of the Cainites and all of the ghouls without difficulty. This one"— she nodded at her captive—"I was only able to wound before the remaining knight, who was much more experienced and skilled than his companions, drew his weapon and engaged me in battle. I fought my best, but I am shamed to admit that he escaped me and fled on his steed. I debated whether to give chase, but in the end I decided to take the wounded Cainite prisoner and bring him here so that we might question him."

"There is no need for shame," Qarakh said. "Nine against one is poor odds; you acquitted yourself well."

"Three against one," Wilhelmina corrected. "The ghouls hardly count."

This time Qarakh did smile. "Nevertheless, I am pleased."

"After I disarmed and bound this one, I set the farmhouse aflame, both to release the family's souls to whatever afterlife awaited them and to conceal how they had truly met their fate. I did not wish the villagers in Burian to think we had begun to kill mortals for sport."

Qarakh nodded. "Another wise move." He gestured toward the bound knight. "Did he say anything of note on the way back to camp?"

"He prattled on in his bastard tongue," she said. "At one point he tried to offer me his purse, I think."

Qarakh burst out laughing, as did Arnulf and Grandfather. Marques looked like a little boy who didn't understand why the adults found him so amusing.

"Translate my words, lore-keeper." The khan turned once more to the captive knight. "You are a fool, Christian, damned by your own hungers. We do not care if a Cainite who travels through our lands feeds while here, but it is forbidden for any-one not of our tribe to kill a mortal."

He turned his back and waited until Grandfather had fin-ished translating. He then raised his voice so that all in the camp—Cainite, ghoul, thrall and villager alike—could hear him. "This man is guilty of participating in the slaughter of an entire family in the west! What should be done with him?"

The villagers looked at each other, uncertain how or even if they should respond. The ghouls and thralls were likewise unsure, but one of the lower-ranking Cainites—Rikard, in fact—shouted, "He must be punished!" His voice was hoarse, but his words were clear enough.

Other Cainites took up the refrain then, chanting, "Punish him, punish him, punish him!"

Deverra leaned close and whispered in his ear. "What are you doing? We need to question him and find out why Alexander has come to Livonia!"

"Don't worry, priestess. I will learn the answers we seek, but the mortals need to see us take a firm hand in this matter. The herd must know that the shepherd protects them." And that was true enough, but there was another, deeper reason for what Qarakh intended to do, even if he couldn't fully admit it to himself: His Beast had been put off long enough.

He turned to Wilhelmina. "Free his hands."

The warrior-maid hesitated for a second, as if she might question her khan's command, but then she drew a dagger from her belt, stepped closer to the mare and began sawing at the leather binding Marques's hands. Within moments, he was rubbing his wrists and looking at Qarakh quizzically, as if he didn't quite know if this turn of events was to his benefit.

The Mongol once more spoke to the knight. "Start riding."

Grandfather translated and when the knight stammered out an answer, spoke to Qarakh. "He says he doesn't understand. Perhaps my French is not up to his standards."

It was Alessandro's turn to speak up. "My khan, I do not know what you have planned, but I beg you to reconsider. If there is even the slightest chance that he might escape—"

"There isn't," Qarakh said gruffly, his voice thickening, growing bestial.

"But if he returns to his lord, he'll be able to tell him the exact location of our camp!" the Iberian persisted. "At the very least we'll have to take down the *gers* and move our camp. I respectfully suggest that we should—"

Alessandro grew silent as Grandfather placed a hand on his shoulder.

"Do not provoke him," the ancient said softly. "He heeds the call of his Beast."

Qarakh heard the two talking about him as if he weren't present, but he didn't care. The world had narrowed to a tunnel at the end of which was Marques and only Marques.

"Ride." The word was barely recognizable as speech. "Ride as if the Devil himself is nipping at your heels." Qarakh smiled, showing teeth grown wolfish. "Because he will be."

The Ventrue knight looked as if he might faint. He understood the khan's intent well enough, it seemed. He grabbed the mare's reins and gave them a yank. The horse turned about and the knight dug his heels into her sides and shouted, "Eeyah!"

With a startled whinny, the mare galloped away at full speed.

Qarakh's body shifted, twisted and reformed until the last semblance of humanity was gone. In his place stood a large slavering gray wolf. The animal let forth a howl and sprang forward.

The hunt was on.

Alessandro watched with mixed feelings as his khan melted into the night. The Iberian had dedicated his unlife to understanding the Beast, had spent decades collecting every myth and legend he could find that might provide insight into how best to handle the undying hunger that dwelt within the heart of every Cainite. He understood why Qarakh needed to deal with the knight in this fashion, and he had to admit that there was a certain benefit in extracting justice in front of the assembled mortals—especially by performing the "miracle" of shape-changing. Still, from a military standpoint, he feared this hunt was a mistake. The khan wouldn't be able to restrain his Beast long enough to question the knight before slaying him, and then whatever information they might have gained from the man would die with him.

Not for the first time, the Iberian wondered at the wisdom of attempting to forge a tribe comprised of those who listened to their bestial natures. Those who traveled that road were most often solitary wanderers, and when they did come together, their raging tempers made certain they didn't remain so for long. Civilization was anathema to them, and what was Qarakh's tribe if not an attempt at feral civilization? And yet, there was much to recommend the tribe. Qarakh had based it on the hunter-herder-nomad model of his homeland. Hunters were free to roam as they saw fit, but the camp and tribal territory gave them a home to return to when they wished. Those who remained in the camp traveled from village to village throughout the region, much as the khan said Mongolian herders followed their animals from one grazing place to another.

Our Beast is unlike a true animal, Qarakh had once said. *An animal follows its instincts, lives by certain patterns of behavior. Not so the Beast. The only boundaries on its hunger and rage are those that an individual Cainite can impose. But the tribe—and the rules we live by—provide a tether for the Beast: one long enough to permit freedom, but not so long as to allow it to run completely wild. Mongols value a principle called* yostoi—*balance. Within my tribe, balance between Cainite and Beast is possible.*

Alessandro wanted to believe in Qarakh's dream of a feral tribe living in *yostoi,* and most nights he did. But this night, watching his khan lope away in the form of a wolf hungry for the kill, he wasn't so certain.

"Damn him," Arnulf growled. "Why should he have all the fun?"

Alessandro turned to the Goth, intending to explain why it was necessary for the khan to go after the Christian knight alone, but before he could speak, Arnulf's form wavered and then a second wolf, this one black and significantly larger than the one Qarakh had become, stood in the warrior's place.

With a yip at Alessandro, Arnulf took off in the direction the knight and Qarakh had gone. The Iberian turned to Deverra and Grandfather. The Telyav priestess seemed worried, but the lore-keeper just shrugged. Wilhelmina watched Arnulf speed away, looking as if she wished she could join the hunt too.

Alessandro sighed. So much for *yostoi.*

Rikard watched as the four remaining members of Qarakh's inner circle went their separate ways. The decrepit lore-keeper shuffled off toward his *ger,* moving as if he felt as old as he looked, and the Telyav witch walked away from the camp in the direction opposite that which Qarakh and the Goth barbarian had taken, shaking her head and muttering to herself. The Hound of Iberia (and what exactly was that sobriquet supposed to mean, anyway?) stood where he was a moment longer before heading over to speak with one of the Cainites standing guard at the edge of the camp. The Norsewoman summoned a ghoul to tend to her horse and then moved into the crowd of villagers to feed. Rikard wasn't quite sure what had just transpired between them—though he was certain it had something to do with the knight Wilhelmina had taken prisoner—and he didn't

really care. It just showed that Qarakh's all-important tribal rules
applied to everyone but the great khan himself. Alessandro—
who did the actual work of running the tribe while Qarakh was
off roving the devil only knew where—was forever drumming
the Tartar's precious rules into the recruits' heads.

Feed when you hunger, but kill only when necessary.

Show your enemies no mercy, but do not torment others needlessly.

He touched his throat. The blood of the girl he'd drained
had healed him (and by Caine, hadn't it been sweet as sin?), but
he could still feel the wound. At least he could speak above a
whisper now.

After Qarakh had cut his throat and shoved him out of the
tree, he'd lain insensate for a time. But he'd managed to wake
up and stagger back to the camp and into the *ger* he shared
with several other recent recruits just as the first rays of dawn
painted the eastern sky.

Do not torment others needlessly... kill only when necessary.
What rubbish! Qarakh had definitely tormented him last night,
and he'd nearly killed him as well. And for what? To teach him
a lesson? How *necessary* was that? And what about hunting this
Sir Marques? Was that torment necessary? His companions and
he had only been feeding. That's what mortals were for!

Being a night creature wasn't about rules. It was about freedom—the freedom to do whatever one wanted whenever one
wanted... and to whomever one wanted.

Rikard considered leaving the tribe that night. With everything going on—the feast, Wilhelmina's return, Qarakh and
Arnulf both off hunting the Frenchman—he could slip away
without anyone noticing. And even if they did notice, he could
always claim that he'd come down with a case of wanderlust.
Half the tribe wandered off like filthy nomads at the drop of a
hat anyway.

He had just about made up his mind to go (after draining
one more child, perhaps a boy this time) when he noticed one
of Qarakh's ghouls walking toward the khan's *ger*. (What was
the man's name? Sasha. That was it.) The ghoul heading to the
tent wasn't unusual—the Tartar actually allowed his ghouls
to share his sleeping space, a practice that Rikard found not

only distasteful but somewhat on the deviant side. What was unusual was the way the ghoul moved. Normally Sasha carried himself with a dignity that, in the ghoul's mind at least, befitted his station. But now he barely lifted his feet off the ground as he walked, and he kept his head hung low, almost as if he were in mourning.

As he watched the ghoul step into the tent, Rikard was at a loss to explain the man's demeanor, but when Sasha came back out of the tent carrying the body of Qarakh's other ghoul—a woman whose name Rikard couldn't remember—the Cainite grinned. The khan had once again broken the rule about killing without necessity. Sasha carried the woman away from the camp, and Rikard, intrigued, decided to postpone his leavetaking long enough to discover how the ghoul intended to dispose of the evidence of his khan's hypocrisy.

And perhaps, Rikard thought as he began to follow, stepping as silently as a stalking cat, *I might be able to pay back my almighty chieftain for giving me this little present.* He rubbed the nonexistent wound on his throat and thought black thoughts as he continued after Sasha.

"How can he be so foolish?"

He only follows his nature.

It was dark here—so dark that even with her night-born eyes Deverra had trouble seeing. There were good reasons this place was called the Grove of Shadows, but the scarcity of light was the least of them.

"His 'nature' might well end up causing the death of the entire tribe! Not to mention destroying everything I have worked so hard to create!"

Death comes to all things—even such creatures as you. I'm surprised you have forgotten this, since you serve the Protector of the Dead. The voice sounded at once chiding and amused.

The rebuke stung. Still, Deverra persisted. "But Alexander—"

Will come, the voice interrupted. *Whether the French knight survives to be questioned or not will make no difference. Even now, the one who escaped the Norsewoman rides toward his master's encampment to report what has befallen his comrades.*

Deverra, though not affected by cold the same way a mortal would be, nevertheless felt a chill run along her spine.

"And what will happen then?" she asked.

The voice was silent for a long moment before answering.

Death. What else is there?

Chapter Five

A sticky coating of blood-sweat covered Marques's skin and soaked the padding beneath his mail. He desperately wished he could stop the flow of vitae—he couldn't afford to lose any strength right now—but there was nothing he could do. He was too scared.

He'd given up simply swatting the mare on the rump to urge her on. Now, he pounded with his fist. She was a ghoul—not one of his, unfortunately, else he might've been able to get more speed out of her merely by willing it—and thus could take the blows more easily than a normal mount. But he was afraid that no matter how fast the horse ran, it would only be a matter of time before they both felt the teeth of their pursuers.

He wasn't sure how close they were. Sometimes their howls seemed to come from miles distant, other times from only a few yards away. There were at least two of them from the sound of it, perhaps more. He had a chilling thought then: what if the entire group of pagans had transformed into wolves and were hunting him as a pack, merely toying with him until their leader gave the command to move in for the kill?

He could well imagine what his liege-lord would say in response to that.

Get hold of yourself, Marques—unless you want your fear to do the savages' work for them!

If he hadn't been so terrified, Marques might have smiled. Fear was alien to Alexander—one of the many qualities Marques admired in his lord. Unfortunately, though Marques had sworn a blood oath to him and thus some small amount of Alexander's blood ran through his veins, fearlessness was not a quality that had carried over. It seemed he was afraid a good portion of the time, though he worked hard to conceal it by projecting a lordly air. He was afraid of not being able to find proper sustenance when he needed it. He was afraid of giving in to his Beast like some savage devil. But most of all, he was afraid of disappointing his lord—and of the punishment such disappointment would bring.

Another high-pitched howl echoed through the night, from somewhere off to his left.

Then again, he had other things to fear right now. Things with fur and claws and far too many teeth.

Marques was an experienced horseman, and riding at night was no problem for him, but he didn't know this land and was traveling too swiftly to note his surroundings. Besides, everything looked the same: tree after tree after tree, the pattern broken only by the occasional grassy plain or marshy expanse. He was well and truly lost, and even if by some stroke of good fortune he managed to evade his pursuers, come morning he would have difficulty finding shelter from the sun's deadly light. He didn't relish digging a sleeping place with his bare hands. He could accomplish the task well enough, but without help, it was difficult to—

He saw a gray blur out of the corner of his eye, and then a heavy form slammed into his side and knocked him off his mount. He crashed into the ground, and only the hardiness of his undead frame kept him from breaking any bones. He tried to rise, but the great gray wolf that had attacked him pinned him down. Its foam-flecked muzzle was only inches from his face, and its eyes burned with a bottomless hunger.

The mare continued galloping, whinnying in terror as she ran. Marques knew exactly how she felt, but he couldn't afford to allow his fear to control him, not if he wanted to survive the night. He grabbed the pagan chieftain by the throat—who else could it be?—with both hands and squeezed. If the wolf had been a mortal animal, he might've hoped to cut off its air, but this was a Cainite in wolfish skin. The best he could hope for was to snap its neck, and as strong as the Mongol was, even that would only slow him down. But during the few moments it would take him to heal, Marques could break a limb off a tree and jam the wood through the beast's heart. Despite mortal legends, such an injury would only paralyze a Cainite, not kill it, but that would be more than enough. With the Gangrel rendered helpless, Marques could make his escape and leave his enemy to the unforgiving rays of the morning sun.

The wolf growled in frustration as it attempted to break free of Marques's grip, but Marques was no weakling. His blood-filled muscles pressed ever harder. He forced the wolf's head back slowly, inch by torturous inch, until he felt vertebrae grind. But then the Mongol pushed back, jaws snapping, eager to find purchase on Christian flesh. Marques's arms began to tremble from the effort of holding the beast at bay. Marques was strong, yes, but not strong enough. He knew it would be mere moments before the wolf broke free from his grip and tore his throat out.

A shadow leaped forth from the darkness and struck the gray wolf in the side. The Mongol was knocked out of Marques's hands, and the impact sent both of them tumbling. When the knight stopped rolling, he quickly scuttled backward on all fours like a crab. There were two wolves now—one gray, one black—and they stood muzzle to muzzle, growling and snarling. They then began to slowly circle one another, gazes locked, animal eyes unblinking as each searched for an opening to attack.

Marques wasn't certain what was going on here—perhaps one of the Tartar's tribesmen had taken this opportunity to challenge his leader?—but he didn't really care. For whatever reason, Providence had granted him a chance to escape.

He got to his feet and started running.

The Gray's first instinct was to attack the newcomer for having the audacity to interfere with his hunt, but even though he was possessed by the fury of the Beast, he still retained enough sense of self to recognize the black wolf's scent.

Kill! shrieked the Beast that shared his soul. *Kill him now!*

The Gray wanted to—but he couldn't escape the niggling feeling that there was some reason he shouldn't. If only he could remember...

But before the memory could return to him, the Black charged. The Beast urged him to meet his attacker head on, but instead the Gray waited until the last instant then darted to the side, nipping the Black on the haunch as he passed—hard enough to hurt, but not hard enough to do any real damage.

No! protested the Beast. *Claw-bite-tear-rip-chew-swallow-bite again! Kill-kill-kill-kill-kill!*

The Black howled more in frustration than in pain, and spun around to attack again. But before he could complete the maneuver, the Gray lowered his head and butted him in the side, knocking him down. The Gray pressed his advantage by leaping atop the Black and fastening his dripping jaws on the other's throat.

Yes!

The Gray's teeth—all of them long and needle-sharp now, not just the canines—dimpled the flesh of the black wolf's neck. All it would take was a bit more pressure, and the skin would be pierced and sweet blood would gush into the Gray's mouth, splash hot and thick on his tongue, slide down his throat and into a belly that was a cold aching pit of endless need.

Do it!

And the Gray almost did. But his nostrils were full of the Black's scent, and a name drifted into his mind to accompany the smell: Arnulf. It was quickly followed by another name: Qarakh.

The Gray released the Black's neck and stepped back. The black wolf's body shimmered, blurred and reformed into that of a large black-bearded man with a scar running across one eye and a huge grin splitting his face.

"Good fight! For a moment there, I actually thought you were going to tear my throat out!"

The Gray vanished and in his place stood Qarakh. "For a moment, I was."

The Goth laughed. He rose to his feet and clapped the Mongol on the shoulder. "What do you say we finish this hunt together, eh?"

Qarakh was irritated at Arnulf for horning in on his hunt, but he understood the Goth's need to periodically test his leader. If he were in Arnulf's place, he would likely do the same.

Qarakh returned the warrior's grin. "If you can keep up."

Seconds later, two sleek wolfish forms bounded off into the night. Soon after, a Cainite named Marques screamed as he was torn apart by two sets of fang-filled mouths.

He didn't scream for very long.

Arnulf licked a smear of crimson from the back of his hand. "Not bad at all."

Qarakh looked away as the Goth warrior continued licking his hand like a cat cleaning itself, lest his Beast be roused again. "His master will not be so easy to fell, I think."

Arnulf lowered his hand and started working on the other, speaking between licks. "Let him come. Him and however many other weaklings he has with him."

Qarakh nodded to the grisly mutilated thing that had once been Marques. "We have no way of finding out anymore, do we?"

"So, will you tend to the ghoul now?" Arnulf asked.

For a moment, Qarakh wasn't certain what the Goth was talking about, but then he remembered Sasha.

"May I join you? It won't be much of a hunt compared to this," Arnulf said as he gestured at the ravaged remains of Marques. "But blood is blood."

Qarakh had been reconsidering killing Sasha, but now he knew that he had no choice. If he failed to slay the ghoul, he would lose face in Arnulf's eyes. As khan, it was vital that he maintain face at all times—especially when it came to a member of his tribe as powerful as the Goth. "Sasha has served me well. I would do him the honor of a swift death at the hands of his master alone."

Arnulf shrugged. "I shall see what other prey might be abroad this night." The Goth exchanged his human form for that of a wolf then melted into the darkness, off on the hunt once more.

Qarakh lingered a moment, looking at what was left of Marques and wondering how Alexander would react to the death of his vassal. Then he too became a wolf and loped off in the direction of the camp.

Sasha touched the flame to the pyre and stepped back. There had been little rain for the last few weeks, and the wood was dry and caught fire easily. He tossed the torch he'd used to set the pyre aflame at Pavla's feet then said a silent prayer to commend her spirit to Telyavel. The growing light from the blaze cast flickering, distorted shadows throughout the clearing, as if the shades of those who had already passed over to the realm of the dead had come to welcome a new soul into their midst.

The smell of burning flesh and hair turned his stomach. He thought that he might vomit, but he swallowed several times and managed not to. He was sure Pavla would forgive him if he did, but he didn't want to spoil her funeral rite, simple and inadequate though it might be.

The life of a mortal servant to the tribe wasn't always an easy one, and on some level he was happy that Pavla had found release. He supposed he had loved her, though it was difficult to say. It was true that they had lain together and had both found pleasure in it, but the act was nothing compared to simply being in the presence of their master, let alone taking in his holy blood. So though he felt sadness at Pavla's passing and anger at their master for taking her life, the emotions were muted and distant, almost as if they belonged to someone else who had only told Sasha about them. He wondered if he'd still feel them tomorrow night, or if he would remember feeling them at all.

Sasha was used to serving his lord at night, and though his senses were nowhere near as keen as those of the khan, he was suddenly aware of a presence in the clearing. At first he thought it might be the priestess Deverra, come to offer a benediction for Pavla. But when he turned, he saw that the newcomer was a male Cainite, one of the recent additions to the tribe.

He smiled at Sasha, though he eyed the burning pyre nervously and kept his distance from it. "It appears that your master has decided that one ghoul is sufficient for his needs."

Sasha didn't respond. Though he was subordinate to any Cainite tribesman, his master was the khan, and that gave him a certain amount of status. He didn't feel bound to answer.

The Cainite's smile turned sly and his eyes narrowed

dangerously. "Shall we see if he can make do without any at all?"

Before Sasha could react, the Cainite was upon him.

Qarakh stood before the smoldering remains of a crude funeral pyre upon which rested two burnt and blackened bodies. After leaving Arnulf, he had returned to the camp where he had picked up Sasha's scent and followed it here. True to his word, the ghoul had taken care of disposing Pavla's body, but it seemed he had also decided to dispose of his own in the bargain. Qarakh should have been pleased. If nothing else, Sasha had done his work for him, as a faithful servant should, but he felt ambivalent. These two had been his only human ghouls, and he had no childer. The bonds of such relationships were difficult for one with a nomad's heart, and they always seemed like cheap imitations of the true love-bond he had with Aajav, one that had started in life as blood brothers and carried over through the half life of drinking Aajav's blood and then into his Embrace. He should have been relieved to be free of such ties, but for some reason he wasn't. Could Sasha have truly cared for Pavla so much that he refused to live without her? Could those servants have shared something as strong as his bond with Aajav?

It was all too confusing. He needed to clear his mind and regain his focus before setting out to parley with Alexander, and there was only one person who could help him do that.

He took wolf form and bounded away, leaving the clearing and the earthly remains of two mortals who had meant more to him than they should have.

As soon as Qarakh was gone, Rikard stepped out from behind the tree where he had been hiding. He had been afraid the Mongol would smell him, but it seemed the stink of burnt flesh had concealed his scent.

Before slaying Qarakh's ghoul, Rikard had *persuaded* the mortal to tell what he'd learned during the Mongol's war council. Servants often overheard more than their masters thought, and the ghoul had been no exception. And thus Rikard had learned a most interesting tidbit of information: Alexander of Paris had come to Livonia.

When he had finished questioning the ghoul—who had little more to add—Rikard drained the mortal dry, then tossed him onto the pyre and remained to watch him burn (from a safe distance, of course). He had still been watching when Qarakh drew near wearing the body of a wolf. While Rikard possessed no such shape-shifting abilities himself, his Cainite hearing was more than sharp enough to detect Qarakh's approach (when he paid attention, that is), and he'd manage to vacate the clearing and make it to the trees in time to hide himself before the khan's arrival. He had watched Qarakh standing before the pyre, face impassive, expression unreadable as always, before the chieftain returned to his animal form and departed.

Rikard was disappointed, though he couldn't say exactly why. He'd known better than to expect any great show of grief from Qarakh over the loss of his ghoul. Killing the kine had been a small act of petty revenge, and Rikard had known it. Still, now that he'd seen how little impact the mortal's death had had on Qarakh, Rikard was filled with a desire to strike back against the Tartar in a way that would, if not destroy him, at least harm him significantly.

He touched his throat before following after Qarakh.

Chapter Six

A cross fields of grass stirred by restless night winds, through stands of trees where shadows danced with darkness, Qarakh ran until he reached a small hill encircled by oak saplings. Deverra had planted the trees herself—as she and her fellow Telyavs had at many sites across Livonia—with the intention that they would one day become a holy grove. But that day was decades in the future, and Qarakh hadn't come here with worship on his mind. He'd come to visit an old friend.

He slowed as he neared the hill and once again took human form. As he walked toward the ring of trees, two wolves that had been lying at the bottom of the hill rose to their feet and trotted to intercept him, warning growls rumbling in their throats. Qarakh was downwind of the wolves, and he knew they couldn't smell him yet, so he spoke to let them know who he was. "It is good to see you again, my friends."

The growls became joyful whines as the wolves bounded forward, eager to greet their master. Qarakh raised his right hand to his mouth and bit through the veins on the back, just below the knuckles. He lowered his hand, and the two ghouls who guarded the resting place of his blood brother lapped up as much vitae at they could before the wound healed.

When he had finished feeding the wolves, Qarakh scratched them behind the ears, first the male, then the female. From her scent, he knew that the female was gravid with pups. Once they were born he would have to destroy them; he couldn't afford to have one of Aajav's guardians become distracted by the needs of younglings.

"And how is Aajav tonight? Has my brother and sire been behaving himself?"

The wolves' only response was to wag their tails, but then they would have done so no matter what Qarakh said. He continued toward the hill, the wolves padding alongside. When he reached the base of the hill, he ordered them to stay. The wolves whined in protest, but they did as their master commanded, circling three times before lying down, heads on paws, tails tucked beneath them.

Qarakh climbed to the top of the hill, then sat cross-legged, hands on his knees, facing the south. As always when he came here, he was struck by how peaceful a location this was: trees all around, but none so close or so tall as to block the view of the night sky, and less than a quarter of a mile away was a small stream. Water was sacred to Mongols—streams, rivers, lakes and oceans were passageways for spirits traveling between the worlds. All together, it made for an appropriate place for his brother.

"I hope you are well, Aajav. It was been too long since we last spoke, and much has happened." Precisely how long it had been, Qarakh wasn't certain. The Mongolian people didn't keep track of time the same way Europeans did, and the passage of the days, weeks, months and years had meant even less to him since his Embrace. "I have seen many things in my travels, and I am eager to tell you of them, but first I must speak of the tribe and of a prince named Alexander."

He told Aajav of all that had happened since his return to the tribe—Deverra's warning, Marques's capture and execution, and his inner circle's speculations on Alexander's motives for coming to Livonia. He also spoke of Rikard's negligence during sentry duty and the bloody lesson it had earned him.

"In many ways, it is Rikard who concerns me most. Not merely him, but what his level of preparedness and dedication tells me about the readiness of the tribe to engage in battle. Alessandro, Arnulf and Wilhelmina are all skilled warriors, and though Deverra is a shaman, her mystic powers would be an asset in a fight. Grandfather likes to present the appearance of an aged elder, but that is only a mask: His experience and cunning make him a most deadly opponent. But the majority of the tribe is made up of ghouls and thralls, and the other night-walkers are mostly untested—and many of them are wanderers who aren't currently in range of the camp. None were trained warriors before joining the tribe, and while Alessandro has done well teaching them, they still have much to learn. Should Alexander attack the campsite, I fear that we will be unable to defend ourselves against him."

He paused, as if giving Aajav an opportunity to answer, though he knew his brother-cum-sire could not. Aajav lay interred in the hill's soil, swaddled in darkness, deep in the torpid slumber caused by terrible wounds. He'd slumbered for years now, and according to Deverra, he might well remain in that deathlike state for decades longer—or more. Many times had the shaman attempted to use her magic to revive Aajav, but so far with little success. Still, her spells had managed to accomplish one thing....

Qarakh put his fingers into his mouth and bit down to the bone. He then pushed his fingers into the ground directly above where Aajav lay and allowed his blood to soak into earth that had been infused with Telyavic enchantments. He closed his eyes and concentrated, as Deverra had taught him, and reached out with his mind.

Aajav?

At first he felt nothing, and he began to fear that Deverra's spell had finally run its course, but then the first tentative tendrils of thought extended toward him, and he knew that the priestess's magic remained as potent as ever.

Though he didn't need to breathe, he nevertheless let out a sigh of relief and waited for whatever message Aajav might have for him.

The night presented a dizzying array of sights, sounds and scents more intoxicating than *qumis* could ever be. Qarakh—newly Embraced—thought he could spend eternity exploring this new world and never grow tired of it—especially if he could continue to explore it with his brother.

"What is wrong with you, Qarakh? You run as gracefully as

a mare about to give birth!" Aajav laughed as he put on a burst
of speed and flew across the plain, his feet barely touching the
ground.

Qarakh tried to concentrate on moving like Aajav, but his
legs felt heavy and clumsy, not much different than they had
when he was mortal. Aajav had told him numerous times that
he was yet an infant to this new life in darkness and should be
patient while he adjusted. But even after the strange apprenticeship of having been Aajav's ghoul, this new state—being a true
night-walker—was like being a baby again: learning how to
eat, how to sleep, how to use his newfound abilities. For a warrior such as Qarakh, who was used to being master of both his
body and his environment, the frustration was at times almost
intolerable.

But this realm of darkness he now inhabited had its compen-
sations. His senses had sharpened to an unimaginable degree—
sounds now had texture and taste. Smells had color and mass.
The wind whispered secrets from the dawn of time, and the soil
beneath his feet spoke of eternities yet to come.

And then, of course, there was the glory of the hunt, the
ecstasy of the kill, and the joy and wonder of blood. Ahead of
him by many yards, Aajav suddenly stopped. One instant he
was a blur of motion, the next he stood still as a rock. Qarakh
caught up with him a moment later, marveling at how he felt no
aftereffects of exertion: no panting breaths, no pounding pulse,
only a light sheen of blood-sweat on his forehead.

"What is wrong?" he asked his sire. "Do you grow tired of
playing chase?"

In reply, Aajav merely pointed, a grim expression on his
face. They stood at the edge of a depression in the plain not
quite large enough to be called a valley. At the bottom lay the
mutilated bodies of a half dozen horses, saddled for riding in
the Mongolian fashion. The stink of animal blood lay heavy in
the air, along with something richer that made Qarakh's mouth
water.

"Anda," Aajav said.

Qarakh saw them then, several desiccated bodies strewn
among the horseflesh. They looked like corpses left out in the

harsh steppe winter, even though it was well into spring. Dried and blackened, their skin stretched taut across bones with little hint of flesh beneath it. They were freshly slain night-walkers, their bodies withering away to dust but not yet eroded.

The smell is their blood, said a voice deep in Qarakh's unbeating heart. *It should be ours.*

Qarakh couldn't imagine who—or what—could have done such a thing to a party of Anda. They were also beings of darkness and lived in secret among the Mongolian tribes. While he was still new to the shadowy existence of night-walkers, Qarakh understood that even though he and Aajav were Mongolian, they were of a different clan from the Anda, a clan called Gangrel. He also knew that while the Anda tolerated Aajav—for he had been Embraced by a wandering Gangrel who had been impressed with his battle skill and the Anda did not blame him for it—they did not fully accept him either. As far as they were concerned, he was not Anda and never would be. The Anda maintained strict control over who was Embraced on the steppe, and when Aajav sought permission to make Qarakh his childe, the Anda had denied him. So Aajav, being Aajav, had done it anyway. The Anda were unaware of Qarakh's existence, and if they learned of it, they would most likely condemn them both to the Final Death.

"We should go, and quickly," Aajav said. Qarakh was surprised to detect a note of fear in his sire's voice. He had known Aajav since they were children, and he had never seen his blood brother display fear toward any man or beast before.

"What is wrong?"

Aajav replied in a hushed tone. "They have been slain by one of the Ten Thousand Demons." He sniffed. "And not that long ago. We must flee before—"

The air next to Aajav rippled like water, and where there had been nothing a moment before, now stood a horse and rider. The rider's features were those of a man from the other side of the Great Wall, nothing demonic about him at all, save that his ears tapered to slight points, and the hairs of his neatly trimmed beard writhed slowly as if they were tiny black serpents. He wore the armor of an eastern warrior, comprised of many interlocking scales that hung down to his knees like a woman's skirt. A horse's mane adorned his helmet, and his armor blazed with reds, oranges and yellows. The warrior's horse was black, but not, Qarakh realized, because the animal had an ebon coat; the creature seemed to be formed from living shadow.

The demon made no move to attack. Indeed, he didn't appear to possess any weapons: no sword, no dagger. He merely sat astride his strange mount—no reins and no saddle either, Qarakh noted—and regarded them impassively.

Aajav interposed himself between the demon and Qarakh. "Back away slowly, my brother. You are still too young in darkness to stand against such a being."

Part of Qarakh was grateful for Aajav's protection, but another part was furious. Not only was Qarakh a warrior born and bred, he was also a dark and terrible master of the night. What had he to fear from a supposed demon that didn't even carry a sword?

This demon slew an entire party of Anda, he reminded himself.

But then the voice inside him spoke again, this time tinged with fury. This, Qarakh realized, was the Beast in his heart. *The Anda were weak; you are strong. Attack and kill!*

Qarakh tensed his muscles and bared his teeth, prepared to spring at this so-called demon, but before he could make a move, the eastern warrior raised his hands and grinned, displaying his own set of fangs. Talons of white bone pierced the flesh of the demon's fingers, lengthening and growing sharper until each was as long as a short sword. Qarakh suddenly understood why the demon (and he now had no trouble at all believing this creature was indeed one) didn't carry weapons of steel. He didn't need them.

The demon sprang from the shadow mount's back and landed on the ground without making a sound. He turned toward the horse, opened his mouth, and took in a deep breath. The ebon substance of the steed broke apart like black fog, and the demon drew the dark wisps into his lungs. Within seconds, the horse was gone, completely assimilated by its master. The demon was larger now, nearly half again the size he had been, as if he had added his mount's strength and mass to his own. His armor had stretched somewhat to accommodate his new form, though it was still constricting.

The demon turned back to face them and then, faster than even Qarakh's undead eyes could follow, plunged the bone claws of his right hand into Aajav's belly. Aajav cried out in pain as the demon, grinning the entire time, lifted him into the air. Black blood gushed from Aajav's belly, but it didn't splash onto the ground. Instead the blood was absorbed directly into the demon's skin, the pores on his hand opening like tiny mouths and drinking greedily. Whatever else this demon was, Qarakh knew that it subsisted on the life fluid of others, just as they did.

Qarakh then forgot that this thing was a demon, forgot that he was, according to Aajav, too young to battle it. All he knew was that the man who was both his bonded brother and his sire in darkness was in agony and losing blood fast. Qarakh rushed around to the demon's side, grabbed the creature's arm with both hands and pulled, hoping to dislodge Aajav from the talons that held him above the ground. But no matter how much strength he put into the effort, Qarakh was unable to budge the demon's arm. In fact, the demon didn't appear to even notice his presence. The fiend was staring intently at Aajav's too-pale face, determined to not miss a single moment of his destruction.

Qarakh released the demon's arm and stepped back. If he couldn't best the monster with strength, he'd try steel. He drew his saber, gripped it with both hands, and swung it at the demon's arm with all his might. The blade sliced through the fiend's flesh and struck bone with an impact so jarring that Qarakh wouldn't have been surprised if the sword had snapped in two. The saber didn't break, but neither did it have much effect on the demon. No blood ran from the injury Qarakh had inflicted, and if the creature was in any pain, he didn't show it. He did, however, turn away from watching Aajav wither and looked at Qarakh with narrowed eyes.

Qarakh attempted to yank his saber free, but it was stuck fast, as if the demon were somehow holding onto the blade with the bone itself. Qarakh swore and released the handle of his weapon and ran to grab hold of Aajav's legs. If the thrice-damned demon wouldn't release his blood brother, then Qarakh would just have to pull him free.

Aajav screamed as Qarakh tugged, and he slipped off the demon's talons with a shower of blood. Both Qarakh and Aajav tumbled backward, and Qarakh made sure to cushion his brother's fall with his own body. Now that Aajav was no longer in contact with the demon, there was a chance his injuries might heal—if Qarakh could keep the demon away from him.

He shoved Aajav to the side, mentally apologizing for being so rough, and leaped to his feet. The demon was looking with amusement at the saber still lodged in his arm. He reached up with his other hand and pulled the sword free. As his wound healed, the demon turned the blade first one way, then the other, as if examining the craftsmanship that went into making it. He then drew his arm back and hurled the saber into the distance. Qarakh didn't bother to see where it landed—it was clearly too far away to do him any good now.

The demon then turned to face Qarakh and grinned so wide that the corners of his mouth split open. His teeth grew longer, wider, thicker, skin peeling away from the mouth in all directions until it seemed to Qarakh there was nothing else left: no lips, cheeks, nose or eyes, just a gigantic tooth-filled maw.

It was then that Qarakh knew he and Aajav were going to die for the second and last time.

Not if you listen to me, said a guttural voice.

The demon came toward Qarakh, claws held at its sides, needle-sharp tips clacking together eagerly as it walked.

Very well, Qarakh thought. *What must I do?*

The voice answered with undisguised glee. *Take Aajav's saber and leave the rest to me.*

The demon was almost upon them now, and Qarakh thought he could see black things squirming behind its oversized teeth.

He didn't hesitate. He bent down next to Aajav, who lay motionless—unconscious or dead, Qarakh couldn't tell—and drew his brother's sword. He gripped it tight, straightened and waited for the voice that was his Beast to keep its promise.

Fury welled up inside Qarakh beyond anything he had ever known. It was as if a raging fire filled his being. No, it was as if he *were* fire… a vast inferno blazing higher and wider than the Great Wall itself, sweeping across the steppe and devouring everything in its path.

Qarakh lifted Aajav's saber, gave forth a bellow that sounded like the combined roars of a dozen Siberian tigers, and charged at the demon. He moved faster than ever before, fast even for one of his dark kind, and before the demon could do more than begin to raise its taloned hands to defend itself, Qarakh swung the saber in a vicious arc and sliced through the fiend's neck.

The demon's head sailed through the air, its maw shrinking as it flew. No blood bubbled up from the wound. In fact, all that was visible inside its neck was darkness, as if the demon were hollow inside. The head hit the ground and bounced once, twice, three times before finally coming to rest on its right ear. Qarakh expected the body to collapse now that it was bereft of a head, but it continued to stand, waiting patiently for whatever would happen next.

The fire that burned so strong and hot inside Qarakh dwindled quickly from an inferno to a mere campfire before extinguishing altogether. Qarakh ran his tongue over his teeth and found them sharper than before. The Beast had left its mark on him.

He started toward the demon's head, intending to destroy it, but before he had taken more than a few steps, the head opened its mouth and a long prehensile tongue snaked out. The tongue split into a fork at the tip, and then the head "stood up" and the tongue walked it back to the waiting body. The body knelt and picked up the head with its claws and gently set it atop the stump. Cut flesh fused together and the head was once more where it belonged. The tongue slithered back into the mouth, and the talons retracted into the fingers from which they'd grown. The demon, fully restored now, looked at Qarakh for a moment before nodding his head as if in a show of respect to a worthy adversary.

In the strange way of dreams of vision, Qarakh was suddenly aware of what should happen next—of what had occurred when this confrontation had actually occurred years ago. The fiend would lean over and vomit a gout of blackness onto the

ground. The inky mass would then rise up, coalesce and solid-
ify into the shape of a horse, and without another look at either
Qarakh or Aajav, the demon would mount the steed and ride off
toward the east. Qarakh would then see to Aajav, who despite
being in desperate need of blood, would refuse to take Qarakh's.
Qarakh would then carry his brother-cum-sire to the corpses of
the Anda and their steeds and help him drink the blood the
demon had left behind.

But none of that happened. Instead, after the demon reat-
tached its severed head, it spoke. And the voice that issued from
his mouth was a familiar one to Qarakh. It was the voice of the
Beast.

"That was the first time you truly gave yourself over to me,
and it saved both you and your beloved sire."

Qarakh experienced a wave of dizziness followed by a sensation of separation, as if his very self were being split down the
middle. One part of him was still the young Cainite who had
barely survived an encounter with one of the Ten Thousand
Demons, but another part was a decade older, khan of a tribe
of Cainites far away from his beloved steppe. The older Qarakh
now spoke face to face with his Beast.

"It was also the last time," he said. After the permanent
physical change that had taken place—the slight sharpening of
all his teeth—Qarakh had realized that giving in completely to
the Beast exacted a heavy toll, one that he was unwilling to pay.
Ever since that night on the steppe, he had worked to keep his
Beast placated so that he might live in *yostoi* with it, and for the
most part, he had succeeded. When fury came, he rode it like a
wild mare, shaping it to its own ends and never surrendering
outright.

The Beast smiled with the demon's mouth. "That does not
mean it will be the *only* time."

Qarakh was rapidly losing patience with the Beast. Though
the older part of him knew this was but a memory that had
given way to a dream-vision, his younger half worried about
tending to his wounded brother.

"I have no time for games," Qarakh said. "I have merely to
will my physical body to withdraw my hand from the earth,

and this spell will be broken. So if you have something to say to me, say it, and speak clearly, without riddles."

The demon's face scowled, but the Beast did as Qarakh commanded. "Before this is all over, you will need me, Qarakh. And when that moment comes, you shall be mine. Forever."

Qarakh didn't have to ask what the Beast meant. "Perhaps I will need to make use of you again, but hear this: I am Qarakh, known to some as the Untamed. No man—or Beast—shall ever be my master."

The demon's mouth laughed and its arm gestured toward the depression where the slaughtered Anda vampires lay. "That is the ultimate fate of those who are foolish enough to believe that they can resist me. My way isn't about *yostoi*; it's about submission, about giving yourself to me completely—mind, body and spirit—so that we can become one."

Qarakh shook his head. "No, that way lies nothing but madness and soul-death."

The demon's mouth stretched into a skin-tearing grin. "Doesn't it sound glorious? But enough talk." The Beast raised the demon's left hand and once more bone talons sprang forth from the creature's fingertips. "It's time I paid you back for decapitating me. A head for a head."

As the demon made ready to strike, the younger half of Qarakh mentally protested. *It was the demon whose head I cut off, not yours!* But the older half knew there was no point in arguing with the Beast. As the talons streaked toward him, Qarakh closed his eyes and willed his physical body to withdraw his hand from the earthen mound...

... and he opened his eyes.

He yanked his fingers free of the earth as if they'd been bitten. He knew that if he'd still been mortal, his heart would have been pounding as if he had suffered through a nightmare. He supposed in a way he had.

He glanced toward the eastern horizon, and though no human eye could've detected it yet, he saw the first faint hint of the approaching dawn. It would still be an hour or so before the light became strong enough to be dangerous, more than enough time for him to assume wolf form and return to his *ger*. If necessary, he could always inter himself within the ground he stood upon when the sun began to rise. He could even sink into the mound and spend the day with Aajav if he wished, though after the vision he had just experienced, he was uncomfortable with the notion.

He continued to sit cross-legged atop the mound and pondered what the vision might mean. He was certain that it meant *something*; all visions held meaning. The trick was interpreting them. Qarakh's vision had begun as a memory of the night Aajav and he had faced the eastern demon on the steppe, and it had ended with what sounded like a threat from the Beast that dwelt inside him.

His Beast had never spoken of such things before. Ordinarily it confined itself to urging Qarakh to give free reign to his fury and to kill without restraint. Qarakh had no idea whether any other Cainites experienced their Beasts as voices in their heads. Grandfather and Alessandro were both scholars of a sort in such things, but as khan, Qarakh felt he could not confide in them. The details of his own struggles were for him alone to know. But why had the Beast chosen to intrude on that particular memory?

Perhaps it hadn't been the Beast that had selected the memory but rather Aajav—and the Beast had insinuated itself in his message. But what could Aajav have been trying to tell him? Why had he chosen that memory above all others?

Perhaps because it had been Qarakh's first time going into battle as a Cainite, and not merely any battle, but one against a foe far more powerful than he. Was Aajav trying to encourage him, to tell him that he had no need to fear Alexander, for he had fought powerful foes before and not only survived but prevailed? True, Qarakh hadn't killed the demon—if such a thing was even possible—but he had kept it from claiming Aajav's life, which surely counted as a victory.

Yes, he decided. That must be it. Aajav had sent him a message to bolster his confidence before he parleyed with the former Prince of Paris, and his Beast had taken advantage of the opportunity to taunt Qarakh in a way it had never done before. There was no more to it than that.

Feeling certain he had interpreted the vision correctly, Qarakh patted the earth in gratitude. "Sleep well, old friend. I shall return to visit you soon and tell you of my meeting with Alexander."

There was no reply, of course. There never was.

Nearly a quarter of a mile distant from the mound, behind a large oak tree that he had used as concealment, Rikard watched Qarakh bound off in wolf form toward the tribe's campsite. He then turned his attention to the two true wolves—ghouls, he guessed—that stood watch over the mound. Once their master had gone, they circled three times and settled down again, heads resting on paws, eyes closed.

Rickard didn't know which dark deity to thank for helping him spy on Qarakh without being detected, but he was most definitely grateful. He had no special Cainite disciplines to draw on to conceal himself, merely stealth and slyness, but they had been sufficient this night.

After the Mongol had left the burnt-out funeral pyre (and the equally burnt bodies of his two human ghouls), Rikard had followed as best he could, but it had been difficult to keep up with Qarakh's wolfish form, to say the least. He'd almost lost the chieftain several times, but he persisted and eventually caught up to him. By the time Rikard had arrived, Qarakh had already reached the mound and was sitting on it cross-legged, eyes closed, as if in the grip of some sort of trance, one hand buried within the earth. Rikard had taken up a position behind the oak where he could see and hear well enough thanks to his heightened senses, which were sharp even by Cainite standards. He'd watched and waited. Not that there had been much to see: Qarakh had sat motionless for some time before finally opening his eyes and withdrawing his hand from the soil with a violent motion, as if he'd been startled by something, though by what, Rikard couldn't say.

He'd listened closely then, hoping Qarakh might give voice to his thoughts, but he said nothing, which had come as no great surprise. The Mongol was not exactly the talkative sort. But then, just before leaving, he said something—two simple sentences that told Rikard everything he needed to know:

"Sleep well, old friend. I shall return to visit you soon and tell you of my meeting with Alexander."

Rikard nearly laughed with delight upon hearing those words, but he managed to restrain himself. Good thing, too—he doubted he'd survive being discovered here.

There were rumors among the lower-ranking Cainites in Qarakh's tribe, rumors that Rikard felt certain were exaggerations at best and outright fabrications at worst. But there was one tale, a story of how Qarakh had first come to Livonia with his sire, another Mongol vampire named Aajav who had fallen into torpor for unknown reasons (at least, unknown to those who passed the tale back and forth) and could not be roused. No one knew for certain what had become of Aajav. Some said that Qarakh had taken him back to the steppe and buried him there, while others insisted that he lay sealed in some hidden monastery or castle deep in the Livonian wilds. But Rikard now knew the truth: Qarakh's sire was interred inside a mound surrounded by a ring of small trees and guarded by two wolves bound by their master's blood. The question remained, however, how he could use this knowledge to repay the bastard Mongol for cutting his throat and leaving him to roast in the sunlight.

He ran his fingers over his neck as he thought, and then it came to him. He had originally intended to leave the tribe tonight. Perhaps he would do so and go in search of a new master, one who might reward him most handsomely for the knowledge he possessed.

A master like Alexander of Paris.

Chapter Seven

Malachite approached Alexander's tent, but instead of announcing himself and asking permission to enter, he hesitated. It would be dawn soon. Perhaps it would be better if he waited to speak with Alexander until after nightfall. Malachite was just about to turn and depart, when a voice called from inside the tent.

"Unless you intend to stand there long enough to greet the morning sun, I suggest you come in."

Malachite hesitated a moment longer, but he couldn't come up with a plausible reason not to do as Alexander bade, and so he stepped inside. The exiled prince's tent—the largest in the camp, of course—contained a bed covered with silken sheets and a goose-down pillow, a highly polished desk and chair with ornate designs carved into the wood, and a large open trunk filled with leather-bound books and ancient yellowed scrolls. A hooded lamp sat upon the desk, its light too dim for mortal eyes to see by, but more than sufficient for Cainites.

Alexander sat at the desk, a map spread out before him. He didn't lift his gaze from it as Malachite walked in. As always, the aura of power that emanated from the slim and youthful-looking prince struck Malachite. The atmosphere around Alexander was charged with barely contained energy, like the air before a violent thunderstorm. Though he had been Embraced as a young man and appeared no more than fifteen or sixteen, in truth he was two millennia old. The steely set of his eyes hinted at his age, but in Alexander's case it was the way he moved— or rather *didn't* move—that revealed how truly ancient he was. There was no wasted motion, no idle tapping of fingers on the

desktop, no head movements as he examined the map, no shift-
ing about in his seat to find a more comfortable position. He
might have been a highly detailed piece of statuary for all the
animation he displayed, and Malachite wondered how long he
could remain sitting like that if it weren't for the necessities of
feeding and sleeping. Nights? Weeks? Perhaps longer?

Though they had remained in this location for two weeks
without incident, and a number of ghouls guarded the camp
while the Cainites rested during the day, Alexander was still
dressed for battle in mail armor and surcoat with his heraldry
emblazoned on the front: a vair, on a pale purpure, with a repre-
sentation of a golden laurel wreath. The background color was
white with repeating patterns of black spots that, if Malachite
remembered correctly, were intended to simulate ermine tails.
Running down the center of the shield was a broad vertical
purple stripe (the color of royalty, of course) and on the stripe
was a gold laurel wreath. Malachite, who had spent most of his
centuries of unlife in Constantinople, recognized the symbols
of imperial power and admitted, despite everything, that they
fit this boyish prince perfectly.

"What do you want, Malachite?" There was no irritation in
his voice, no feeling of any sort for that matter. Alexander displayed emotion only when he wished to. He continued to stare
at the map before him.

"May I ask what you are doing, milord?" Malachite asked.

Alexander's head swiveled on his neck as he turned to
look at Malachite, but the rest of his body remained statue still.
"Surely you haven't come here merely to satisfy idle curiosity."

"I have come for another reason, but my curiosity is never
idle, milord. We Nosferatu are archivists of a sort. To us, all
knowledge—no matter how seemingly insignificant—is power."
It hadn't been such in Constantinople. No, there Malachite
had status and respect and no need to hide in shadows and
trade scraps of rumor like his cousins in the West. But then,
Constantinople was now a relic of its past glory.

Alexander smiled. The effect, as always, was mesmerizing.
He was a handsome "youth" with curly black hair and deep
brown eyes: a dark Greek god cast in unliving flesh. Malachite

experienced an urge to avert his gaze, as if looking into Alexander's eyes was like staring at the sun itself. But he didn't look away, for he knew the prince would take that as a sign of weakness, and there was nothing Alexander of Paris despised as much as weakness.

"If I have learned one lesson in my long existence, my dear Malachite, it's that *power* is power." He looked at the Nosferatu for a moment longer, his expression unreadable, before finally turning back to his map. "If you must know, I'm looking at a map of Christendom and pondering the different ways it might be reshaped."

"In your image?" Malachite asked.

Alexander grinned. "Who else's?" He looked at the map for another moment before rolling it up and placing it in the trunk with his other documents. He closed the lid and turned to Malachite. "If you have something to say, Nosferatu, you'd best get to it. Dawn draws nigh."

Though Alexander had referred to Malachite by the name of his clan, there was no derision in his voice as there often was in the voices of other Cainites. The tainted vitae that ran through the veins of all Nosferatu twisted and distorted their forms, making them into hideous monsters and unliving lepers. Malachite knew that the disgust others displayed toward his clan was primarily because their physical appearance was the Mark of Caine made manifest, reminding them that, no matter what any individual Cainite looked like, all were damned. When around others—Cainites and mortals alike—Malachite usually kept the hood of his black robe up to conceal his features, or he used the gifts of his blood to take on a more pleasing seeming, but he didn't bother to do so in Alexander's presence. The ancient didn't care about Malachite's appearance one way or another. Malachite supposed the prince had seen worse sights in the last two thousand years.

"We have lingered here for the better part of a fortnight now," Malachite said.

Alexander didn't respond right away. He sat on the edge of his bed and gestured for Malachite to take the desk chair. The Nosferatu hesitated as he considered the proper etiquette for this situation. Should he take the seat that was offered or should he remain standing? Technically, he wasn't one of Alexander's sworn followers, though he certainly was not the prince's equal either. Malachite doubted that Alexander considered any creature, mortal or immortal, his equal. To him they were all either pawns to manipulate or obstacles to surmount.

The merest hint of a crease appeared in the skin between Alexander's eyebrows, and Malachite knew the prince was becoming irritated. Unsure which was the wisest course—but knowing that keeping the ancient waiting much longer surely wasn't it—he turned the desk chair around to face Alexander and sat down.

Alexander's delicate lips formed a small smile, and Malachite sensed he had just failed some sort of test.

"As you say, it has been two weeks since we made camp here, but I fail to see the significance of the fact. Don't tell me that you've grown restless, Malachite. For our kind, two weeks pass as swiftly as two hours do for mortals. Perhaps it's the... simplicity of our accommodations? The wilds of the Livonian countryside hardly provide the same comforts that you once knew in Constantinople, do they?"

Malachite knew Alexander was baiting him, but he still felt a surge of anger at the gibe. He felt the need to take a breath—not because his undead lungs craved air, but out of reflex remembered from a time when his body breathed deeply to calm itself. He managed to keep from inhaling, though. He'd already failed one of Alexander's tests. He didn't relish failing another.

"When you asked me to accompany you to Livonia, it was my understanding that I was to serve as your advisor." Malachite allowed himself a smile. "It is somewhat difficult to perform that duty when the one I am to advise does not share his thinking."

Alexander looked at him, not moving, not blinking. When he finally spoke, his tone was amused, though there was a coldness in his eyes. "As I recall, it was *you* who asked to accompany *me*." He held up a hand before Malachite could respond. "Your point is well taken. But there is a simple reason why I haven't told you more than I have: There is as yet nothing to tell."

Malachite frowned. "I'm afraid I don't understand."

Alexander's chuckle sounded almost human. "I'm being disingenuous. I should say rather that I am still in the process of gathering information. When I have acquired enough, I shall it mull it over, and then when I am ready, decide what my next move shall be."

"While I understand the need to perform a certain amount of reconnaissance, how much is truly necessary in this situation? We have come here at the behest of Lord Jürgen to subdue pagan Livonia which, from what little I have seen, is nothing more than an expanse of trees and grasslands broken only by the occasional human settlement." At least, that's why Alexander had come to this land. Malachite had a far different reason—one that he had no intention of sharing with the fallen prince.

At the mention of Jürgen's name, Alexander grimaced as if he'd just tasted disease-ridden blood. "I've come here for my own reasons, not to serve a petty German prince." He spoke the word *serve* as if it were an obscenity. "And subduing this land won't be as easy as you imply. We are here to deal with this Tartar chieftain Qarakh who seems to have established a Cainite tribe of sorts here. He defeated a band of Black Cross knights and Sword-Brothers last year. I must know more about the size and strength of the Tartar's tribe before I can effectively plan my strategy."

Malachite was unable to keep the frustration out of his voice. "I don't see the need for any elaborate plan of attack. It is my understanding that Tartars are like the Turks we Greeks faced in Anatolia: savage raiders, yes, but little more than wild men and nomads. They can't possibly match the skill and experience of your men. I would think—"

"But you are *not* thinking. That is the problem."

Malachite had survived a very long time as a Cainite, and he knew better than to judge his kind by their apparent age. Nevertheless, given Alexander's youthful appearance, Malachite couldn't escape the feeling that he was being reprimanded by a child. The anger and frustration that had been roiling within him now threatened to fuse into a blazing fury, and he knew his Beast was close to breaking the mental chains with which he kept it bound.

Evidently Alexander sensed it too, because Malachite felt waves of calm emanating from the former Prince of Paris. Cainites were always wary of the Beast rising in others, for it could provoke theirs to come to the fore as well. Alexander's personality and will were so strong that he could inspire emotions in others with relative ease, be it submission, courage or calm. It was one of the things that made him an effective leader.

Malachite felt his Beast recede into the back of his mind, where it would lair and wait, ever vigilant for the next opportunity to escape.

Alexander continued as if nothing had happened. "As you pointed out earlier, you understand the value of information. Why then should it seem strange to you that I am biding my time?"

"Because it is unlike a lord at the head of a force of knights," Malachite admitted, though he feared Alexander would be insulted. "I would expect you to march your forces straight into the enemy's territory and demand that he fight or surrender."

Alexander shook his head, the motion so slight that it was almost undetectable. "Ah, chivalry. God and the Devil save me from that foolishness."

Malachite winced at the blasphemy. Though he was one of the Damned, he nevertheless considered himself a Christian. Many Cainites believed their condition was a test—or punishment—delivered by God, while others thought their kind was created by Jehovah to shepherd humanity. Malachite believed both were true, and that the divine will had seen its culmination in a wondrous city where Cainites and mortals both could thrive, a lost dream called Constantinople. Malachite was determined to see that dream reborn—no matter the cost.

"In all honesty, I suppose I might very well do as you suggest once I've established the location of this Tartar's haven," Alexander said. "That is, if my ultimate goal were indeed conquest." He smiled then, as if enjoying a private joke.

Malachite thought for a moment upon the prince's words. "You are seeking allies."

Alexander's smile grew wider. "There are powerful Cainites who lair in these marches, Malachite. Qarakh is one of them in

Livonia, but there are Tzimisce *voivodes* who claim lands here as well, and others besides. If I can forge alliances with any or all of them…"

"You shall be in far better position to retake Paris," Malachite said softly, impressed by the prince's raw ambition. Jürgen—on whose behalf Alexander was technically leading this crusade—had warred with the Tzimisce of Hungary for several years. To hear Alexander talk openly of seeking alliance with them, it was clear he would never rest until he regained Paris, which he deemed to be rightfully his.

"Isn't that the way of our kind, to take the strength of others and add it to our own?" Alexander said.

"That is how we feed."

"No, that is how we exist."

Malachite didn't subscribe to such a bleak worldview, but he knew this wasn't the time to argue the finer points of philosophy with Alexander. "And what if you discover that someone doesn't wish to become your ally?"

Alexander shrugged. "Then I shall engage them in battle, defeat them, and the triumph shall add to my reputation, ultimately helping me regain my throne."

Malachite was in awe at the simple audacity of it. "And what if you have to fight them all—Qarakh's tribe and the *voivodes* both?"

"What if I do? I will take them on as they come—singularly or collectively—and I will destroy them." There was no pride in his voice, no boasting. He said it as if it were a simple statement of fact, no more remarkable than saying that the sun revolved around the Earth. *Or in his case*, Malachite thought, *around Alexander of Paris.*

"I apologize, milord," Malachite said.

Alexander frowned. "Whatever for?"

"For having the audacity to believe that I could ever advise you."

Alexander laughed with delight, and for an instant he seemed as youthful as his countenance. "Do not despair, my dear Malachite. The time will undoubtedly come when I shall have need of your counsel. Until then—"

Before Alexander could finish his thought, Brother Rudiger—a Cainite garbed in a mail hauberk and a tabard emblazoned with the black cross of the Teutonic Knights— entered the tent. While Alexander was the ultimate leader of his army, Brother Rudiger commanded the knights in the field. All of the knights were members of the Order of the Black Cross, a secretive brotherhood of Cainites and ghouls hidden within the mortal Teutonic Order and loyal to Lord Jürgen. As a means to gather influence, such orders within orders were not uncommon among Cainites, but Malachite had to admit that the Order of the Black Cross was among the most entrenched he had encountered. Jürgen seemed able to use the cover of the Teutonic Knights (and their allies, the Livonian Sword-Brothers) with unparalleled ease.

Much of this was due, Malachite thought, to the fact that the unliving Black Cross knights had much in common with their mortal counterparts and cat's-paws. They were true believers in the campaign to extend Christendom and fight the scourges of heresy and paganism, all for the glory of God. That they enlarged their order and lord's domains in the process, and that many living Christians would consider them devils, was sec- ondary to their crusading zeal.

Brother Rudiger, though of Ventrue blood like Alexander, could not have been more different from the exiled prince. Though he tried to conceal it, he loathed the secular-minded Alexander for his hypocrisy in using the Church for his own ends. Malachite had witnessed the two interact on a number of occasions, and while Rudiger always deferred to the prince and carried out his orders, the Nosferatu thought there might well come a time when he would refuse to do so. And then there would be trouble indeed.

"A rider draws near the camp," Rudiger said. The knight was of medium height, broad-shouldered and somewhat stocky. He had a round face with neatly trimmed brown hair and a beard to match. His mouth was set in a firm line, and Malachite had the impression that he was fighting to keep his lip from curling in distaste at being in Alexander's presence.

The prince's eyes glittered like shards of broken ice. For an instant, Malachite thought that he would spring off the bed and fall upon Rudiger for entering without being announced. If the Black Cross commander noticed Alexander's reaction, he gave no sign; he merely stood calmly and waited for a reply.

"Why do you disturb me with this news? Are your knights incapable of dealing with a lone rider?"

Rudiger's eyes narrowed, but his tone remained even. "Of course they are capable, but I thought you'd want to be informed of the rider's identity at once. It's Lord István—and he's alone."

Alexander was silent for a moment before responding. "Bring him to me as soon as he arrives."

"I shall do so." Rudiger withdrew. Malachite noticed that the knight had departed without speaking an honorific: no *Yes, your highness* or *At once, milord*. Definitely a sign of trouble to come.

Malachite started to rise, but Alexander gestured that he should remain seated. "Stay. I would have you hear what István has to say."

Malachite inclined his head. "As you wish, milord."

Their wait wasn't long. Within moments, they heard István ride up. Outside, Rudiger ordered a ghoul to tend to the Cainite's horse. Then Rudiger and István entered the prince's tent, the latter giving Malachite a quick look as if to say, *What are* you *doing here?* before bowing to his liege. He was a slender Magyar with black hair that fell to his shoulders and a neat black beard. He wore mail beneath a tabard that was ripped in several places and stained with dried blood. He hailed from yet another line of Ventrue but had sworn many an oath to Alexander. Malachite thought they'd bonded over a shared penchant for cruelty.

Rudiger, Malachite noted, did not bow. Nor did Alexander remark upon this.

István straightened and began speaking rapidly. "Your highness, I have returned from my reconnaissance mission with troubling news. I—"

All Alexander did was raise an index finger, but the gesture was enough to make István stop talking and close his mouth with an audible click. The prince turned to Rudiger. "You may leave us, Commander."

"I think it would be best if I—"

"It's not your place to think. Your place is to see that my orders are carried out on the battlefield. Do you understand?"

Rudiger looked at Alexander for a moment before bowing his head. "Yes, milord." The knight's voice was wire-taught with barely suppressed rage. He turned and walked out of the tent.

Alexander gave a small smile, clearly enjoying Rudiger's obvious displeasure at having to submit to the prince, before looking to István once more. "When you rode out of camp a week ago, you did so alongside several others. Or have you forgotten?"

István's eyes narrowed, and Malachite knew he was calculating how best to respond.

"Of course not, your highness! I merely—"

Another lift of an index finger, another click of a mouth closing.

"Tell me what happened, István." Alexander's voice was barely above a whisper, but the tone of command it held was undeniable. "Tell me clearly and concisely, *and* without exaggerating your own merits."

István seemed ready to protest this last comment, but then he nodded and began relating his tale, precisely in the manner his prince had commanded. When the knight was finished, he stood quietly, back straight and chin up to preserve his dignity, but his trembling hands spoiled the effect.

Alexander stood and István flinched, as if he expected his prince to strike him across the face—or worse. But Alexander, an inch or two shorter than his subject, merely looked up into István's eyes. "Did you *have* to slaughter the farmer and his entire family? The Tartar will take that as a personal insult."

István frowned in confusion. "I don't understand, my prince. They weren't members of Qarakh's tribe; they were only mortal pagans."

"The deaths of the kine mean nothing to that savage," Alexander said. "It's a matter of territory. We killed in his lands without his permission. Would you let others pick from your herd, István?"

"No, milord." It was clear from István's expression that he

still didn't comprehend how this had become his fault.

Alexander looked at István for a moment, as if he were trying to decide what to do with him. Malachite had the impression that the prince could just as easily dismiss him as tear off his head. In the end, Alexander chose the former.

"Dawn is near and you need rest after your ordeal."

Looking as if he couldn't believe his good fortune, István bowed low then withdrew from the tent without bothering to disguise his haste.

As soon as the knight was gone, Alexander said, "The entire party slain... and by a woman, no less." He shook his head in disgust.

"István survived," Malachite pointed out—not that he thought it any great compensation—"and from his story, it appears that Sir Marques did as well."

"It has been two full nights. If Sir Marques were able, he would've returned by now."

"István just returned. Perhaps Marques will too.

Marques is skilled, resourceful and truly loyal to me—far more so than István. I fear there are only two possibilities: He is being held captive by the savage, or he is truly and finally dead."

Malachite remained silent and waited to see what Alexander would say next. He was surprised when the Ventrue smiled.

"This is not the way I would have arranged events myself, but perhaps things shall work to our advantage in the end."

"Milord?"

"I had intended to approach the Tartar when the time was right, but now—thanks to Marques, István and the others— Qarakh will undoubtedly come to us. After all, that's what I would do if our positions were reversed."

"And if you were in his place, would you come to talk or to fight?" Malachite asked.

Alexander's smile became a outright grin. "All existence is a battle, my dear Malachite. The only difference is what weapons you choose to fight with: words or steel."

Now it was Malachite's turn to smile. "I believe you are actually looking forward to the Tartar's arrival."

"Oh, I am." A faraway look came into Alexander's eyes, and Malachite knew the prince was already busy plotting his strategy. "I am indeed."

Chapter Eight

"Do you really think this is wise, my khan? I beg you to allow Arnulf, Wilhelmina, and myself to accompany you."

"I ride alone as a sign of strength and confidence. Alexander will know that I—and by extension, my tribe—must be mighty indeed for me to face him on my own. As well, it shall be a clear signal that we do not intend to war with him. At least, not yet."

"Then permit us to follow at a distance, so that we will be close by should the need arise."

"Your desire to ride with me does you credit, Alessandro, but the Ventrue will undoubtedly have scouts that would know if you came too near his encampment, and he would take your presence as a sign of weakness on my part. I need you and the others to remain here, for I would not leave the tribe unprotected while I am away."

"Then there is nothing I can say that will make you change your mind and take someone with you?"

"Nothing."

"Lost in thought?"

Qarakh turned to Deverra. The priestess rode bareback upon a piebald mare, the reins held loosely in her hands. She didn't truly need them to control the steed and held them only because she didn't know what else to do.

"Merely riding," Qarakh lied. "On the steppe, the wind is often so loud that speaking is difficult, even when side by side. Because of this, my people tend to travel in silence, communicating only when necessary."

Deverra reached up with one hand, pulled back the hood of her robe and shook out her long red hair. "Is that a hint?"

Qarakh frowned as he tried to determine whether the Telyav was truly offended or merely toying with him—or perhaps a bit of both. "No, only an explanation."

The priestess didn't respond right away, and they continued westward across open grassland, the night sky above them clear and full of ice-bright stars. Qarakh rode the same dusky gray mare that had been so close to collapse only a night ago. Now, thanks to some rest and a few swallows of her master's vitae, she was ready and eager to travel once more.

He would've made better time traveling alone in wolf form, but Deverra did not possess the ability to alter her shape as he did, so he was forced to go on horseback. In the end, it would probably prove the best choice, anyway. These Christian Cainites rode among mortal knights and thought of themselves as noble-blooded, supposedly above low and animalistic creatures like Qarakh. Arriving as a wolf would have only reinforced this attitude in Alexander, and perhaps lessened Qarakh in his eyes. The Mongol cared not at all what the former Prince of Paris thought of him, but he was too shrewd to allow the man's prejudice to lessen his own bargaining power.

After a time, Deverra said, "I thought perhaps that your silence grew out of your displeasure."

Qarakh groaned inwardly. He wished for once that the woman would say exactly what she meant. "Of what displeasure do you speak?"

"You were not happy that I insisted on accompanying you."

"At first," he admitted. "But I have thought over your reasons." Deverra had argued that as the Telyavs' high priestess, not only was it her duty to represent her clan when Qarakh parlayed with Alexander, but that her presence would be a symbol of the strong alliance between Qarakh's tribe and the Telyavs.

Deverra smiled. "Are you saying I was right?"

A night breeze whispered through the grass around them. Maintaining a straight face, Qarakh said, "My apologies. I was unable to hear you because of the wind."

Deverra's laugh was loud, full of life and joy. The sound

stirred echoes of feeling that Qarakh thought had died with him the night Aajav had visited his *ger*. Qarakh realized that the priestess's laugh reminded him of what it had been like—no, what it had *felt* like—to be truly alive.

"You still call the Mongols your people," Deverra said. "But you are far away from those lands. Are we not your people now?"

Qarakh said nothing.

Holding onto the bridle of Aajav's horse, his blood brother slumped in the saddle beside him, an arrow in his neck and one between his shoulder blades, wounds swollen black with poison. Steppe ponies running hard, hooves striking the ground like rolling thunder, arrows whistling through the air around them, and riding in pursuit much closer than Qarakh would like, a half dozen Anda vampires, bows drawn, faces twisted into masks of hatred and death.

Qarakh scowled and forced the unbidden memory away. "Being a Mongol is more than riding on the steppe. It is… a way of thinking, of knowing one's place in the world at all times. Of—"

"Living in *yostoi*," Deverra finished.

Qarakh nodded. "Or at least attempting to do so. *Yostoi* is even more important for our kind. The Beast that dwells within us all can never completely be caged or controlled, but it can be kept in its place, if one knows how to give it what it needs instead of what it wants. By remaining true to the Mongol way, I find the clarity of mind and strength of spirit to live with my Beast instead of despite it."

"I see why Grandfather respects you so, Qarakh. There are many Cainites far older than you who do not know their Beasts half so well." Deverra smiled. "If you were a mortal youth, I might be tempted to say you were precocious."

"I am merely Mongolian. There is nothing special about me."

Deverra looked at him with a penetrating gaze that Qarakh couldn't quite read. "Oh, I think there is, Qarakh the Untamed, though you aren't aware of it. I believe that if the need for battle arises, you will not only be able to stand against Alexander, but also defeat him."

Qarakh chuckled. "I appreciate your confidence in me, priestess, but while I fear no man alive or undead, I would just as soon avoid having to fight a two-thousand-year-old warrior."

"Do you think—" Deverra broke off before she could finish her question. Her head whipped to the right and then she leaped from her horse. Lifting the hem of her robe so she might run more easily, she dashed off into the darkness.

Startled by her actions, Qarakh leaned over, grabbed the reins of her horse and brought both mounts to a halt. He quickly tied the piebald's reins to those of his gray, for though both horses were ghouls, he knew for certain that his horse would not budge from this spot unless he commanded it. He then dismounted, drew his saber and ran off after Deverra. He heard the sounds of a struggle followed by a high-pitched animal cry of pain, and then all was silent.

When he caught up to Deverra, he found the priestess crouched over the body of a stag, her face buried in the ragged wet ruin of its neck. Realizing what had occurred and that there was no danger, he sheathed his sword and watched her feed. He knew that he should turn and walk away so that Deverra could have privacy, but he was too fascinated. She gnawed the deer's flesh as she drank, shaking her head back and forth in the manner of a wolf. It was so unlike the priestess's usual calm and serene manner that he knew he was seeing her Beast at work.

After a time she looked up, saw him and frowned, as if she didn't quite recall who he was. Then recognition filled her gaze, and she lowered her eyes in shame.

"I wish you hadn't seen me like this." She drew the back of her hand across her mouth to wipe away the stag's blood, but there was so much that all she succeeded in doing was smearing it around. "I must use my own vitae in order to cast spells, and after working an enchantment to determine the location of Alexander's camp..."

"You need to restore what you have lost," Qarakh finished for her. "There is no shame in that."

"But to drink the blood of an animal..."

"The steppe is sparsely populated. A Cainite can go for days, sometimes weeks without seeing a single mortal. All of our kind who live there—including myself—have drunk from the veins of animals." He hesitated for a moment and then stepped forward and knelt on the other side of the stag, facing Deverra. They looked at each other for a time without speaking, and then as if reaching an unspoken agreement, they lowered their mouths to the deer's carcass and fed.

Qarakh wished that he could stop and lash Aajav more securely to his saddle, for with each strike of his pony's hoof, he was in danger of falling off his mount. Should that occur, the Anda would be upon them in moments, and Final Death would follow soon after.

He had no idea what manner of poison the Anda used to coat the tips of their arrows—demon blood, perhaps?—but whatever it was, it was potent. One strike had been enough to make Aajav lightheaded, and the second had rendered him nearly unconscious. Qarakh feared his blood brother would not survive a third strike.

Coward! Stand and fight!

Qarakh did his best to ignore the voice of his Beast, but it wasn't easy. It galled him to flee, but he didn't know what else he could do. If he hadn't needed to keep hold of the bridle of Aajav's horse, he could turn around and loose his own arrows at their pursuers, not that the shafts would do much good since the tips weren't smeared with poison. But at least he would be fighting instead of running.

There was little to mark the Anda horsemen as different from any other Mongols. Indeed, in mortal life each had belonged to one of the nomad tribes that wandered the plains. They carried sabers and bows, wore leather helmets and leather coats, and rode hardy steppe ponies. The only indication that they weren't human was the color of their skin: instead of a healthy dark brown, it was pale and washed-out. The color of death.

The Anda ruled the night world of the steppe, and they strictly regulated who could be Embraced and who could not. Aajav was not Anda, but they had accepted him after a fashion.

As he had lived as a Mongol, he had been allowed to survive and hunt among them, but never as an equal. Again and again, he had had to surrender territory and feeding rights to his supposed betters. The Anda permitted him to sit in on their councils, but he was not allowed to speak. Most of all, Aajav was not permitted to create any childer.

But Aajav had, and while he'd been able to keep Qarakh's transformation into one of the undead a secret for close to two years, the Anda had finally gotten wind of it and set a trap for them—a trap Aajav and Qarakh had fallen into far too easily. Now they were fleeing for their unlives.

They rode southward, and Qarakh glanced to his left, toward the east. The sky was a lighter shade of blue near the horizon, indicating that dawn wasn't far off. Should the sun begin to rise before the Anda had caught up to them, they would all seek shelter from its searing rays by interring themselves as well as their horses in the ground. They would slumber in the embrace of the earth until sunset when they would rise to resume the hunt once more. And if the Anda should rise before Qarakh and Aajav—or if Qarakh was unable to help his blood brother wake—the Anda would have them.

Qarakh knew he had to do something, and swiftly, but what?

They approached a small depression in the steppe, and Qarakh knew that they would be hidden from the Anda's view for a few precious seconds as Aajav and he rode down into it. The question was how to make those seconds count. And then it came to him. He would use the Anda's own trick against them. He had no idea if it would work, but he could see no other choice if his blood brother and he were to live to see another nightfall.

As they came to the top of the rise, Qarakh released his hold of the piebald's bridle and shouted, *"Tchoo! Tchoo!"* In response to the command, both ponies increased their speed, and Qarakh grabbed hold of Aajav's left arm and launched himself from the saddle, pulling his blood brother with him. As they fell backward, Qarakh—still holding tight to Aajav's arm—concentrated on becoming one with the earth. Instead of striking the ground, they slipped beneath it as easily and gently as if it were water.

When they were successfully interred, Qarakh released his grip on his blood brother's arm and listened for the Anda's approach. There were six of them, and he could feel the vibrations from their horses' hoofs judder through the soil as well as the substance of his interred body. The vibrations increased in intensity as the hunting party drew near, and when Qarakh judged they were close enough, he envisioned himself rising from the earth and drawing his saber.

He rose up beneath a sweat-slick horse belly, and before he was halfway out of the ground, he swung his saber in a sweeping arc. The blade sliced into the belly of one steed, then two, then three before the swing was completed. Flesh and muscle parted. Blood and loops of animal intestine spilled upon the steppe. The wounded ponies shrieked in agony. Their front legs buckled, and they stumbled forward.

Their riders fought to maintain control, but it was impossible. The three Anda went down with their mounts. The remaining riders continued on, not yet aware their companions had fallen.

Nostrils flaring at the scent of equine blood, Qarakh rose the rest of the way out of the earth and stepped forward. As the Anda struggled to get to their feet—two were pinned by their ponies and one was simply stunned—Qarakh swung his gore-slick saber three times, and three Anda heads rolled upon the ground. Vitae gushed from their neck stumps, and Qarakh's Beast screamed for him to drink before the sweet blood was wasted on the hard rocky soil of the steppe. But Qarakh resisted. There were still three more Anda to deal with.

As the surviving hunters turned their mounts around and headed back to attack their ambusher, Qarakh sheathed his sword and bent to pick up one of the decapitated Anda's bows. As was the Mongolian custom, the riders approached side by side, for only a defeated party rode in single file, and Qarakh had an excellent shot at each. He drew a poisoned arrow from a quiver, nocked it, took aim and let the shaft fly. The hunter on the right stiffened as a poisoned arrow pierced his eye and buried itself in his brain. Before the wounded hunter could fall out of his saddle, Qarakh had nocked another arrow and fired.

One more arrow, one more twang of a bowstring, and all three riders were down.

Frightened, the hunters' ponies ran off. Qarakh dropped the bow and started forward, intending to draw his saber and lop off the remaining Anda's heads to ensure that they were truly dead, but then he felt a tingling sensation on the back of his neck and a cold fluttering in the pit of his belly. He looked to the east and saw a splash of faint rose pink on the horizon, and he didn't hesitate. He sank into the ground where he stood, and moments later he heard screams as the first rays of dawn kissed the flesh of the three Anda he had brought down.

Satisfied that Aajav and he were safe for the time being, he fell into the darkness of day-sleep.

Roots curling toward him, tendrils pushing through soil like thick wooden worms. Tips touching his face, caressing it, before undulating toward his temples and gently piercing the skin.

Another's presence in his mind, but not the Beast, not this time.

This presence he welcomed.

"We shall rest here, and when dawn draws nigh, I shall inter us in the soil, and we will sleep." He didn't expect a response. It had been weeks since Aajav had so much as twitched an eyelid, let alone spoke.

Aajav lay on his back, eyes closed, face pointed toward Tengri, arms and hands at his sides—just as Qarakh had arranged him. They were in a clearing, surrounded by pine and oak trees, the sky above them clear and filled with stars. A nearly full moon glowed greenish white. Their mounts were untethered and grazed contentedly on the grass the clearing had to offer. Qarakh sat cross-legged next to his blood brother and sire, and tried to think of what to do next.

This new land was very different from the steppe; there was so much life here. Though it was night, birds still sang and flew from tree to tree. Small animals scurried along branches and rustled through leaves. Larger animals—rabbits, foxes, deer and wolves—moved through the forest as they hunted or avoided being hunted. Even the ground was teeming with life: Insects crawled in the grass, and earthworms burrowed through the soil. The steppe had these things too, but there everything was spread out across miles upon miles of barren plain. Here, it was too much, too close....

He heard a word then, spoken by a feminine voice in a language he didn't understand. Before whoever it was could speak again, Qarakh stood, drew his saber and turned to confront her.

A brown-robed figure emerged from the shadows between two trees and began walking toward Qarakh and Aajav. He sniffed, trying to catch her scent, but the air was a confusion of unknown smells, and he couldn't tell which—if any—belonged to her.

Perhaps she's a spirit, a voice whispered inside his head, *and therefore doesn't have a scent.*

Qarakh gripped his sword more tightly. He did not know what strange spirits or demons inhabited this land, or if his blade would prove effective against them, but he would stand and protect Aajav, even unto the Final Death.

As the woman drew closer, she lowered her hood to reveal delicate features, curly red hair and smooth alabaster skin that almost shimmered in the moonlight. She smiled as she came toward them, but Qarakh knew better than to let his guard down. Did not a predator bare its teeth just before attacking? When she came within twenty feet, she stopped. Not quite within fighting distance, but still close enough to talk, Qarakh noted.

She spoke again in that odd language, and Qarakh pointed to an ear with his free hand and shook his head.

The woman acknowledged the gesture with a nod, and then reached into a leather pouch hanging from her belt. Qarakh tensed, ready to spring to the attack in case she should bring forth some manner of weapon, but all she withdrew was a handful of dried leaves. She then knelt and pulled up some blades of grass and a bit of soil from the ground. She crushed the leaves and added them to the other ingredients, then opened her mouth—displaying the sharpened canines that marked her as one of the undead—and bit her tongue. Vitae welled forth and she lowered her head over her cupped hands and gently spit a stream of blood into them. She whispered words that Qarakh didn't understand, but he did note that one word in particular was repeated several times: *Telyavel*. She dipped her tongue into the mixture and swirled it around—three times to the right, then three to the left. Afterward, she rubbed her hands together and applied some to her ears, then wiped the remainder off in the grass.

When she was finished with this strange ritual, she stood and looked at Qarakh.

"I am Deverra, high priestess of Telyavel, Protector of the Dead," she said in unaccented Mongolian. Or perhaps that was merely how Qarakh heard her words.

He scowled and didn't lower his saber. "You are a witch?"

She smiled. "I suppose your people might call me a shaman."

Qarakh considered this for a moment, and then he nodded and lowered his sword, though he did not sheathe it. "I am called Qarakh, and this"—he gestured to his blood brother—"is Aajav."

"You are both Cainites, yes?"

"I do not understand."

"Those who do not breathe, who feed on the blood of the living and sleep during the day," the priestess explained.

Qarakh nodded. "And you?"

"Yes, though I wager I am from a different clan."

"We are of the tribe known as Gangrel. I am of Aajav's blood, and he is of the hunter Oderic's."

The priestess nodded as if she'd expected as much. "What is wrong with your sire?"

"He is not merely my sire," Qarakh said with some irritation. "He is my bonded brother. Our souls are linked now as they were in life. As to what malady has gripped him, I cannot say."

After Qarakh had slaughtered the Anda hunting party, the clan elders had put a high blood price on his head. And though he was a strong and fearless warrior, he wasn't a foolish one. He knew he could never hope to stand against all the Anda in Mongolia—not alone and certainly not while caring for the ailing Aajav. So they had left the steppes and ridden westward, searching for a place where they not only would be out of the

Anda's reach but also removed from civilization. They had made it as far as the forests and grassy plains of this land—whatever it was called—before Aajav could ride no longer, not even bound to his saddle.

Qarakh debated how much he should tell the priestess. "Five weeks past, he was struck by arrows coated with poison. He began to recover after a few days, but now..." He trailed off, as there was no need to explain further. Aajav's still form was all the explanation necessary.

"May I examine him?" the priestess asked.

Qarakh hesitated before giving her permission. Even so, he kept his saber in hand as the priestess walked over and knelt next to Aajav. She gently pried open his eyelids, then opened his mouth and peered inside for a few moments. Afterward, she examined his fingernails and then removed his boots so she could get a look at his toenails. When she was done with that, she put his boots back on and lowered her face to his head and sniffed his hair.

She looked up. "I need to taste his blood. A drop or two should be sufficient."

Qarakh didn't like it, but he pressed the tip of his saber to the back of Aajav's left hand and pushed slightly. The blade tip punctured the flesh, and a thick drop of crimson welled forth. She dipped her finger in the blood and then touched it to her tongue. She closed her mouth and looked thoughtful for several moments. She nodded to herself and then pressed her fingers to his cheeks. She closed her eyes. Qarakh tensed, wondering if she was attempting to cast some sort of foul spell on Aajav. He decided he couldn't afford to take any chances and was just about to cut off the priestess's head when she withdrew her fingers and stood.

"I could detect only the faintest traces of poison in his body," she said. "Not nearly enough to affect a strong young Cainite like him. I believe that while his body has purged the poison from his system, his mind has retreated into torpor."

Qarakh had only been a childe of darkness for five years, and he did not know to what the priestess referred. He didn't wish to appear ignorant, though—especially since he was—so he nodded as if he understood.

"Some Cainites retreat into deep slumber in order to rest while healing from severe injuries. Others lapse into the state as a result of some terrible trauma, while for some it is a last, desperate escape from the tedium of eternal life. As to why Aajav has fallen into torpor..." she broke off and shrugged.

Qarakh looked upon the face of the man who was both brother and father to him and sheathed his sword. "Is there nothing that can be done for him?"

The priestess considered the matter for some time. "We can provide a comfortable place for him to rest, somewhere he will be both safe and undisturbed. I can continue to pray to Telyavel and search for a magical remedy, thought I must be honest with you: I cannot guarantee that Aajav will ever rise again. Some Cainites emerge from torpor after only days or weeks, while others never do. Still, if you are willing to accept my help, I will do everything in my power to restore your brother to you."

Qarakh looked into the priestess's eyes and tried to gauge whether he could trust her. He saw no guile or deception in her gaze, only kindness and concern.

He bowed his head. "On behalf of Aajav and myself, I am both honored and grateful to accept your aid, priestess."

"Please, call me Deverra."

Qarakh woke to the sensation of warmth. He was lying naked beneath a bearskin blanket, and he wasn't alone. His bedmate shifted position next to him, and he felt the smooth curve of a feminine behind press against his side. He thought he—they— were inside a *ger*, but the fire was little more than smoldering embers and didn't provide enough light to see by, so he wasn't certain.

Qarakh wasn't fully awake yet, but he knew something was wrong. He remembered riding toward Alexander's camp with Deverra... remembered stopping when the eastern horizon began to grow light. They'd tied their horses to the low-hanging branches of a sapling and then walked to a majestic oak that Deverra had chosen. Using her Telyavic powers, the priestess had merged with the tree, and therein she would sleep untouched by the sun's rays. Since one patch of earth was much the same as another to Qarakh, he elected to inter himself in the ground at the base of the oak. He remembered sinking in the soil and succumbing to the darkness of slumber, and then...

And then he'd dreamed of fleeing the Anda hunting party, and of his first meeting with Deverra. So was this another dream? It couldn't be anything but, and yet... it felt so real. He reached over and slid his hand along the smooth skin of a woman's hip and smiled. It felt more than real—it felt good.

The woman made a purring sound deep in her throat and rolled over to face him, but when Qarakh saw who it was, he jerked his hand away as if he'd been burnt.

"I like that. Don't stop." She sounded amused.

"What is this place?"

She shrugged and the bearskin slipped down to reveal a bare shoulder. "A place of the mind, a pleasant illusion, a shared dream. It is all these things, and more... and less."

"Make sense, woman!" he snapped.

"I am still sleeping within the oak tree, and you remain interred in the ground at its base. I used magic to reach out through the tree roots and connect us, mind to mind."

Qarakh remembered the sensation of wooden tendrils stretching toward him, brushing against his temples before burrowing into his flesh. If he concentrated hard enough, he could feel the roots protruding from his skin.

"If you wish, I can end the spell." Deverra shifted slightly, and the blanket slipped farther down to reveal the curve of her breast.

Qarakh thought for a moment before answering. "Tell me more about this place."

She smiled. "As I said, it is a shared dream. Here, we can be together as man and woman. As a *mortal* man and woman."

Now Qarakh understood why his vision couldn't easily penetrate the dimness within the *ger*. For the first time in years, he was seeing through mortal eyes. It was strange, but at the same time, it was... exciting. There were many advantages to being a Cainite, but for everything gained by the casting off of morality—enhanced senses, increased strength, the power to heal wounds that would slay a human—something was lost.

One of these things was the ability to perform the physical act of love. Cainite bodies could go through the motions, but they were undead bodies, and as such could only engage in a hollow mockery of the most life-affirming act of all.

But now, here in this place of dreams, such limitations no longer applied.

Qarakh smiled, showing teeth that were small, blunt and altogether human. Then Deverra came into his arms, and they gave themselves over to a sweet ritual older than even Caine.

Chapter Nine

When Qarakh rose from the earth the next evening, Deverra was already up and waiting for him. At first, it was something of a shock to perceive the world once again through Cainite senses—in varying ways they were both more keen and more limited than mortal ones—but within moments he had readjusted and was ready to continue on to Alexander's camp.

Deverra had prepared the horses for travel, and as Qarakh approached her, she handed him the reins of his dusky gray mare.

"Sleep well?" she asked, a twinkle in her eye.

Qarakh took the reins from her and climbed into the saddle in a single smooth motion. "Yes, though I did have some strange dreams."

Deverra mounted her piebald and turned to look at him. "Truly? I never recall my dreams upon awakening." With a mischievous grin, she turned away, gave the reins a shake, shouted *"Tchoo!"* The piebald immediately launched into a gallop.

Qarakh shook his head as the priestess rode off. No matter how long he might ultimately continue to stalk the night, he doubted he would ever fully understand the ways of women.

"Tchoo!" he called, and the gray set out in pursuit of the piebald.

Alessandro strode away from his *ger*, the skin on his left wrist a ragged, dripping ruin. He wasn't concerned about the wound; it would heal soon enough. But he *was* troubled by the manner in which he'd received it. He'd been feeding Osip, one of his ghouls, when suddenly the young man—who up to that point had been contentedly sipping vitae from a small cut on his master's wrist—bit down on Alessandro's flesh and began tearing at it like a starved animal. Alessandro had cuffed Osip once, but though the blow had been less than gentle, it hadn't been enough to dislodge the ghoul. Alessandro's anger had risen then, along with his Beast, and he'd grabbed a fistful of Osip's hair and yanked. He'd managed to pull the youth away from his bloody wrist, but Osip had continued snarling and snapping, ravenous for more blood, until finally Alessandro was forced to strike the ghoul hard enough to render him unconscious.

He'd nearly pounced upon Osip then, but despite how much his Beast had wanted to rip the little bastard apart for having the temerity to insult his master's flesh, Alessandro had held back. He knew it hadn't been Osip's fault—before Qarakh had departed with Deverra, the Mongol had ordered every Cainite with a ghoul (human or animal) to increase the number of feedings so they might be at full strength should Alexander choose to attack. But ghouls' intake of vitae had to be carefully managed or they became aggressive and disobedient. Even so, Alessandro still might have killed Osip if it hadn't been for what had happened to Qarakh's two ghouls. The khan hadn't said anything before he departed the previous evening, but when Sasha and Pavla hadn't shown up for martial training, the other ghouls began talking and the truth soon came out.

Of course, Qarakh's ghouls were his to do with as he pleased, but knowing how much the Mongol hated waste, Alessandro believed it likely that his Beast had gotten the better of him, and that had given Alessandro the strength to resist his own Beast when Osip lost control.

Pavla and Sasha hadn't been the only ones who failed to attend martial training; Rikard had also been missing. Alessandro had checked Rikard's *ger* then asked around camp if anyone had seen him lately, but the answer was always the same: not since the feast the previous night.

In and of itself, Rikard's disappearance wasn't remarkable. A number of the tribe's members—including its khan—were ultimately nomadic, and came and went with little warning. But Rikard wasn't overly fond of traveling. In fact, he seemed to enjoy little about tribal life. Perhaps the possibility of a coming battle with Alexander's forces had finally convinced him that it was time to move on. If so, Alessandro doubted there would be many tears shed over his departure—not that the tribe could afford to lose anyone at a time like this.

Alessandro wasn't superstitious by nature, but he was beginning to wonder if these events weren't in truth ill omens, and if so, what they might portend for Qarakh's meeting with Alexander. The Iberian decided to seek Grandfather's counsel on the matter, and he found the lore-keeper in a nearby field watching Arnulf and Wilhelmina instruct the lesser warriors of the tribe in the finer points of swordplay. The students had formed a wide circle, and in the middle the two teachers faced each other, weapons drawn, feet planted in battle stances. Alessandro took a position next to Grandfather and decided to observe the lesson.

Wilhelmina spoke loudly so all could hear. "Many Cainites believe that their strength and speed alone will win battles for them. And often they will—should your opponent be mortal." She flicked her sword toward Arnulf's face, but the Goth easily intercepted the blow with his ax. "But if your opponent is a Cainite, he—"

"Or she," Arnulf added.

Wilhelmina lowered her sword and bowed her head in acknowledgement. "He *or* she will most likely be equally as fast and strong, if not more so. Look at the two of us: Arnulf is obviously taller and more muscular than I, and his ax seems a far more formidable weapon than my sword."

A number of students murmured agreement, but most simply continued to watch with silent interest.

"But we all know that appearances can be deceptive when it comes to our kind. I might well be a great deal older than Arnulf, or perhaps the vitae that runs through my veins came from a more powerful sire than his. But for the sake of argument, let us say that all is at it appears, and Arnulf truly is faster and stronger than I."

Arnulf grinned. "Was there ever any doubt?"

A few students chuckled—*Probably new to the tribe,*

Alessandro thought—but the rest remained quiet.

Up to this moment, Grandfather hadn't given any sign that he was aware of Alessandro's presence, but now the lore-keeper turned to him and whispered, "Have you noticed Arnulf's eyebrows?"

Frowning, Alessandro took a closer look at the Goth warrior's face. The brow (for now the two met in the middle) was darker and bushier than it had been before Arnulf had run off after Qarakh and the Ventrue knight that Wilhelmina had captured. Though Alessandro had understood the necessity of it at the time, he now wished that Qarakh hadn't ordered—and carried out—Marques's execution. There was much information they might've gained from questioning the knight, especially if Deverra could've employed her magic, or even if Alessandro had been given the opportunity to use some of the more effective techniques of persuasion he'd learned during his time as one of the fanatical Lions of Rodrigo. A pity—and perhaps another omen, along with the change in Arnulf's eyebrows?

"I hadn't noticed," Alessandro admitted.

Steel rang on steel as Wilhelmina tried a different attack on Arnulf, and the Goth once again easily deflected it.

"I'll grant that it is not a huge change, but it is often the minor ones which are the most disturbing," Grandfather said.

Alessandro didn't need the lore-keeper to explain any further. Like all Cainites, the Iberian understood only too well. Surrendering completely to the Beast, even for a short time, always left its mark on Cainites one way or another. For Gangrel, that mark was physical, a bodily feature turned permanently bestial. Alessandro glanced at Grandfather's fur-covered hands and not for the first time wondered when and how they had gotten that way; Grandfather, more successfully than anyone the Iberian had ever met, lived in harmony with his Beast.

"Do you think Arnulf is beginning to lose himself?" Alessandro asked.

Before Grandfather could reply, Arnulf let out a surprised grunt and Alessandro turned his attention back to the demonstration. Wilhelmina had sidestepped Arnulf's latest attack, and the Goth stumbled forward, unbalanced. Before he could right himself, Wilhelmina planted a foot against his backside and shoved. Arnulf took a couple more stumble-steps forward before crashing to the ground.

More laughter from the students, louder this time.

"Sometimes a Cainite's speed can be a drawback," Wilhelmina said. "Because Arnulf was able to swing his ax so swiftly, when his blow didn't find its target, the power of the swing put him momentarily off balance." She grinned. "And for a cunning warrior, a moment is all that is required."

While Alessandro listened to Wilhelmina's words, he kept his gaze on Arnulf. The Goth warrior lay on the ground, teeth gritted, hand clenched so tightly around the haft of his ax that it appeared the knuckles might burst through the skin any second. Alessandro thought he heard a low growling coming from the man's throat, but he wasn't certain. Then, with a speed that belied his large form, Arnulf was suddenly on his feet and swinging his ax in a sweeping arc toward Wilhelmina's neck.

Alessandro wanted to shout a warning, but knew he wouldn't be able to get it out in time to save Wilhelmina. However, just as the ax blade was about to make contact with the tender flesh of the Viking maid's neck, Arnulf halted his strike.

"If you manage to gain an advantage over your opponent, do not hesitate to make the most of it," Arnulf said, grinning with a mouthful of sharpened teeth. "For the tide of battle can shift in less than a moment."

Ax head a fraction of an inch from her throat, Wilhelmina stared into Arnulf's eyes, her jaw muscles clenching and unclenching, sword arm quivering, eager to swing. Finally, in a husky voice, she said, "Indeed." Arnulf kept the ax to her neck for a moment longer before lowering it and stepping back, nodding once to Wilhelmina who hesitated before returning the nod.

Grandfather turned to Alessandro. "Does that answer your question?"

It certainly did. Alessandro decided to keep an even closer eye on Arnulf as the tribe continued to prepare for the possibility of war. "Grandfather, could I speak with you—away from the others?"

"Of course. We've already witnessed the most interesting part of tonight's lesson, for after this Arnulf and Wilhelmina will both be keeping their Beasts on shorter leashes. Come, let us walk." And though Alessandro was sure the ancient Cainite had no need to do so, Grandfather put his hand on the Iberian's arm for support, and together they walked away from the training field as Wilhelmina began to pair the students up for sparring practice.

As the sound of clashing steel rang through the air, Grandfather said, "What is on your mind, Alessandro?"

Now that he was in the presence of the lorekeeper, Alessandro felt foolish discussing his concerns about omens, so instead he asked, "What is your assessment of our tribe's strength?"

A small smile played about Grandfather's lips. "There are many kinds of strength. Could you be more specific?"

"Our fighting strength."

"Of course you do." Grandfather didn't continue right away, and Alessandro began to think the elder might decline to comment, as he sometimes did. Others, Arnulf especially, took this habit as a sign of a wandering mind due to the lore-keeper's age, but Alessandro knew differently. Grandfather simply preferred to keep his own counsel on certain matters.

But after a time, Grandfather sighed. "In the end, there's very little difference between us, you know. Cainites and mortals. Just as a grown man isn't all much different from the boy he once was, so too are we not as far removed from the living beings we once were as we might like to think. It's been the same story since the beginning of time... tribe against tribe, leader against leader. There may be different pretexts for war—territory, religion, honor, power—but in the end, it always comes down to the same thing: feeding the Beast."

"For mortals as well?" Alessandro asked.

"Of course. Where do you think our Beasts came from?" Grandfather broke off and patted the Iberian's arm. "Please forgive an old man for rambling. You asked what I think of our tribe's strength. Our tribe is young and still in the process of growing, but we count among our number many powerful

Cainites who are no strangers to battle."

"Many of them are off wandering, though." Alessandro glanced over his shoulder at the training field. "And the majority of those who remain are young and unskilled."

"The young will learn, and in time the wanderers shall return."

"But that's just it: time. Will there be enough for our messengers to locate the wanderers and tell them they are needed back home? Will the young ones learn the battle skills necessary to keep them from Final Death, let alone to defeat Alexander's army?"

"These are questions only time may answer," Grandfather said. "But if it's reassurance you seek, remember that word spreads fast among night-walkers and that our people can travel quite swiftly when needed. Several wanderers have already returned since the call first went out, have they not?"

"Only three."

"That is three more than we had two nights ago, and still more will come. And while the young ones might not be battle-hardened veterans yet, at least they now know which end of a sword is which." He smiled. "Most of them. And all shall continue to improve."

"But Alexander's men are no doubt highly trained and experienced. I don't see how we can hope to stand against them."

"It might not come to that, depending on how Qarakh's meeting with the prince goes. After all, what is a parley but a battle of words? But in the end, when two tribes go to war, victory is determined by one thing alone: the strength of the leader. Would you like to hear a story?"

Alessandro was surprised by this sudden change of topic, but he agreed out of respect for the ancient Gangrel, if nothing else.

"Two shepherds tended their flocks at opposite ends of a valley. It was a large valley, and fertile, so the few conflicts that arose between the shepherds were minor and easily resolved. But then one day a lone wolf came into the valley and began preying upon the flocks, first taking a sheep from one and then from the other. Both shepherds were saddened and angered by their loss, and though they had always tended their flocks with care, they vowed to do so with even greater diligence in the future. But the wolf was a crafty devil, and despite the shepherds' best efforts, they were unable to prevent him from continuing to take sheep from the two flocks.

"The first shepherd was so angry that he gathered together all of his friends and relations and set out to hunt down and destroy the wolf. The second shepherd, though also angry over his losses, was a more pragmatic man. He understood that the wolf wasn't a demon sent to plague him, but rather an animal simply following its nature. So the second shepherd chose his best remaining sheep and slaughtered it. He left a portion of its meat in a place where he knew the wolf roamed and would be sure to find it. The next day, the shepherd returned and found the meat gone, so he left a second piece.

"Meanwhile, the first shepherd and his hunting party searched throughout the valley, but as I said before, the wolf was a clever creature, and they did not find him. The shepherd, who now thought of himself as the hunter, become increasingly frustrated, for not only couldn't he track down the wolf, but he continued to lose sheep from his flock to the beast's hunger.

"The second shepherd hadn't lost any more sheep, except for the one he sacrificed to feed the wolf. And since the wolf was content with the meat as the shepherd doled it out, the shepherd was able to keep the animal placated for a fortnight before he was forced to kill another of his sheep, thus saving all the others the wolf would've taken otherwise.

"The hunter continued his search, but before long his friends and relatives grew weary and departed one by one until only the hunter was left to carry on his quest for vengeance. And then, one night, the hunter's prayers were answered when he found himself face to face with the wolf that had been preying on his flock for so long. So long, in fact, that there wasn't much of a flock left. The hunter, whose only weapon was a spear he had carved himself from a cedar branch, prepared to strike at his most hated enemy. But before he could even raise his spear, let alone cast it, the wolf attacked him and tore out his throat. That night, the wolf did not go in search of sheep, nor did he eat the meat offered to him by the shepherd, for he had far more than enough to fill his belly."

Alessandro waited for Grandfather to continue, but when the lore-keeper said nothing more, he realized that the tale was finished.

"Forgive me, Grandfather, but I do not understand."

"It is a simple story with an equally simple message. One man died because he thought he could dominate the beast, with another man lived and managed to protect his flock because he came to understand the beast and learned how to live with it."

"I must be thickheaded tonight, for I do not see how this story applies to Qarakh and Alexander."

"As I said before, victory will go to the tribe with the strongest leader. Which of the two men in my story would you say was the strongest? The hunter who had many friends to help him—at least at first—and a weapon to slay the wolf, or the shepherd who had only himself, his understanding and the willingness to sacrifice?"

Alessandro didn't have to think about it for long. "The shepherd, I suppose. Though at first he seems weaker, at the end of the story he is still alive, as is most of his flock. More to the point, he knows how to continue to protect them."

Grandfather nodded, as if he were a teacher pleased with the progress of a student. "Now which of those two men would you say is Alexander and which is Qarakh?"

Alessandro suddenly understood. "Alexander is the first shepherd, and Qarakh is the second."

"Alexander may be stronger than Qarakh in the ways that most Cainites measure power, but the khan of our tribe understands the ways of the Beast like few others I have encountered—and I speak of myself as well. Despite what some of the Damned would like to believe about our kind's destiny and our ultimate purpose, a Cainite's existence can be boiled down to one undeniable truth: Will he succumb to the Beast or will he learn to live with it? And if one can fully learn to do the latter, he possesses a strength that no other Cainite, no matter how ancient, can ever hope to match."

Alessandro considered Grandfather's words for some time

as they walked. "I believe that I understand your lesson, and I find it reassuring. But there is one thing that troubles me. In your tale, the shepherd had to select and sacrifice one of his sheep in order to protect the rest of his flock."

"Yes."

"Then if your story should prove prophetic, which of us will Qarakh sacrifice in order to defeat Alexander?"

Holleb coughed—a deep, barking sound—and his tiny body shuddered as he struggled to draw in breath.

"Hush, sweetness. It's not far to Lechsinska's." Tears rolled down Rahel's cheeks. She knew she shouldn't cry, that tears would only blur her vision and make it harder to see in the darkness, but she couldn't help herself. She wrapped the blanket tighter around her baby brother and quickened her pace.

Rahel also knew she shouldn't be out at night. Hadn't her father told her often enough? *You might fall and break a leg—or your neck. You might become lost in the forest and never find your way out again. There are wolves abroad at night, and worse things.*

No matter how many times Rahel asked, her father would never say what those "worse things" were, only that she wouldn't want to meet one alone on a dark trail. So where was she now? Alone on a dark trail, of course.

Holleb wheezed, coughed, struggled for breath. No, she wasn't alone, and she was here for a good reason. Her baby brother was ill, and she was taking him to see Lechsinska, the healer woman who lived in the forest. Many people believed Lechsinska was a witch and claimed that she cast spells to spread illness so that the afflicted would then come to her for "healing." Rahel knew better, though. Her father was a woodcutter, and they lived in a small cottage on the edge of the forest. Rahel had visited the old woman many times as she was growing up—much to her parents' displeasure—and she knew that Lechsinska's abilities didn't stem from black magic, but rather her knowledge of herbs and their healing properties. She'd spent many an afternoon helping the old woman gather mushrooms and blossoms, all the while listening as Lechsinska enumerated their benefits.

This one is good for gout… and this one will help a barren woman conceive… and this one…

But even though Rahel was thirteen now and almost a woman herself, her father had forbidden her to have anything more to do with Lechsinska. The healer had acted as midwife during Holleb's birth: a birth their mother hadn't survived. Rahel didn't blame the old woman. She understood that herbs and knowledge could only do so much, but her father had been so devastated by the loss of his wife that he accused Lechsinska of killing her with witchcraft, and delivering unto him not a son, but a demon in the form of a human infant. He cast Lechsinska out of his home, buried his wife and then intended to slay Holleb, but Rahel stood up to her father and said that if he killed her brother, he would have to kill her, too. And for a moment, she thought he would, but then he turned away from her, walked to the straw-filled pallet that had once been his marriage bed, lay down alone and cried.

From that day on, he would have nothing to do with Holleb or Rahel. Oh, he made certain there was enough food for them—even goat's milk for the baby—but he would barely look at either of them, let alone talk to them. Rahel tended to her brother and told herself that her father would return to his former self once his grief ran its course, but as the days turned to weeks and then months with little improvement on his part, she was no longer so sure.

With no older siblings, grandmothers or aunts to turn to, Rahel become both sister and mother to Holleb. She had cared for the little one as best she could, and though it hadn't been easy, she was happy to do it, not only because she loved her brother but because he was all she had left of her mother.

So when he had come down with the croup in the middle of the night, she had bundled him up and gone outside, leaving her father sleeping in their cottage. Despite the dangers the night held, they held far less terror for her than the thought of losing her brother.

She continued along the path to Lechsinska's hut, almost running, when a figure detached itself from the shadows and stepped onto the trail, blocking her way. She gasped and only

just managed to stop before bumping into the man—if indeed
it *was* a man.

"Good evening to you, child." The man's voice was soft and
kind, but with a mocking edge that frightened Rahel. "What
brings you to the forest at such a late hour?"

Rahel was too scared to speak, but then Holleb answered
for her with one of his barking coughs.

"Ah, taking the little one to see a healer, I wager. Surely
he can't be your child, though. You are too young. A brother,
perhaps?"

The best Rahel could manage was a nod, and though it was
dark and she could not make out the stranger's features, for
some reason she knew he could see her just fine.

Holleb coughed once more.

"I can see how badly the little one needs medicine, so I won't
keep you much longer. I am searching for the encampment of a
man named Alexander. I am confident that he is in this part of
the country, but I am unsure as to his exact location. Have you
heard anything about him, or if not him specifically, about a
group of knights that has come to Livonia?"

Rahel tried to reply, but her mouth was dry as dirt and she
could not speak.

Holleb coughed again, and the man stepped forward and
placed his hand over the baby's mouth.

"If you do not answer me, I'll make sure the whelp never
coughs again."

Rahel found her voice then. "Please, sir! Do not hurt my little brother! I'll—I'll do anything you ask!" She had a good idea
what a strange man might want from a young girl she encountered in the forest at night, and while the thought frightened
her, she was determined to do whatever it took to safeguard her
brother's life.

The man removed his hand and Holleb took in a wheezing
breath. She expected the baby to begin crying from fear, but he
merely whimpered, too sick and exhausted to do more.

"Very well. I promise that I shall not harm the child. *If* you
tell me what I want to know."

"My father is a woodcutter. A week ago we took a wagonload

of wood to the village of Kolya. Some of the men there were talking about a group of Christian knights that had made camp a day's ride west of the village."

"And what did they say about these knights?"

"Some feared that they came here to force us to worship their god at swordpoint. Others said that the knights do not walk in the light of day, that they are demons who have come to plague our land."

"And what do you think? Are they demons?" She couldn't see his face, but she could hear the smile in his voice.

She shrugged. "Men tell many stories."

The man leaned his face close to hers. Despite the darkness, she could make out his sharp teeth.

"Some of the stories they tell are true."

When Rikard was finished with the girl, he dropped her lifeless body to the ground and continued along the trail. He intended to find the girl's home, slay her father and take their horse—for surely they had one to draw their wagonload of wood when they went to the village.

Ever since leaving the tribal camp, Rikard had been traveling by foot. He would've taken one of the tribe's horses, but knowing how much Qarakh valued the animals, Rikard feared they might come after him. Now he was tired of walking and eager to reach Alexander's camp and see what sort of deal he might be able to work out with the Ventrue prince.

Behind him, lying on the ground not far from his sister's corpse, the infant burst out with a wracking cough. Rikard had been true to his pledge; he had not harmed the child.

He continued on to the woodcutter's cottage.

Chapter Ten

It was well after midnight by the time Qarakh and Deverra approached Alexander's camp. The ancient's standard flew above tents pitched in the middle of flat, featureless grassland. Deverra remarked that she was surprised Alexander would choose such an exposed camping ground.

"Here he can see in any direction, and there is no cover for an attacking force," Qarakh explained. "It also sends a message to anyone who comes near."

Deverra frowned. "Which is?"

"'I have no need to hide, for I am mighty enough to defeat all comers.'"

The priestess smirked. "He certainly doesn't lack for confidence, does he?"

"If he has survived for two thousand years, his confidence is well earned."

Deverra didn't reply, and they continued riding in silence.

As they drew near the camp, Qarakh began making preliminary judgments about Alexander's military capacity. He counted seventy-eight tents, each with the capacity to house four people apiece, perhaps five. Most would belong to mortals—stable boys, cooks, blacksmiths, laundresses and camp followers of all kinds—who would also serve as the Cainites' food supply. The number of fires throughout the camp attested to just how many mortals there were. Cainites detested fire, and they had no need of it to cook or see by. There would likely be a number of human warriors as well—a mix of knights, men-at-arms and mercenaries—while the remainder of the fighting force would be made up of Cainites and ghouls. The higher-ranking vampires would sleep two to a tent, and of course Alexander would have his own quarters. Qarakh then counted the horses and wagons before doing a quick mental calculation. Around thirty Cainites, fifty or so ghouls, perhaps two hundred mortals. Three hundred all together, he decided.

Of those thirty Cainites, Qarakh doubted all were equal in power. Much depended on their age, individual skill and experience. Alexander was undoubtedly the most powerful, and the Ventrue would make certain to surround himself with the strongest Cainites that he could. But Alexander was a deposed prince, and because of this most likely had to take whatever warriors he could get. There would be a small inner circle of loyal followers that had accompanied their master into exile—made up primarily of Alexander's childer, Qarakh guessed—and they would be deadly fighters to a man. But the remaining Cainites, while certainly competent, would not be up to the level of the others. In which case—

He realized that Deverra had just said something. "Yes?"

"I said, don't you hear it?"

Qarakh listened. "I hear only the normal sounds of a camp: men talking while they tend to armor and weapons, horses whickering restlessly and pawing the ground, eager to be loosed from their fetters."

Deverra shook her head in annoyance. "No, beneath all that."

Qarakh listened again, more intently this time, and now he thought he heard something more than camp noises. It was a soft shushing sound, like ocean waves breaking on a distant shore. He gave Deverra a questioning look.

"It's the wind whispering through the grass," she said. "And I don't like what it's saying."

"I hear no words."

"You hear them, but you don't understand. There are two words, one spoken overtop the other, as if they were one. The first is Alexander's name."

"And the second?"

Deverra hesitated a moment before answering. "The second word is 'death.'"

Qarakh wasn't certain how to take this, but before he could think more about it, a rider left the camp and headed in their direction.

Qarakh brought his mare to a halt and gestured for Deverra to do the same.

As the rider drew closer, the Telyav priestess stiffened. "Shouldn't you draw your saber or nock an arrow, just in case he intends to attack?"

"If Alexander wished to kill or capture us, he would've sent more than a lone horseman. We are being greeted."

"So what do we do?" she asked.

"We wait. This is, after all, why we came, is it not?"

Deverra nodded, but she continued to eye the rider warily as he approached. Qarakh wondered if the wind and grass were saying more to her than she admitted.

The rider slowed as he reached them and brought his mount to halt. He addressed the two in a language Qarakh did not understand, but the Mongol thought he could sense an undertone of distaste in the man's voice. The Christian surely felt it beneath him to be addressing the newcomers as equals.

"He speaks German," Deverra said. "He bids us welcome on behalf of his highness, Prince Alexander."

The rider—a knight, Qarakh guessed—was brown-bearded and wore a helmet and a mail hauberk. On his tabard was a black cross, and Qarakh wondered at the significance of the symbol. The knights they had faced in previous years—the Livonian Sword-Brothers—wore a similar tabard but with a red cross and a sword emblazoned upon it. These were of a different order, then.

Qarakh replied in Livonian. "I am Qarakh, and this is the priestess Deverra. We have come to parley with your master."

Deverra translated and the knight replied in German again. His expression remained neutral for the most part, but his nose wrinkled and his upper lip twitched, and Qarakh knew precisely how he felt about them.

"His name is Brother Rudiger," Deverra said, "Commander of the Brothers of the Black Cross. He wears the tabard of a mortal order of monkish knights called the Teutonic Order, and I think the Black Cross must be a Cainite part of that order."

Qarakh heard her words, but another voice imposed itself: *Slay him!* urged the Beast. The words were accompanied by a mental image of Qarakh plunging taloned fingers into the soft jelly of Rudiger's eyes. It was tempting, but Qarakh restrained himself.

Then the Black Cross knight turned his mount and began riding back to the camp at a trot.

"He wishes us to follow," Deverra said to Qarakh, and gave him a questioning glance. He nodded, and they followed after Rudiger.

As they entered the camp, Qarakh sensed a power permeating the atmosphere, as if the air itself crackled with barely restrained energy. He knew that Alexander was near. Deverra felt it too, perhaps even more strongly than he, for she kept glancing around like a rabbit that knows a predator lurks near. Qarakh felt an urge to reach out and touch her, to reassure her, but he kept his hands on the pommel of his saddle. Such an expression of tenderness was not only inappropriate because he was khan, but here it would be taken as a sign of weakness. Neither he nor Deverra could afford that.

They slowed their mounts to a walk as Rudiger led them toward the center of the camp. As they passed, Qarakh noted how no one—Cainite, ghoul or mortal—looked at them. They merely continued going about their business as if their camp had visitors every night. Qarakh wondered if Alexander had ordered them to display such nonchalance, or if they were so confident in their prince's power that they were truly unconcerned with who these newcomers were and what they wanted.

Careful. That's exactly what Alexander wants you to think.

As they approached the center of the camp,

Qarakh smelled the stink of burning wood and light stung his eyes. He squinted and managed to make out a slim figure sitting in a wooden chair before a blazing fire. Alexander of Paris.

Rudiger brought his horse to a halt. When he spoke, Deverra rapidly translated: "Your Highness, may I present for your pleasure Qarakh and the priestess Deverra." There was something about the knight's posture and tone that made Qarakh think Alexander didn't completely command the man's respect. If so, that was useful to know; any discord between the prince and his knights could only be an advantage.

"Thank you, Rudiger," Alexander said, and Deverra translated. "Would you dismount and join me by the fire?" Alexander's smile was thin and cruel. Qarakh soon saw why: Small beads of blood-sweat erupted on Rudiger's forehead as he stared at the flames. Cainites possessed an almost animalistic fear of flame, which reminded them of the killing fire of the sun.

The Mongol warrior was no exception. The Beast inside him recoiled at the sight of the flames, but Qarakh continued to sit calmly in his saddle. He understood that Alexander was testing him, and he would not give the Ventrue the satisfaction of seeing him react to the fire. He wondered how Deverra was faring, but he didn't look at her; he could not take his gaze off Alexander lest the prince think she was more to him than a simple ally.

Alexander looked at Rudiger, smiling cruelly as the knight demure from approaching the flames. He then turned to Qarakh and Deverra. "Welcome. Perhaps the two of you shall join me?" The Ventrue spoke in nearly flawless Livonian, his tone polite and reserved, but Qarakh could sense the power behind the elder's words. He wasn't making a request so much as issuing a command.

Qarakh paused a moment to let Alexander know that he chose to dismount of his own volition before he did so. Out of the corner of his eye, he was pleased to note that Deverra did likewise. Two ghouls came forward to lead their horses to the camp's stable, and Alexander dismissed Rudiger, who was clearly relieved to remove himself from the proximity of the campfire.

Qarakh stepped toward Alexander and the fire. His eyes had adjusted to the brightness, and he could see that the Ventrue appeared relaxed despite the nearness of the flames. Physically, he wasn't impressive, at least from a martial standpoint. His body was that of a boy-man, not a child but not an adult, either. But Alexander's power came from his blood and millennia of experience, and together they made him almost unimaginably strong. He wore a purple tunic, black leggings, black boots and a flowing purple cape. Qarakh knew that Europeans thought of purple as the color of royalty, and he was certain Alexander had chosen it for that very reason. Qarakh noted that the Ventrue wore no armor beneath his tunic and carried no weapons: a sign both of hospitality and of strength. Despite himself, Qarakh approved.

As he approached the prince, Qarakh caught a whiff of ancient decay, like old bones buried for untold centuries and finally unearthed. He knew it was the scent of Alexander, the smell of time itself.

The prince gestured to a pair of empty wooden chairs set up next to his (but not *too* close), and with a nod, Qarakh accepted the invitation and took the one on Alexander's right. Waves of heat rolled off the fire. Qarakh's Beast whimpered like a frightened cur, but he ignored it. He was a Mongol, born to the harsh life of the steppe. He had endured far worse than a little heat in his time.

He expected Deverra to take the remaining seat, but the priestess held back and stared at the fire with wide, fear-filled eyes. Qarakh understood that she was fighting her own Beast, attempting to force it into submission so that she might come near the flames, but she was losing the battle.

"If it would make your companion more comfortable, she is welcome to stand behind us next to Malachite," Alexander said, gesturing over his shoulder.

Qarakh looked in the direction the prince had indicated. Thanks to the glare of the fire, he hadn't noticed before, but standing ten feet behind Alexander was a man garbed in a black robe. His hood was down, revealing the misshapen, distorted features of the Nosferatu. Many Cainites found them repulsive and shunned them like the lepers they resembled, but Qarakh knew better than to judge by appearances. Few things were exactly as they seemed.

Deverra gave him a look that was half apologetic and half pleading, and he nodded his assent. With a grateful smile, she backed away from the fire and, giving it a wide berth, walked over to stand beside the Nosferatu. Rather than viewing Deverra's choice with disapproval, Qarakh saw it as a fortuitous development. Whoever this Malachite was and whatever his relationship to Alexander, he might be more talkative standing apart from the Ventrue, thus giving Deverra a chance to learn much more than if she merely sat next to Qarakh while he and Alexander parleyed.

"You are a Tartar, are you not?" Alexander asked. Without waiting for an answer—which was good, since Qarakh thought it was a foolish question and had no intention of replying—he continued. "You are the first of your people I have ever met face to face, so you will forgive that we converse in Livonian and not your tongue, I hope. You'll also overlook Rudiger's reluctance to learn even that language, I hope. He can be somewhat stubborn."

"Yes. Livonian is fine."

"Excellent. Now, first a gift to establish our good intentions." Alexander gestured and a ghoul came forward, leading a family of mortals: a man, his wife and their three children. Their heads were bowed, as if in supplication—or fear. "I understand that a few of my people overindulged themselves at a farmhouse in your territory. Please accept these mortals as replacements for those who were lost. You may do with them as you see fit."

Qarakh understood now why the humans were so frightened: They feared they were going to die. In truth, he *did* thirst—the Beast sent him a cascade of sensations: gushing crimson, terrified screams, life essence pouring down his throat hot and sweet—but he resisted the urge to fall upon the mortals and begin tearing at their flesh with his teeth. This prince and his men likely already thought of any Gangrel as an animal. Qarakh saw no need to reinforce that perception in Alexander just now.

"I thank you for your most gracious gift," Qarakh said. "They shall accompany us back to our camp when we depart."

Alexander turned to the ghoul who had brought the family and spoke something in German. The ghoul bowed low, turned and walked away, the family following close behind, all of them looking relieved and somewhat surprised to still be alive.

Whether Alexander knew it or not, according to Mongolian

custom, it was now Qarakh's turn to proffer a gift. He reached into a leather pouch that hung from his belt and drew forth a shock of light brown hair bound at one end by a strip of hide. He tossed the hair to Alexander, and without appearing to move the Ventrue caught it in the air. First his hand was at his side, then it was holding the shock of hair, without seeming to cross the intervening distance.

Alexander raised the roots of the hair to his nose and sniffed the sticky black residue coating them. He then looked at Qarakh and though when he spoke his tone was even, his gaze was winter cold. "Marques."

"I thought you might wish to have something to remember him by," Qarakh said. "I would have brought more, but this was all that remained."

The prince and the warrior locked gazes for a long, tense moment, and then Alexander smiled. It was an easy, natural smile, and Qarakh almost believed it.

"Poor Marques. He wasn't the strongest or brightest, but he was a faithful enough servant." He tossed the hair into the fire, where it crackled as it burned, filling the air with an acrid stink that Qarakh found at once repulsive and enticing.

"Now that we've dispensed with the pleasantries—not to mention Sir Marques—to what do I owe the pleasure and honor of your visit?"

Alexander's words were velvet-wrapped steel, and Qarakh knew better than to believe them. "I've come to learn the reason for your presence in Livonia. I would think there is little in this land to interest a prince—certainly nothing worth assembling an army for."

"Anything and everything is of interest to me... provided I can find a way to use it to my advantage." Qarakh was somewhat taken aback by this sudden honesty on Alexander's part. Perhaps the Ventrue was only attempting to seem forthcoming in order to deceive him. Or perhaps he truly was being sincere now so as to set up a later deception. This thinking in circles was maddening; Qarakh had to suppress a growl of frustration. He was almost tempted to draw his saber and attack the prince, caution be damned. But he doubted he'd catch Alexander off guard—he recalled how swiftly the Ventrue had moved when he'd caught Marques's hair—and even if he should somehow gain the upper hand against him, Qarakh doubted he could slay the prince before his knights came to their master's rescue. So he forced himself continue talking. If he had to fight Alexander using double meanings and veiled threats instead of steel, tooth and claw, so be it—for now. "And what have you found to interest you here?"

"You, of course. The chieftain who has repelled the Sword-Brothers and Rudiger's fellows among them. Some of the locals speak of you as divine. They say you travel in the company of priests and gods."

Qarakh looked to Deverra to see if she had any reaction, but she was too engrossed in a whispered conversation with Malachite to have heard Alexander's comment. He wondered how much the Ventrue knew about the Telyavs.

"I take it that your interest in my tribe and our land is due to more than curiosity. One does not need to gather an army just to learn the answers to a few questions."

Alexander grinned, revealing small, almost delicate incisors more suited to a child than a being two millennia old. "I suppose that all depends on the nature of the questions, doesn't it? Still, you are correct in your assumption. I have not come merely to learn about you: I have been dispatched to… deal with you."

It took an effort of will for Qarakh to refrain from reaching for his sword. "The way you say *deal* makes it sound as if you mean *destroy*."

"That may be why I was sent here, but that doesn't mean it is my intention. If I can, I'd prefer to strike a bargain instead."

Despite himself, Qarakh was intrigued. "Go on."

Five years ago, word first came to us that there was a chieftain in Livonia who claimed to be a Tartar. From that point on we heard of reversals for the Christian crusaders in these parts. A year and a half ago, Cainites allied with the Sword-Brothers came here to put an end to that opposition. Instead, they ran into you."

"While I enjoy listening to a well-told story as much as any man, I already know how this one ends," Qarakh said. "These knights sought to remake our herd into theirs and we repelled them."

"*Repelled* is hardly the word. You destroyed them. Only a single knight survived to carry news of their defeat to the ears of Jürgen the Sword-Bearer, Prince of Magdeburg."

Qarakh was now certain that Alexander knew little or nothing about the Telyavs' skill with sorcery, else he would've mentioned it during his tale. Good. That gave his tribe an advantage.

"I have heard of this Jürgen."

Alexander gave Qarakh a puzzled look, as if the Mongol had just uttered the most unnecessary sentence in the history of the spoken word. "Of course you have. Lord Jürgen was kind enough to offer his hospitality to me after my leave-taking from Paris. When news of the your tribe's victory reached him, he became concerned, and I offered to take a force to Livonia—"

"And *deal* with us," Qarakh finished. "Indeed."

"But now that you are here, you wish to bargain." A slow smile spread across Qarakh's lips. "Is my tribe so impressive that you are willing to give up without a fight?"

Alexander's face betrayed no emotion, but the fingers of his left hand twitched. For a being of such self-control, this was tantamount to a frenzied outburst. Qarakh had the impression of pressure building behind his eyes, of Alexander's gaze boring into him. The pressure increased to the point of pain, and Qarakh's Beast howled for Alexander's vitae. The Mongol warrior felt the itching sensation of fur sprouting on the backs of his hands, along his arms, neck and face, and he knew that this time his Beast would not be denied.

But then, just as suddenly as it had come, the pressure was gone. Qarakh struggled to keep from assuming wolf form, and though it was a near thing, in the end gray fur subsided into his skin, and the Beast remained tethered to its leash… for the moment.

When the Ventrue responded, his voice was cold and completely devoid of emotion, and Qarakh knew he was hearing the true Alexander—the undead creature that had lived for two millennia—speak for the first time. "Make no mistake, Tartar: I fear nothing in this world or beyond it. And if I desire something, I pursue it relentlessly. I do not give up."

Qarakh glanced past Alexander and saw that Deverra and Malachite had broken off their discussion and were watching the two warlords intently, waiting to see what they would do next. Qarakh wondered if Deverra would be able to cast a spell before Alexander or Malachite could attack. He had no doubt she had one already in mind, but the question was whether she could make her preparations in time. He decided it was unlikely.

"Give up? Perhaps not," Qarakh said. "But as a warrior, I'm sure you understand the concept of tactical withdrawal—especially when it suits your ultimate purpose."

Alexander looked at him for a moment, face expressionless, and Qarakh wondered if he had pushed the deposed prince too far, but then Alexander threw back his head and laughed. The sound had a youthful quality to it, at once musical and boyish, and for an instant Alexander seemed as if he really were only as old as he appeared.

"True enough! You're a bold one, Qarakh." Alexander turned to look at Malachite and gave the Nosferatu a nod. Reassured all was well, Malachite returned to his conversation with Deverra. "I respect that. Perhaps we *can* make a deal after all. Just because Jürgen sent me here to bring you to heel doesn't mean I intend to do so. It should come as no surprise to you that I desire to reclaim that which is rightfully mine: the throne of Paris. To be frank, I care not a whit for Livonia and who rules here, nor do I wish to spread the holy word of Christ to the pagans who inhabit this land."

"Are you not a Christian knight?" Qarakh asked. "What I am," Alexander said, "is a man who was born as a mortal and reborn as one of the Damned before Jesus was a gleam in Jehovah's eye. But I am also a pragmatic man, and I use whatever resources are available to me. As far as I am concerned, Christianity is merely one more weapon in my arsenal: a tool to use when I have need of it, and one to discard when I do not."

"Why do you tell me these things? We have only just met."

"We are kindred spirits, you and I—warriors who take what they want without hesitation or apology, with the courage to dare all and the strength to succeed where others would surely fail. We are extraordinary men, even for our kind, and because of this we should be allies instead of enemies."

Qarakh understood that Alexander's words were nothing more than flattery designed to sway him, backed by the Ventrue's raw will. Qarakh felt tendrils of that will stretching forth from Alexander, testing his defenses, probing for weaknesses, searching for any avenue of ingress they could find. And though he knew all this, Qarakh still found himself half-believing what Alexander was saying.

"You are well spoken, Prince, but you have already told me that you are a pragmatic man who will use and discard whatever tools he needs. Perhaps my tribe and I are merely tools to you. How can you be trusted?"

"I can always be trusted to act in my own best interests. That is how I have survived for so many centuries, and why I shall continue to survive for many more to come, perhaps even unto the end of time itself." Alexander's gaze became distant for a moment, as if he were peering down the long tunnel of eternity toward whatever unguessable fate lay waiting for him at its end. "I believe an alliance would not only benefit me, but you and your tribe as well. I can return to Magdeburg and report to Jürgen that the threat posed by your tribe was overblown and easily dealt with. I can then work to discourage others from mounting campaigns on Livonia. Jürgen can be redirected to Prussia." The Ventrue's words took on a slight mocking tone. "Thereby safeguarding your pagan utopia."

"And what would you expect in return for your... patronage?" Qarakh asked.

"When the night comes for me to retake Paris, you and your tribe will fight alongside the rest of my forces. And when I have retaken my throne, I shall do everything in my power to see to it that Livonia remains free from outside interference of any kind."

"Including yours?"

Alexander smiled. "I am a creature of the city and look to the Ile de France above all. I do not desire to rule over distant grasslands and forests."

Qarakh considered the Ventrue's words, trying to gauge the

depth of their sincerity—if any—and wondering what treachery might lie beneath them. "I see that you still do not believe me. What can I do to convince you?" Alexander glanced at the fire. It had burned down some since they had begun talking, but the flames were still full and strong. "I guess that Tartars take matters of honor and pride very seriously, and that they do not give their word lightly."

"This is true."

"I will not suggest a blood oath, for we both know the insidious powers of that humor upon us. So we must find other ways of proving our commitments and pledging our loyalties." Without warning, Alexander plunged his right hand into the fire. Immediately the skin began to sizzle and blacken, and the stink of burning flesh filled the air.

Behind them, Deverra gasped and Malachite called out Alexander's name. But Qarakh didn't turn to look at either of them; he kept his gaze fastened on the Ventrue's face. His brow was furrowed, his jaw muscles bunched tight, but despite the agony he surely was experiencing his eyes were clear and calm. "I pledge to you, Qarakh who is called the Untamed, that should you enter into an alliance with me, I shall never attack your tribe, and I shall use all my power and influence to protect it." Alexander's voice was strained, and blood-sweat had broken out on his brow, but still he did not cry out in pain.

Qarakh considered for another moment before putting his own hand into the flames. White hot agony blazed along his undead nerves, and the Beast inside him screamed.

"I accept your pledge, Alexander of Paris, and in turn I vow to consider your offer and give you an answer within a fortnight. May the flames of this sacred fire bind us both—for as long as each remains true to his word."

The two Cainites stared into each other's eyes as their burning flesh hissed and popped. For an instant it seemed as if Alexander might say more, but then he nodded and pulled his ruined, blackened hand from the fire. Qarakh waited one more moment and then withdrew his.

Deverra and Malachite were at their sides then, as if they both wished to give aid but were unsure exactly what to do.

Alexander grinned and then called out, "István!" A Cainite that had been standing in the background came forward and bowed. "Yes, my prince?" The man's Livonian was accented, but passable. Apparently, he didn't share Rudiger's stubbornness on the matter of language.

"Bring us bowls of blood in which to soak our hands. Bleed only the strongest and healthiest mortal you can find for Qarakh. As for myself… you know my needs. Bring two flagons full as well so that we might slake our thirst and drink to our new friendship. Bring flagons for Malachite and the priestess as well."

István bowed even lower this time, and Qarakh had the impression he was striving to be more attentive than normal, as if he were trying to make up for some transgression. "At once, my prince."

István straightened and started off to do his master's bidding, but before he could get far, Alexander said, "One more thing."

István stopped and turned back around. "Yes, my prince?"

"Bring a bucket of water and put out this damn fire."

Chapter Eleven

"Must you be going?" Alexander said, though he didn't sound all that unhappy at the prospect. On the Ventrue's right stood Malachite, to his left was István and Brother Rudiger.

"I should return to the camp and hold council to discuss the matter of our alliance," Qarakh said.

They stood at the edge of Alexander's camp. Qarakh and Deverra's horses had been prepared for them, and they held the reins in their hands, ready to mount and ride. Both horses pawed the ground restlessly, as if anxious to start the return journey. Qarakh had already sent ahead the human family that had been Alexander's gift to him, with directions to drive their wagon east. The Cainites would be able to catch up with them easily on horseback—a fact that would prevent the mortals from taking advantage of their lead to try and escape.

Qarakh extended the burned fingers of his hand and then curled them into a fist. Thanks to a good soaking in blood—both internal and external—his hand was mostly healed, though the flesh was still shiny and pale pink, like that of a mortal infant. Alexander's hand, however, was completely restored—a testament to his age and power.

Alexander glanced toward the east. "Dawn is not far off. Perhaps you should spend the day here and get a fresh start tomorrow evening."

"I appreciate your hospitality, but unlike you, Deverra and I are creatures of the forests and plains. We shall have no trouble finding resting places along the way."

"So be it. Then there is nothing left for me to do but wish you good traveling."

"One moment, my prince, if I may." The exhalation from Malachite's speech tainted the air with the odor of rot, and Qarakh had to keep from wrinkling his nose at the smell. This one too had learned the language of the Livs.

Alexander turned to the Nosferatu with a puzzled look. "Yes?"

"Deverra has told me something of how her tribe is structured, and I am curious to see it for myself. I find the notion of Livs adopting Tartar tribal patterns and behaviors most fascinating. I believe there is much to learn by directly observing their tribe."

In and of itself, Malachite's curiosity wasn't suspicious. Despite their monstrous appearance, Nosferatu had a reputation for being scholars; they also could be adept at concealment and moving without detection when they wished—perfect attributes for a spy. Qarakh was about to deny Malachite's request when Deverra caught his eye. The priestess nodded almost imperceptibly, and Qarakh, though he did not know why Deverra wished the Nosferatu to accompany them, nevertheless kept his objections to himself. He trusted Deverra's judgment as much, if not more, than he did his own.

Ghosts of emotion drifted across Alexander's face, too faint and subtle to read clearly. If Qarakh had to guess, he would say the Ventrue was experiencing a mixture of surprise, anger and disbelief. It appeared that Malachite's request was unplanned, but Qarakh knew better than to trust appearances—especially where Alexander of Paris was concerned.

The Ventrue turned to Qarakh. "Do you have any objection to Malachite accompanying you?"

"No. He may ride with either Deverra or myself, if he wishes."

"Nonsense. I can afford to spare a horse for my good friend Malachite." Alexander ordered István to fetch a steed, and the Cainite nodded and hurried off, almost but not quite running. Rudiger watched István go, amusement dancing in his eyes.

Qarakh tried to gauge the Nosferatu's response to obtaining Alexander's permission, but his face was nearly as expressionless as the prince's. There was a glint of anticipation in

Malachite's eyes, though, and Qarakh wondered if he'd made a wise decision in agreeing to take the Nosferatu with them.

While they waited for István to return, Qarakh addressed Malachite for the first time since entering Alexander's camp. "Deverra and I shall have no difficulty finding shelter from the sun as we travel. Will sleeping in the open be a problem for you?"

Malachite shook his head. "I have been traveling for many years since I left Constantinople." The Nosferatu's mouth twisted into an approximation of a smile. "I've learned how to make do." There was a sadness in Malachite's voice that hinted at a story behind his words.

István returned then, leading a roan gelding. Qarakh and Deverra mounted their steeds. While István held the gelding's bridle, Malachite climbed into the leather saddle with more grace than Qarakh expected.

"Farewell, my new friends," Alexander said. He fixed Malachite with a stare. "And farewell to my old one. I shall look forward to our eventual reunion."

"As shall I, your highness."

Qarakh noticed the Nosferatu kept his tone carefully neutral. Whatever the precise nature of the relationship between Alexander and Malachite, it was obviously more complex than it appeared on the surface. *Perhaps the Nosferatu has more than one story to tell*, Qarakh thought.

"Farewell to you, Alexander of Paris," Qarakh said. "Our meeting has given me much to think on—and perhaps act upon as well."

Alexander smiled, upper lip curling away from his smallish incisors. "I couldn't have said it better myself."

"Do you truly believe that was wise?" Rudiger asked. Alexander watched as the Tartar, his priestess and

Malachite rode off at a trot. The Nosferatu didn't look especially comfortable on horseback, and Alexander thought it was a good thing he possessed the preternatural healing abilities of a Cainite. The way he sat in the saddle, he'd need them.

Alexander didn't look at the knight as he replied. "Could you be more specific?"

"I speak of your allowing the Nosferatu to accompany those pagans." Rudiger didn't bother trying to conceal his disgust for them.

"I couldn't very well deny him in front of Qarakh, not after the oath I made with the Gangrel." Alexander thought Malachite had chosen his moment well, but the man's intentions were still unclear. Alexander supposed it was possible that Malachite's request was exactly what it seemed, but he doubted it. In his own way, the Nosferatu could be just as devious as any prince. Whatever Malachite's game was, Alexander was confident he would eventually uncover its true nature, and then he would find a way to turn it to his advantage. He always did.

Then he thought of Geoffrey, his childe, who now sat upon the throne of Paris.

His throne.

And he thought of a woman named Rosamund.

Some games, he told himself, *take a little longer to win than others*.

"Then the Tartar believes you truly intend to ally with him?" István asked.

"Fool!" Alexander snapped. "Qarakh believes nothing of the sort. He knows better than to trust me." He heard the Gangrel's words once more: *May the flames of this sacred fire bind us both— for as long as each remains true to his word.* Clever, that last bit. "And while that normally would be a wise decision, I am quite serious about forging an alliance with Qarakh and his tribe." *At least a temporary one*, he added mentally. "In time, I hope he comes to see that."

"Perhaps Malachite will help to convince him," István offered.

"Perhaps." But whatever reason Malachite now rode with Qarakh the Untamed, Alexander doubted it had anything to do with playing the role of ambassador. "Still, we must prepare in case the alliance fails to come to fruition." He turned to Rudiger. "Come to my tent after complin tomorrow night so that we might plan strategy."

"Yes, your highness." Rudiger bowed his head and departed. As he walked away, Alexander looked at István.

"Tell me, are you aware of anyone... new?" Ventrue didn't like to speak openly of their tastes in blood, but István was a loyal clansman. Moreover, he was already aware that only the blood of women in love could satisfy Alexander—just as István himself was restricted to feeding on mortals in pain, and Rudiger on the ill.

István thought for a moment before answering. "There is a young laundress barely into her womanhood whom I noticed earlier this night. She was watching one of the mortal squires with keen interest."

"Is she pretty?"

"I'm afraid she's rather plain, your highness."

Alexander sighed. "I suppose one must take what one can get when in the wilderness. See that this laundress is brought to my tent after Vespers." He paused. "And tell Rudiger to wait a while after comping to visit me. I prefer to talk strategy with a full stomach."

As Rudiger walked toward his tent, he ground his teeth so hard that his incisors pierced his lower lip, causing two thin streams of blood to dribble into his beard. Everyone—mortals, ghouls and Cainites alike—hastened to get out of his way when they saw the furious expression on his face.

Despite his great age, Alexander was a fool. Worse, he was a blasphemous, unbelieving fool who viewed the Church as nothing more than a tool to further his own ends. If Lord Jürgen hadn't tasked Rudiger with carrying out Alexander's orders... But he had, and since Jürgen was the *Hochmeister* of the Order of the Black Cross, Rudiger was sworn to obey his every command—regardless of how he felt about it.

Rudiger knew full well that Alexander had ordered a fire built for his parley with the Tartar so that the knight would be unable to remain and listen. All Cainites feared fire to one degree or another, but Rudiger was absolutely terrified of it. It was his one true weakness, visited upon him by God to keep him humble, he believed. He also knew that Alexander intended to ally with the pagan tribe for his own reasons, and not as a tactic designed to eventually lead to its destruction.

Rudiger was tempted to compose a missive to Lord Jürgen informing him of this development, but he would not. As much as it galled him, Alexander was his master—for the moment, at least—and it was his duty to serve the exiled prince to the best of his ability, whether he liked it or not.

But he would keep watching, and if he found incontrovertible proof that Alexander intended to betray Jürgen, then he would do what he had to. And if that meant harm must come to the former prince, then God's will be done.

Smiling, Rudiger wiped the vitae from his beard, then licked his fingers as he continued on to his tent.

Dawn tinted the eastern sky as Rikard—tired, hungry, irritable and afraid that he was going to have to spend another day burrowed in the earth like a mole—rode into view of Alexander's camp.

Finally! He should have just enough time to reach the camp before sunrise. He'd beg shelter in one of the tents, sleep, and when darkness fell, he'd seek an audience with Alexander of Paris. And then…

He grinned. And then.

He cracked the reins and kicked his horse into a gallop.

Qarakh swung his saber in a vicious arc, and the edge sliced across the knight's face before the mortal could even think about raising his own sword to deflect the blow. The Mongol's strike had nearly severed the man's jaw. As blood gushed from the wound, the knight staggered back in agony and shock, but he still managed to keep hold of his sword. Qarakh was impressed; most mortals would have fallen by now. It seemed the Sword-Brothers' reputation for being mighty warriors was well earned. Out of respect, Qarakh decided to grant the man a swift death. He plunged the point of his saber into the knight's right eye, and the mortal stiffened as steel pierced his brain. Qarakh gave the blade a quick twist before yanking it free, and the man fell to the ground, dead but still gripping his sword.

Wilhelmina and Arnulf fought back to back, their blades

moving so swiftly that they were blurs even to Qarakh's eyes. Steel rang on steel, metal bit into flesh, screams of pain echoed through the night, and fountains of blood—mortal, ghoul and Cainite—sprayed the air.

Though his Beast urge him to keep fighting, Qarakh paused a moment to consider strategy. If all the knights of the Livonian order were of similar mettle, it was fortunate that there weren't many Cainites among their ranks this night. He doubted that Arnulf or Wilhelmina shared that view. The two lived for battle—Wilhelmina so she could slay as many Christians as possible, and Arnulf... well, the Goth warrior just loved to kill, whoever the foe and whatever the reason. Mortals and ghouls provided little sport for either of them; they'd much prefer to go up against other Cainites.

Alessandro, though no less deadly a fighter, was more calculating. Instead of hacking at anything that came within range of his sword, he moved across the battlefield, selecting his targets with care. A handful of Cainite knights fought alongside the mortal Sword-Brothers, and while there were far fewer of them, they posed a much greater threat. Alessandro sought out the unliving knights and dispatched them with surgical precision, striking swiftly and without a single wasted motion. The Iberian's face was composed and expressionless, but his eyes blazed with the controlled bloodlust of his Beast.

Grandfather stood well away from the battle, along with Deverra and several other Telyavs, at the edge of a grove of oak trees. The tribe had chosen this moment for battle in order to defend one of the Telyavs' groves, one that had grown around a sacred fire tended by Deverra's acolytes. For nearly a week the knights had marauded through the forest, killing as many of the locals as they could. Now Qarakh and his tribe were here, and the battle had been well and truly joined.

Not that the Telyavs were helpless to defend their grove. Grandfather and Deverra had been conferring for much of the battle, and now the high priestess spoke to several other Telyavs. They then bared their wrists, bit open the veins and formed a ring around one of the largest oaks, clasping hands to form a tight, unbroken circle. As vitae dripped from their wrists onto tree bark, the Telyavs began to chant in a language unfamiliar to Qarakh.

Despite its importance to the Telyavs, the clearing was a small one, not large enough to accommodate fighting on horseback, and almost all of the combatants on both sides had dismounted. The Telyavs' chanting increased in volume and intensity until finally, throughout the clearing, tree roots burst forth from the ground and coiled like serpents around the knights' legs. Not all the knights, though—only those who were Cainites. The coils tightened, and their captives were thrown off balance. Some fell, others struggled to remain standing, and still others began to hack at the roots with their swords. Qarakh knew his people had only moments until the vampiric knights cut themselves free, but that was all the time they needed.

He raised his saber and bellowed a command in Livonian. "Kill the bound ones!"

While some of the newer recruits looked around in puzzlement, the rest of his warriors understood and obeyed. Wilhelmina bellowed a war cry, dashed for the nearest struggling knight and decapitated him with a single blow. Arnulf dropped his sword as he shifted into wolf form and leaped for another trapped knight, fangs bared and jaws flecked with foam. Alessandro stepped calmly toward the bound knight nearest him and laid open the Cainite's throat with a swift, efficient sweep of his blade.

Qarakh felt a moment's pride in his warriors before surrendering to the urgings of his Beast and rejoining the battle.

It was over all too soon.

Most of the knights—mortal and undead—had been slain, while only a few tribe members and Telyavs had been lost. Several of the Christian knights had fled the clearing, but Wilhelmina and Arnulf were in pursuit. Qarakh was confident their hunt would prove successful.

"But it wasn't, was it? One knight survived to tell Jürgen what occurred."

Qarakh did his best to ignore the voice. All around him, Cainites were bent over the corpses of mortal, ghoul and vampire alike, feeding to dispatch the wounded and restore their own strength. Qarakh approved; he despised waste. Deverra and the other Telyav enchanters were among the most ravenous of the feeders, for they had sacrificed a great deal of their own blood to enchant the tree roots.

"They may have helped win a single battle, but the war goes on."

Qarakh told himself to ignore the voice, but he couldn't. As if controlled by an outside force, his body turned of its own accord to face the owner of the voice. At his feet lay the corpse of a mortal knight he had killed by skewering through the eye. Qarakh could've sworn he'd slain the man in a different part of the clearing. Still, in the thick of battle, it was easy to become confused about details, and really, what did it matter precisely where he'd killed the mortal? The man was dead, wasn't he?

"You're a fine one to talk about being dead. You died years ago, but you're walking around. Why do you find it so difficult to believe that I can still talk?" The voice emanated from the corpse's mouth, but neither its tongue nor lips moved. And there was something familiar about the voice, something that Qarakh couldn't quite...

"You came to the aid of the Telyavs, but in so doing you drew attention to yourself and your tribe. And now, a year later, Alexander of Paris has come to Livonia, and he has brought an army with him."

Qarakh frowned. A year later? Alexander? He lowered his saber and inserted the tip into the corpse's mouth. "Whatever foul sorcery has granted you speech, I wonder if it shall continue to work after I cut out your tongue."

"Go ahead." The voice sounded unconcerned, as if the corpse might have accompanied the words with a shrug if it were still capable of moving its shoulders. "I will simply find another vessel through which to speak."

Qarakh looked around and saw that no one else in the clearing was moving. Deverra, Alessandro, all the rest... they stood, kneeled or crouched as motionless as the bodies of the dead that littered the field. The clearing was silent, the air itself still and lifeless. Qarakh looked up at the sky and saw that the stars were gone. He sensed they weren't hidden by sudden cloud cover, but were truly no longer there, had perhaps *never* been there. All that remained was vast, unbroken, infinite darkness.

He looked back down at the corpse, but it was no longer that of the mortal knight. It was Aajav. He shared the knight's wounds—the slashed throat and ruined eye—and he was clearly dead, not merely in torpor, but nevertheless it was Aajav, his blood brother and sire, lying on the ground before him.

"You were a fool to pledge oath to the Ventrue. He will turn on you faster than a striking snake." Though the face was Aajav's, the voice was not.

Qarakh knew now that it was the same voice it always was: the voice of hunger, rage and endless need. The voice of the Beast.

Qarakh frowned in confusion. He had taken an oath with someone named Alexander? He could almost remember, but how was that possible? It hadn't happened yet—or had it? If only the damnable Beast would be silent and let him think... The tip of his saber remained inside the corpse's—inside Aajav's—mouth, and Qarakh nearly rammed the blade all the way in then, but he resisted. He knew there was little point, for the voice came not from Aajav, but from inside himself, and the only way to silence it would be to greet the dawn and find Final Death. But this he would not do, for he would never give the Beast the satisfaction of claiming the only victim it truly wanted in the end: him.

Besides, even though he knew this was some manner of enchantment or hallucination, the face was still that of his brother, and he couldn't bring himself to ravage it. He gently removed the sword and lowered it to his side.

A shard of memory came back to him then. "I have merely pledged to consider an alliance with the Ventrue," Qarakh said, sounding more defensive than he liked. "Nothing more."

"Alexander is a hundred times older than you are," the Beast said. "You cannot hope to best him, neither in a battle of wits, nor in a battle of arms. And have no doubt: It shall come down to the latter, and sooner rather than later."

"No matter the opponent, there is always a way to win. A warrior need only find it."

"There is only one way to defeat this foe, Qarakh, and *I* am that way. Give yourself over to me, and I shall grant you victory over Alexander of Paris."

Qarakh felt fear, then—not of the Beast, but rather of himself and his own need to protect his tribe and their Telyav allies If the Beast could truly do what it claimed, perhaps... perhaps it would be worth the price he would have to pay.

Tempting though it might be, giving himself over to the Beast that dwelled inside him would not be living in *yostoi*. He would be surrendering to his basest impulses and desires, allowing himself to be subsumed until there was nothing left of Qarakh the man and all that remained was the hunger and fury and lust of the Beast.

Qarakh's reply was simple. "No."

The corpse that looked like Aajav (because it couldn't be Aajav, it *couldn't!*) moved for the first time since it had begun speaking. It turned its head so that it was clearly looking at Qarakh with the one eye it still possessed. Its mouth stretched into a hideous parody of a grin, and this time when it spoke, its mouth moved.

"What makes you think you have a choice?"

The mouth opened wide then, impossibly, cavernously wide. Inside was a darkness beyond anything Qarakh had ever imagined. It wasn't merely the absence of light and color. It wasn't simply nothing, for the concept of nothingness always implied *something*. It was the lack even of lack itself. It... wasn't. Air rushed in to fill the great yawning void, screaming past Qarakh, tearing at him, thrusting him forward, toward and into, and then he was falling, but not falling, for falling was something, and since this wasn't nothing, there couldn't be something, so he couldn't be falling, but he was, he was, he—

Chapter Twelve

Qarakh awakened. Swaddled in the cool, comforting embrace of earth, he was tempted to stay there, to close his eyes and return to sleep and hope that there would be no more memories, no more dreams that changed all too easily into nightmares. A sluggish weariness settled into his body. His limbs felt heavy, leaden, as if they were no longer flesh and not quite stone, but rather some transitional state between. An overwhelming sensation of peace welled up inside him, and he felt himself slipping away... But before awareness completely deserted him, Qarakh realized what was happening: He was surrendering to the same torpor that had claimed Aajav.

With a supreme effort of will, he surged free of the earth and stood once more in the open night air. He felt dizzy and weak at first, but with each passing second, vertigo ebbed and strength returned to him.

"Is something wrong?"

Qarakh nearly sprang upon the Nosferatu standing in the forest glade and holding the reins of three horses, but then he remembered—this was Malachite, their new traveling companion.

"No." He couldn't believe how easily he had almost given in to the temptation of torpor. It had felt so natural, so right, so effortless to allow himself to sink into the oblivion it offered. Is that what it had been like for Aajav? If so, Qarakh could understand now why his brother had so far refused to wake from his sleep within the sacred mound of the Telyavs.

Malachite evidently had been in the process of readying the horses when Qarakh appeared, for the three mounts were already saddled. The Nosferatu must have noticed Qarakh's scrutiny of the horses, for he said, "I fed them, too."

Qarakh glanced upward at the patches of sky he could see between the overhanging tree branches.

The sun had gone down, but not so long ago that the stars were visible. "I'm surprised you had the time—that is, unless you have discovered a way to walk in sunlight."

Malachite gave Qarakh a thin smile. "Not quite, but the tree cover in this part of the forest is especially thick, and members of my clan *are* skilled at keeping to the shadows. When the forest gloom became dark enough, I rose and—since both you and Deverra remained sleeping—I decided to put my time to good use and prepare the horses for travel." When Qarakh didn' t respond right away, Malachite frowned. "I hope I haven't done something wrong. I know little about your customs, and if there is some proscription against someone else touching your horse..."

Qarakh waved away the Nosferatu's concerns. "I am glad you did. The sooner we start riding, the sooner we shall reach the current campsite."

Malachite opened his own mouth then, presumably to ask a question, but before he could speak, Deverra emerged from a nearby oak tree, separating herself from the wood as easily as another being might move through air. She gave Qarakh a smile. "Sleep well?"

He found himself wishing that Deverra had used her magic to connect their spirits during the day. Not because he desired her again—at least, not only—but because her presence would have been a comfort to him as he slept and might well have prevented his nightmare, or at least made it easier to bear. Still, they had agreed she should conserve her strength and perform enchantments only when necessary—a wise, if not particularly satisfying, decision.

If the Nosferatu hadn't been present, Qarakh might have told her the truth about his dream, but as it was, he simply responded with a curt nod.

She frowned and gave him a look that said, *We'll talk about it later*, before turning to Malachite. "And how was your slumber?"

Malachite brushed a bit of dirt and mold off the left sleeve of his robe. "I've spent the day in worse places than beneath a fallen tree, but I must say that I envy your ability to inter yourself within living ones. I don't suppose I can convince you to tell me how it's done?"

"It's quite simple, really," Deverra said with a grin. "All one has to do is renounce Christ and embrace the worship of Telyavel."

Qarakh expected the Nosferatu to take offense at this, but instead he smiled back.

"Is Tremere blood sorcery truly so simple?"

Deverra's grin fell away. "I am not Tremere," she said, her voice taut with anger. "I am Telyav."

Malachite made a half-bow and then straightened. "My most sincere apologies. I have heard whispers that there were members of that sorcerous clan in these far lands. I made an unfounded assumption."

Deverra said nothing for several moments, and though her face remained composed, her eyes reflected the fury that raged inside her as she struggled to come to terms with her Beast. Finally, her gaze cleared and when she spoke, her tone was relaxed, if melancholy. "I was Tremere once, but that was some time ago. It is, as they say, a long story."

"I gather we have something of a ride ahead of us," Malachite said. "A story will help make the time pass more swiftly, not to mention more pleasantly." Deverra considered for a bit, but finally she said,

"Why not?"

Qarakh was surprised. Not so much that she would choose to share such a story with Malachite when they'd only met last evening, but because he was actually jealous of the Nosferatu.

"Let's mount up and be off, then," Qarakh said, the words coming out more gruffly than he intended. Deverra looked at him and, though he wasn't certain, it appeared she was trying to suppress a smile. Qarakh wondered if some fraction of the link they had shared that heady day remained, still strong enough to allow her to sense his feelings. Then again, perhaps his feelings were so obvious that she needed no witchery to divine them.

"Very well." Deverra climbed into her saddle, and Qarakh and Malachite did likewise, and the three of them rode off at a trot, headed northeast, in the direction of the tribal lands. And as they rode, Deverra began her tale:

"I was born to my mortal life in Livonia. My father was a village blacksmith, and I grew up to the whoosh of bellows, the crackle of fire and the ringing of hammer on steel. To my father, his work was a sacred task. Telyavel is not only the Protector of the Dead. He is also the smith god, the Maker of Things. My father believed that a smith worked with the basic elements of creation itself—air, fire, water and earth—and molded them as he saw fit. To him, being a blacksmith was not only a way to honor the gods, it was a way to know, in a limited fashion, what it was like to *be* them.

"Perhaps it was my father's outlook that sparked my own interest in the secret functioning of the world. I studied the flows of the elements and learned to draw secrets from them. When the village livestock got sick, I was able to find the secret of curing them. Some called me a witch then, but most of the village agreed that as a smith's daughter I had been blessed by Telyavel.

"And so time went on, my father working at his forge, and I using my paltry knowledge to make life a little better for our people. I was not long into my young womanhood when a solitary stranger came to our village, a wise man garbed in robes of amber and brown. He spoke to the villagers, telling them that he heard rumors of a girl who demonstrated impressive skill at the mystic arts, and they of course directed him to my father's forge. The man introduced himself to my father as Alferic and they spoke for some time. Later that night, my father told me a great scholar was going to take me on as his apprentice, and I would leave with him in the morning.

"I was saddened at the thought of leaving my family, but I was also excited by the prospect at learning more. So excited that I didn't notice the glassy-eyed stare in my father's eyes or the listless monotone of his voice. Years later, I realized that Alferic had ensorcelled my father to make him agree to give me up. The Tremere can be quite aggressive when it comes to finding and taking on apprentices. And the more potential a child has, the more aggressive they can be. My father was fortunate that he was weak-minded enough to succumb to Alferic's spell, otherwise my soon-to-be teacher would likely have slain him in order to obtain me.

"I went away with Alferic. Over the next several years, he introduced me to the world of the mystic scholars of House Tremere. We traveled from chantry to chantry, through Hungary, Bavaria, Saxony, Bulgaria... and if I found it odd that the magi preferred to sleep during the day and be active at night, I put it down to simple practicality. After all, so many spells and enchantments must be cast in the dead of night—or so Alferic taught me.

"Slowly, step by step, Alferic led me deeper into the realms of dark sorcery until I considered it commonplace to offer up my body as part of a mystic rite or plunge an obsidian dagger into the breast of a willing—or often not-so-willing—participant. I learned my lessons well, and by the time I entered my full womanhood, my apprenticeship was at an end. And during the ceremony wherein I was officially to become a full-fledged magus, I learned the final secret of the Tremere when Alferic Embraced me. The exchange of vitae was presented as merely another mystic rite, and I had no idea what its true purpose was—not until I changed.

"I suppose on a certain level I wasn't surprised, for the revelation that the Tremere were in truth vampires explained a great many things about them, but I was horrified and furious that I had been transformed without my consent. And I soon discovered that I was not the only one among the Tremere who felt this way. Ordinary mortals would've had little choice but to accept their new state of existence, but we were magi, and we believed that what had been done to us could be undone, so we secretly began searching for a way to reverse the Embrace.

"Ultimately, the undead Tremere weren't so very different from many mortals. They considered blood sorcery and even the Curse of Caine itself to be nothing more than avenues to greater power. They valued knowledge only as a means to an end and knew nothing of true wisdom.

"Those of us seeking a remedy for our condition met with little success but plenty of suspicion from our fellows. We therefore decided to break off from the clan and search for a cure on our own. I knew my homeland was a place of great power, so I led our little splinter group to Livonia. We didn't find a way to reverse the Embrace, of course—I'm no longer sure that such a thing is possible—but we found something else: a new home and new purpose.

"Telyavel was Protector of the Dead and so we sought a new bond with the god. He accepted our worship and guided us to act as priests and serve the land and people. The blood rites became part of the people's worship, and the Telyavs were born."

"You said that the Tremere knew nothing of true wisdom," Malachite said. "What do you think true wisdom is?" There was no mockery in his voice. He seemed genuinely interested in Deverra's answer.

She thought for a moment, then looked at Qarakh and gave him a smile. "To live in *yostoi*." Before Malachite could ask, she explained. "It's a Mongolian word that means 'balance.'"

"A balance of what?" the Nosferatu asked.

"Of life and death, the Self and the Beast, killing out of necessity instead of mere bloodlust," Deverra said. "*Yostoi* is the path of true harmony between the desires of the flesh and the needs of the spirit."

Malachite smiled. "Our beliefs are not that dissimilar after all."

Qarakh sniffed. "Yours is a religion of civilization—of buildings that close you off from the world, of laws that force you to act against your own nature, and of priests who tell you the greatest glory is to force your god on others at sword point."

"Merely because one proclaims himself Christian doesn't make it so," Malachite said, "any more than I can become a falcon by simply stating that I am."

Qarakh was about to argue the point, but then he remembered what Alexander had told him, how the prince used Christianity as a tool and nothing more. The Mongol wondered how many other "soldiers of Christ" held the same view—not that it mattered overmuch. In the end, an enemy was an enemy regardless of how sincerely he practiced his professed religion.

"We should be far enough away from Alexander's encampment by now for you to speak freely," Qarakh said to Malachite. "Why don't you tell me the true reason you wish to accompany us?"

Malachite hesitated before responding. "It is, as Deverra said a while ago, a lengthy story."

"You said that a story can make time pass more swiftly," Qarakh said.

Malachite smiled. "I did say that, didn't I? My tale begins with a dream—*the* Dream—a dream called Constantinople."

"Your Highness?"

Alexander sat sideways on his bed, head bent over the body of a young woman in a plain brown peasant dress lying next to him. He looked up from the wet crimson ruin that had been the laundress's neck and glared at István. Alexander didn't liked to be disturbed when he was feeding. He was a civilized man—after all, was he not a child of Greece, the greatest civilization the world had ever seen?—and civilized men didn't speak to their servants while in the process of fulfilling their most basic needs. Alexander no more wished to be interrupted while feeding than a mortal man would wish to be disturbed while using a chamber pot.

"What is it?"

For an instant, it appeared as if István might withdraw from his lord's tent rather than risk the full force of Alexander's wrath, but then he cleared his throat—a sign of nervousness rather than any physical need—and continued. "A Cainite has entered the camp and wishes to see you. His name is Rikard. He claims he is a deserter from the Tartar's tribe. He says he has information for you."

"Does he now? How interesting." Alexander looked down at the laundress' savaged neck. Had he meant to kill her? Oh well, she was tasting flat anyway. With one hand he lifted the girl's corpse and tossed it at István's feet. "Dispose of this trash." He licked his bloody lips. "Give me some time to make myself presentable. Tell this Rikard I shall see him."

István picked up the girl's body and tucked it under his left arm. "Yes, your highness," he said, relief evident in his tone. He bowed his head, then turned and left.

"Well, well, well." Alexander smiled, displaying blood-flecked fangs. "My new friend has himself a Judas."

Chapter Thirteen

"And so you came to Livonia with Alexander in hope of finding this bishop?" Qarakh asked.

Malachite nodded. "It is my belief that Archbishop Nikita might have information on how I can locate the Dracon."

To Qarakh, it sounded a fool's dream at best and a lunatic's delusion at worst. The Nosferatu sought a supremely powerful Cainite called the Dracon—whose existence Qarakh was skeptical of—so that he might restore the city of Constantinople which, to Malachite's mind at least, somehow signified a kind of paradise on earth. It didn't make any sense to the Mongol. Only a creature of civilization could equate a city—a conglomeration of stone and wood—with a state of spiritual enlightenment.

Deverra, however, took the Nosferatu seriously. "While you parleyed with Alexander, Malachite told me of his search for Nikita. In turn, I told him that if anyone might know where this man hid, it would be you, for you have roamed wide across Livonia and neighboring lands."

Qarakh glanced up at the stars, then sniffed the air. He scented rain coming; not tonight, but soon. He judged they would reach the camp before the next sunrise, but not long before. They'd caught up to and passed the mortal family in their wagon a bit ago, and Qarakh had been pleased to see that they were still headed in the right direction. He was now confident that they would complete the remainder of the journey without trying to escape. Not that a few mortals more or less would make that much difference to his tribe, but a wise shepherd knew that he could always use a few more sheep in the herd.

Qarakh turned to Deverra. "Do the Telyavs know of this preacher?"

Deverra shook her head. "No. This Nikita may be a powerful Cainite able to mask his presence from us. Sorcerous sight is not always better than the traveler's own eyes."

Malachite rode on Qarakh's right, Deverra on his left as their mounts proceeded at a trot across the grassy plain. The Nosferatu leaned over in his saddle to speak with Qarakh—so far, in fact, that the Mongol wouldn't have been surprised if Malachite fell off his horse.

"Have you encountered such a place, or at least heard tell of it?" There was an eagerness in the Nosferatu's voice, and a gleam in his eyes that spoke of barely restrained fanaticism.

Qarakh wasn't sure how to answer—or for that matter, *if* he wanted to answer. After all, what did they truly know about Malachite? Deverra seemed to trust him, but even if he proved trustworthy, Qarakh wasn't certain helping the Nosferatu would be a good thing.

"You are Christian, and we are what you would call pagans. Deverra reveres Telyavel—"

"Among other gods," the priestess put in.

"—while I honor Father Tengri, Lord of the Sky. It is the way of the Mongols to tolerate the beliefs of others, but you Christians extend no such courtesy. The Sword-Brothers look to subjugate all Livonia to their faith. And Alexander, though he may not truly believe in your savior, nonetheless uses His name to further his own ambitions. Why should we help you in your quest?"

Qarakh expected Malachite to come back with an angry defense of his religion, but instead the Nosferatu grew thoughtful for a time, and the three Cainites continued riding in silence, save for the sound of their mounts' hoofs. Eventually, Malachite spoke once more.

"I could say that both mortals and Cainites are imperfect creatures, and that one shouldn't judge an entire religion by the actions of its worst adherents—or of those who adhere to it in name only. And I could say that a central part of the Dream is to create a place where Cainites and mortals can live in peace together and follow God's will, and not man's confused and sometimes self-serving interpretation of it. I could say that it was crusaders like the Sword-Brothers who sacked Constantinople and restoring the Dream would be a defeat for them. I could even say that the will of God Himself is against you, and you can no more hold back the spread of Christianity than you can postpone the changing of seasons. And while I believe those are all valid points, I also believe that none of them will sway you. In the end, you will help me because you choose to, or you will not help me at all."

Malachite fell silent then, and it was Qarakh's turn to think. The Nosferatu had shown no signs of deception or intolerance so far, and moreover, there was much information about Alexander and his forces that he could share. But Qarakh doubted Malachite was generous enough—or foolish enough— to provide such information without cost.

He glanced at Deverra, and she gave him a slight nod.

"It was several years ago, during the winter...."

Qarakh glided like the shadow of a passing cloud over frost-covered grass. The night wind was cold and biting as sharpened steel, but the frigid air had little effect on his undead flesh. He had left his horse tethered to a small tree a few miles back. He could move more swiftly and silently on foot. This night called for stealth.

He had been roaming throughout Livonia for the better part of a month now. Since arriving here with Aajav the previous year, and meeting Deverra, he had made this land his new home. The Telyav still worked diligently to revive Aajav and in return he was determined to help her resist the encroaching Christian knights and missionaries who threatened her faith. But her role as priestess among mortals had given him larger ideas. If she could establish such a relationship here, he wondered if he might build something more: a tribe, or even a tribal nation in the Mongolian sense. Livonia was a lush, unspoiled land of plains and forests, yet with enough mortal inhabitants to provide good feeding stock. In addition, the Livs were a pagan people who had resisted the encroachment of

Christianity for centuries. A nation of night-walkers could be established here, a place where vampires might be able to live freely and openly, without being forced to hide in the shadows like ghostly wraiths.

To this end, he had been scouting the length and breadth of the land to determine if there were any hidden powers—Cainite or otherwise—that might oppose him. The Telyavs had no objection, according to Deverra. In fact, they welcomed the thought of an alliance with such a tribe as Qarakh might create, for while the Telyavs were skilled at witchcraft, they were not proficient in the arts of war. There were others to consider, however.

On his long trek from the far eastern steppe, Qarakh had faced the man-wolves on several occasions. These Lupines—men cursed to assume the shape of wolves under the right conditions—were ferocious warriors who held their own territories in the deep woods. They could hunt by day or night and had little love for Cainites, even Gangrel who could take wolf shapes as well as they. There were packs of these werewolves in Livonia, and Qarakh had sought them out, primarily to determine where the man-wolves drew the boundaries of their territory, and to learn if they might be amenable to an alliance with his tribe—once it was established. The most restrained response he'd received to his inquiries was a set of fangs buried in his shoulder, while the most violent response had come close to delivering him unto the Final Death.

No potential alliances among the Lupines then, to put it mildly, but he discovered that if he remained out of their territory deep within the thickest part of the forests, they took no notice of him. The Lupines would never be friends to his tribe, but at least it appeared they wouldn't be enemies. There were other powers in Livonia, however. The land practically reeked of magic, but these other creatures—fey folk and spirits that neither man nor Cainite had names for—all took the Lupines' attitude of separation from night-walkers.

But Qarakh wasn't so sure of the beings that inhabited the stone structure he now approached at a loping run.

Several nights ago when he had first passed by this

place—high wall, courtyard, a main building of simple construction and design, no ornamentation to the stonework, plain wooden shutters covering the windows—he'd experienced a strange sensation. A feeling that someone was watching him, but not from any specific vantage. It was as if whoever (or *whatever*) was observing him from every direction at once. But as disturbing as that had been, there was more.

It was subtle at first, an almost unnoticeable itching or tingling on his skin, thousands of phantom insects crawling all over his body on tiny invisible legs. The feeling became more intense the closer he rode to the stone building until it felt as if the ghostly insects were now digging their pincers into his flesh and tearing off small hunks by the hundreds... no, by the thousands. Before long, the pain had become so unbearable that Qarakh, no stranger to pain, hadn't been able to stand it any longer. He'd turned the horse—which hadn't noticed anything wrong save for her master's sudden and atypical clumsiness with the reins—away from the building and kicked her into a gallop. The pain had instantly begun to lessen, and it continued to abate with every yard they put between themselves and the cursed place.

But now Qarakh had returned, coming swiftly and silently on foot, hoping this time to approach unnoticed. Whatever the nature of the power that was associated with the building, Qarakh needed to know precisely what it was—and whether it would prove friend or (more likely) foe.

He was within a dozen yards of the outer wall now, and it appeared his attempt at stealth had been successful. He didn't feel he was being watched, and he experienced no sensation of pain. Perhaps the attention of whatever lay behind the wall was elsewhere this night.

"Or perhaps you have been allowed to approach."

Qarakh stopped running and whirled to face the owner of the voice. The stranger was male and garbed in a black robe. His aspect was that of a man in his middle years—brown hair gray at the temples, cheeks verging on being jowls, eyes beginning to recede into the sockets, the flesh beneath them puffy and dark—but his eyes glittered as if made of ice, their glassy surfaces catching the light from the stars above them and casting it back as tiny pinpricks of cold fire. For an instant, Qarakh had the impression that the light wasn't a reflection but instead emanated from somewhere behind those eyes. But he dismissed it as nothing more than a trick of the nocturnal light.

"It's a cold evening to be abroad, even for creatures such as we." The man smiled, almost deliberately, revealing long sharp incisors, as if to confirm that he was indeed a Cainite. "But then you're a stubborn one, Qarakh the Untamed, else you would not have returned after the warning I gave you the other night."

Qarakh was surprised that the man knew his name, but he fought to keep his expression neutral. "Who are you and what is this place?"

The man cocked his head slightly and looked at Qarakh for a moment, as if he were not only seeing the Mongol's physical aspect but looking beyond that, into whatever remained of his once mortal soul.

"This is a simple monastery, and I am naught but a humble brother." The man's tone contained the merest trace of amused mockery, as if he were an adult speaking to a naughty but precocious child.

Normally Qarakh would have responded to such treatment with rage, but the Beast inside him remained silent, almost as if it had retreated to a far corner of his mind and huddled there, shivering in fear. Qarakh realized that his Beast was hiding because it had for the first time encountered a predator far greater than itself.

Still, Qarakh was a warrior, and warriors did not run unless there was no other choice, and even then they only did so if it might lead to a later victory. Instead, he nodded, accepting the man's nonanswers.

The stranger went on. "I know why you have come here, my son, and while I cannot offer you an alliance, I can assure you that neither I nor any of mine shall interfere with you and the tribe you will create. We are contemplatives and scholars. The Obertus order is not a threat to you."

Qarakh knew better than to accept a stranger's word without question, but in this case he had no doubt whatsoever that the man was speaking truth, though he didn't know *how* he knew this. He just did.

"I have one other thing to tell you," the man continued. "Should you wish to hear it."

The stranger made this statement in an offhand manner, but there was something in his voice that told Qarakh he was being given a choice—one that would shape the course of his future for better or for worse. Qarakh had never backed away from a challenge and did not intend to start.

"I do."

A faint hint of a smile—perhaps of approval, or amusement—moved across the man's lips then was gone.

"Victory is in the blood, my son. Thus it has ever been, and thus shall it ever be." The man then gave Qarakh a look that was a mixture of affection and sadness. "Now go."

Sudden terror welled up inside Qarakh—unreasoning, overwhelming terror. His Beast sprang out of hiding and shrieked for Qarakh to flee, flee, *flee!* Without thinking, without even being truly aware of it, Qarakh turned, shed one form and donned another, and bounded away on padded paws. He ran with no other thought than to put as much distance as he could between himself and the dark-robed man whose eyes held the whole of the night sky. Qarakh was still running hours later, when the first rays of dawn came stabbing out of the east, and he dove into the sheltering embrace of the frozen winter earth only seconds before the sun would have taken him.

Nestled safe within earth and ice, he closed his eyes and prayed he would not be afflicted by dreams. This time, at least, his prayers were answered.

"I might know of a place for you to search," Qarakh said to Malachite. "A monastery. And perhaps I shall tell you of it... in time."

The Nosferatu opened his mouth as if he intended to protest, but then he closed it and merely nodded.

The three Cainites continued riding toward the camp in silence, each alone with his or her own dark thoughts.

"Your name is Rikard."

Rikard wasn't sure whether Alexander expected an answer or not, so he merely nodded. The Ventrue sat a table in his tent, a map spread out before him. He didn't look up from it as he spoke. Rikard found this annoying, but he knew better than to say anything about it.

"And you have come here because you wish to betray your master."

Rikard had no doubt that he should respond to this statement, but he also knew that he had to do so carefully. He sensed that Alexander, for all his seeming indifference, was listening quite closely.

"I have come to betray no one. I wish to enter into your service—if you will have me, that is." Rikard congratulated himself; a little touch of humility never hurt.

Alexander continued examining the map, now tracing his fingers over blue lines indicating rivers. He still didn't look at him, but Rikard could sense the prince's increased interest.

The Ventrue was nothing like he had expected. He looked to have been Embraced while barely out of boyhood. He was slight of build, his features delicate, almost feminine. Instead of wearing the mail armor and tabard of the military orders, he was dressed in a purple robe a bit too large for his body. Rikard thought it made Alexander look ridiculous, like a child playing dress-up in his father's clothes.

The prince's brow wrinkled in contemplation, and for an instant Rikard feared Alexander had read his thoughts. But then the Ventrue's brow smoothed. Rikard tried to relax, but not fully. Doing so in the presence of a Cainite of such age and power as Alexander of Paris would be tantamount to committing suicide.

"Why would you wish to do such a thing?" Alexander asked. He now ran his fingertips over the letters of place names on the map. Rikard noted that he avoided touching Paris. "If serving Qarakh was not to your liking, what makes you think you shall be any more satisfied in my service?"

Rikard had anticipated this question and had a ready

answer. "Qarakh is a cunning warrior, I'll give him that, but he's not much of a leader. Besides, his whole notion of creating a tribe comprised entirely of feral pagans is ludicrous."

"Indeed?" Alexander looked up from his beloved map at last and fixed his penetrating gaze upon Rikard. "What makes you say that?"

The intensity of the prince's gaze was such that Rikard felt an urge to take a step backward, but the power of those eyes kept his feet fastened firmly where they were. "Most of the tribe are wanderers who come and go as they please. Livonia is a place they visit upon occasion rather than their home."

"Really." There was something in Alexander's tone that urged Rikard to continue, so he did.

"Yes, and the new members that Qarakh manages to recruit"—Rikard had to resist the urge to add *like me*—"are mostly outcasts and troublemakers. And even after all the training they've been given, they still barely know which end of a sword goes in their hand and which goes in their opponent." Rikard knew he was exaggerating, but he wanted to make certain that Alexander believed that his sole motivation for coming here was to join his forces instead of using the Ventrue to take revenge upon Qarakh. He doubted Alexander would take kindly to being used.

"Go on." Alexander's tone had hardened, and Rikard began to worry that he had said something to make the prince angry. Nevertheless, he did as Alexander commanded. On a subconscious level, he knew he didn't have any choice.

"I suppose it's not all Qarakh's fault. The witch Deverra has him under some kind of spell, and it's muddled his thinking. Whenever the Tartar is in Livonia, she's never far from his side, and he listens to her as if she were his equal. It must be sorcery— why else would he trust the counsel of a Tremere usurper?"

"*What* did you say?"

Rikard blinked. One instant Alexander had been sitting at his desk, and the next he was standing toe to toe with Rikard, looking up at him with eyes full of death. Rikard turned pale— even for a Cainite—and he desperately wished he could flee the tent, the camp, the whole damn country, but he remained standing where he was, unable to so much as lift a foot, let alone turn and run.

In his terror, Rikard couldn't recall what he had said to so upset Alexander. "I... I don't..."

"Are you telling me that the priestess that counsels Qarakh is a member of Clan Tremere?"

"That was one of the rumors around camp. Not only Deverra, but all the Telyavic priests. Supposedly they broke off from the Tremere some time ago and came to Livonia. Why, I don't know."

"And do these Telyavs still possess the mystical knowledge and abilities of their former patrons?"

"I'm not sure. I don't know a great deal about the Tremere, but Deverra definitely wields magic, and I believe the other Telyavs do as well, to greater or lesser degrees."

Alexander swore in a language Rikard didn't recognize, and then his serpentine gaze bore into the traitor's eyes, and Rikard had the feeling that the prince was digging into his mind, sifting through his memories with unimaginable speed to determine whether or not he was telling the truth. Rikard felt pressure building within his head, growing more intense and painful with each passing second, until it felt as if his Final Death were at hand.

But then, just when Rikard thought he could take no more, the pressure let up.

Alexander stepped back and Rikard saw that he was smiling. "You've been an immense help to me, Rikard, and I especially appreciate the tidbit of information that you were holding in reserve. You tried so hard to keep it from me, but I'm afraid your mind proved too weak. One of the weakest I've encountered in two thousand years, actually. Do you have anything else to offer me before I dismiss you?"

Rikard did not. He felt like a hollow vessel that had been well and truly emptied. With some effort, he managed to shake his head.

"I thought not. Very well, then. Despite the fact that I personally appreciate and am grateful for your treacherous nature, long and too often bitter experience has taught me that men like you are best disposed of once you've fulfilled your purpose."

Rikard's thoughts were sluggish, fragmented and confused, as if Alexander's less than gentle probing had damaged his mind. He wasn't sure if he fully understood what the prince had said, but he decided to smile anyway.

"In a moment, I want you to leave my tent and seek out the Cainite who brought you here. His name is Lord István. I want you to give him a message. Are you listening carefully?"

Rikard nodded, eager to please his new master.

"Tell him that you are his to do with as he pleases. Cainite pain will surely taste even sweeter to him than the mortal suffering he must subside on. Repeat the message, please."

Rikard did so, and he must have gotten the words right because Alexander said, "Very good, now do as I told you."

Rikard was saddened at the thought of leaving his beloved master, but he wouldn't be a very good servant if he disobeyed, so he turned, grinning like an idiot, and left in search of István, repeating Alexander's message to himself in a whisper over and over and over and over and…

Damn them all to hell! How could he have been foolish enough to believe rabble such as Qarakh and his tribe would make suitable allies? They were animals and nothing more—chaotic, savage and equally likely to turn on him or desert him. Qarakh might fancy himself a man of honor, but in the end he was just another beast in Cainite's clothing.

But Alexander was far more disturbed by the discovery that the Telyavs were an offshoot of the damnable Tremere. He had known about the Tartar's tribe—after all, that was the reason he had marched on Livonia in the first place—and while there had been some rumors swirling around Jürgen's court that the pagans possessed a certain degree of mystic powers, Alexander had dismissed them as inconsequential. After all, every Cainite had blood gifts of one sort of another. But the Tremere were power-hungry sorcerers of the worst type, diablerists and schemers who routinely violated the traditions of high blood. Sorcerers were interested in one thing only: increasing their own power. It was a motivation that Alexander well understood, and he might have been tempted to explore the possibility of an alliance with the Telyavs anyway... *if* they hadn't been members of the thrice-damned Tremere. Goratrix and his clan had supported Geoffrey in his theft of the Parisian throne, and it was quite possible that these "Telyavs" were in Livonia for the sole purpose of drawing him here and luring him into a trap. Such scheming would be just like his traitorous childe.

And like Rosamund?

Two thoughts followed this one: simultaneous, intertwined.

Rosamund wouldn't do this. Rosamund would do this to me.

Without being aware of it, Alexander bared his teeth, looking as much like an animal as any Gangrel. Plots within plots, wheels within wheels, motives within motives... Two thousand years of unlife, and what did he have to show for it? His entire existence was one mirror facing another reflecting a reflection reflecting a reflection reflecting a reflection, on and on forever, until it was impossible to determine what the *real* image, what the *truth*, really was.

In that situation, there was only one way to determine what was real and what wasn't: smash the mirrors to pieces.

There was no point in waiting for Qarakh to make a decision about an alliance—either he was a willing partner in the Telyavs' trap or merely their pawn. Either way, Alexander had no intention of allying with the Gangrel now. The fallen prince... no, the once and future prince... would instead attack swiftly in order to catch his enemies off guard. He would crush them and use the victory to build his political capital in the Cainite community and, perhaps most importantly, send a clear message to Geoffrey—and Rosamund. He would not be stopped.

He walked out of his tent and almost called out for István, but then he remembered. István was likely busy right now with his new playmate. He waved over one of the ghouls who served him as attendants and ordered him to inform Rudiger that his prince was ready to speak with him.

There were plans to make.

Chapter Fourteen

The first thing Qarakh did upon returning to the campsite was call a council, a *kuriltai*. Alessandro, Wilhelmina, Arnulf and Grandfather joined Deverra and their khan at the usual meeting place away from the tents. Malachite had looked disappointed when it became clear that he was not going to be invited to sit in on the council, but he contented himself with talking to one of the Cainites who had returned to the tribal lands since Qarakh and Deverra had departed for Alexander's campsite. Qarakh was pleased to note how many had returned, and how many of the tribe's allies had come as well. Eirik Longtooth of Finland was here, as was Karl the Blue. From Prussia, where they led the Gangrel resistance to the Teutonic Knights, came Borovich the Grim and Tengael. From Lativa, Lacplesis the Beastslayer and the Tzimisce Vala, and from Uppsala, the Gangrel leader Werter. Some had brought Cainite and ghoul warriors with them, while others had come alone. Qarakh didn't care; he was glad to see them all. If things did not go well with Alexander, every one of them would be needed.

As soon as they sat down on the fallen logs, Qarakh related the details of his parley with Alexander. When he was finished, he asked, "How strong are we now?"

Alessandro answered. "At last count, forty-seven Cainites— including us—and thirty-two ghouls."

"Did you count the Nosferatu?" Arnulf growled.

Alessandro looked at the Goth warrior and frowned in puzzlement. "I assumed he was merely a visitor, but if you think I should—"

Qarakh held up a hand to silence his second-in-command.

"There is no need. Your assumption was correct." He looked at Arnulf. The Goth held his ax in one hand and slowly ran the thumb of his free hand along its razor-sharp edge, slicing the finger to the bone. He then paused for the wound to heal before doing it again. He was obviously unhappy, and Qarakh didn't have to ask why. It was because he had brought Malachite—a stranger and perhaps a spy for Alexander—into their camp. The question wasn't whether or not Arnulf was going to make an issue out of it, but how much of an issue, and how soon.

"How many warriors does Alexander have?" Wilhelmina asked. The eagerness in her voice indicated that she hoped there were quite a few and that they were all Christian.

"We did not see the entire camp," Qarakh said, "but from what we observed, I would guess that he commands thirty Cainites, and twice that many ghoul and mortal knights. Perhaps more."

"Ninety versus seventy-nine," Grandfather said. "And Alexander's warriors will be highly trained to a man, while many of ours have yet to see their first battle."

"More warriors reach our camp with each passing night," Alessandro pointed out. "Our strength will continue to increase, while Alexander's will not."

"Perhaps none of this will ultimately matter," Deverra said. "Not if Alexander is serious about seeking an alliance with us."

Arnulf snorted, but said nothing.

Sooner, Qarakh thought. *Definitely sooner.* "How much feeding stock do we have in camp?"

"Not counting the ghouls?" Alessandro asked.

Ghouls could be fed off of when necessary, but their primary function was as servants. "Trained to fight or not, the ghouls will be needed if battle comes."

"In that case, we have… fifty-six."

"Fifty-five," Grandfather corrected. "One of our tribesmen seemingly ran all the way from Scotland in wolf form, and was so in need of nourishment that he immediately drained one of the mortals to death upon arriving."

Qarakh didn't bother asking the name of the Cainite who had killed the mortal. Ordinarily, slaying one of the herd while feeding—whether purposefully or not—was punishable by a year's exile from Livonia or becoming blood-bonded to the khan, whichever the guilty party chose. But this was hardly the time to be concerned with enforcing tribal law, not with the possibility of war looming on the horizon.

Fifty-six mortals could support thirteen or so Cainites, perhaps a few more if the humans were rationed. But for a force of Cainites as large as theirs had become, they would need five times as many. Even at that number there would be no pretense of remaining hidden, and many mortals would grow weak and ill from recurrent draining.

"When we finish the *kuriltai*, we shall take down our *gers* and move our camp to within a quarter mile of the mortals' village so that we might feed more easily."

"As you will, my khan," Alessandro acknowledged, "but I doubt there are very many mortals in the village—especially since a number have joined us here at the *ordu*. With your permission, I will send riders to neighboring villages and farms to gather those they can and bring them here."

Qarakh nodded. "See that it is done."

"I take it then that you're dismissing the idea of an alliance with Alexander?" Deverra asked.

"No. But better to prepare for a war that doesn't happen than to be caught at less than our full strength." Qarakh took a moment to look at each member of his inner circle in turn, his gaze holding Arnulf's for a second or two longer than the others'. "Before I decide about Alexander's offer, I would hear your words on the matter."

As one they turned to Grandfather. The oldest among them, it was his right to speak first. "High-blooded princes like Alexander normally have little use for our kind as anything other than servants, or as in the case of certain sorcerers, subjects for experimentation." He glanced at Deverra. "I do not speak of the Telyavs, of course."

Deverra acknowledged his words with a nod.

"I therefore find it difficult to believe that Alexander wishes to do anything more than use our tribe to further his own ambitions—and when we have served our purpose, he will seek to destroy us."

Arnulf nodded vigorously at this.

Qarakh wanted to ignore the Goth, but he knew he couldn't this time. "You agree?"

With a flick of his wrist, Arnulf released his ax. The weapon spun through the air, and the head buried itself in the ground between Qarakh's feet with a dull *thunk*. Qarakh didn't flinch, nor did he take his eyes off Arnulf.

"Alexander is our enemy. Instead of wasting our time sitting here and talking, we should attack!" Arnulf punctuated this last word by slamming his fist against his leg. There was a *crack* of breaking bone, followed by softer grinding and popping sounds as the injury healed.

"Aye!" Wilhelmina said, her voice thick with battle lust.

Qarakh understood what was happening. Their Beasts were talking to them, urging them to give in to their anger. He turned to Alessandro. Though the second-in-command could be as savage as the rest—indeed, his blood boiled over into rage with frightening speed—Alessandro nevertheless had a keen mind for tactics. He would be more levelheaded here, away from the actual battlefield.

"It is possible this displaced French prince is sincere in his offer of an alliance," the Iberian said thoughtfully. "I doubt he wishes to establish a kingdom for himself in Livonia. In his eyes, it would be poor substitute for Paris."

"He is a Christian," Wilhelmina said. "Their kind spread across the land like a plague simply because they can."

"Alexander told me himself that he is no Christian," Qarakh said. "He merely uses the religion as a tool."

Wilhelmina shrugged. "Perhaps the religion is using *him* and he is unaware of it."

"And if he sees his religion as nothing more than a means to an end," Grandfather put in, "then why would he view our tribe any differently? Or his oath, for that matter?"

Before Qarakh could respond, Arnulf jumped in. "He will attempt to conquer us because he is a conqueror. He can no more deny his nature than we can." He scowled at Qarakh. "Though some find it easier to try to deny their nature than do others."

Qarakh reached down and plucked Arnulf's ax from the

ground. He held the massive weapon lightly, as if it weighed nothing. And image flashed through his mind—the ax blade biting into Arnulf's skull, cleaving flesh, bone, and brain, spraying a fountain of vitae mixed with chunks of gray matter into the air.

The Mongol gritted his teeth and tossed the ax back to its owner. Arnulf caught the weapon by the haft and tightened his fingers around it until the knuckles were bone white.

Qarakh turned to Grandfather once more. "I would have you finish your council, wise one."

"If Alexander had his way, he would be sitting upon the Parisian throne this very moment. In order to reclaim what he believes to be his rightful place, he will do whatever is necessary. He will ally with us or seek to destroy us—whichever he ultimately believes will be to his best advantage. He does not care for Livonia, not does he care about us. I doubt he even cares about Paris, deep down. All Alexander cares about is fulfilling his own desires."

"The same could be said of any Cainite," Alessandro pointed out.

Deverra had been silent for a time, but now she spoke. "Some of us have learned to live *with* our hungers—both physical and spiritual—instead of *for* them."

Qarakh turned to his tribe's shaman, his... he almost thought *companion*, but he couldn't bring himself to. Such relationships were an aspect of mortal life, and not for creatures such as they. Deverra was his shaman, one of his advisors, an important ally as leader of the Telyavs—nothing more.

"What do you think?" he asked her.

"When working magic, one often employs dangerous materials, energies and entities that are liable to turn on the caster if the ritual goes awry. But if one prepares thoroughly and performs the enchantment with care, the rewards can be well worth the risk. I view our current situation as much the same. Yes, Alexander is powerful, dangerous and duplicitous. But he also might be the key to securing our future. So far, we have managed to hold out against the encroachment of their civilization. But we all know that it is only a matter of time before the

Christians—eager to spread the word of their god and extend their worldly power—descend upon our land in full force. Indeed, the Sword-Brothers are in Livonia to do just that to the mortal herd; without those whom we feed upon, we are lost. If Alexander is true to his word, he might be able to help prevent that from happening."

"*If,*" Wilhelmina said. "You seem to forget that Alexander is in the company of some of those very same Sword-Brothers and other monks in knight's dress. He would have to keep their conquering zeal in check as well as his own. And even if he did, allying with Alexander would be like making a pact with a demon."

"So?" Deverra said. "It wouldn't be the first time I have done such a thing."

Qarakh wondered if Deverra were speaking metaphorically or literally. He decided he didn't want to know.

"I acknowledge that the risk is a great one," the shaman went on, "but the potential benefits to Livonia make it a gamble worth taking. Still, I believe we should continue to shore up the tribe's strength while we explore the possibility of an alliance with Alexander." She smiled at Qarakh. "If only to be prudent. I have already sent a message on the night wind for my fellow Telyavs to gather here as swiftly as they can. Some will arrive in the next few days, and the remainder should be here within a week's time, two at the most."

"And what if Alexander chooses to attack before then?" Arnulf demanded.

"Then we fight him as best we can," Deverra said, unconcerned.

Arnulf leaped to his feet, and Qarakh—fearing the Goth had finally lost control of his Beast and intended to attack Deverra— jumped up and put himself between them. Arnulf locked gazes with Qarakh, and the Mongol saw that the Goth's eyes had gone feral and yellow.

"I was only going to ask the witch if she had any weapons in her arsenal stronger than mere words."

Qarakh struggled not to respond to Arnulf's challenge, but he couldn't help himself. He was also khan, and he couldn't allow Arnulf to get away with this.

Qarakh's voice came out as a low growl. "She is not a witch, and if she chose to waste her powers on the likes of you, she could slay you where you stand without lifting a finger."

Arnulf didn't take his eyes off Qarakh. "Perhaps, perhaps not. But what of you, Mongol? Do you have what it takes to slay me? You—who bargains with our enemy, who brings a Christian spy into our camp, who would rather talk than fight?" The Goth warrior leaned closer until their noses were almost touching. "You disgust me, Qarakh the *Tamed!*"

Qarakh felt Deverra's hand on his shoulder. "Do not do this. Not now. We need to—"

But the rest of her words became nothing more than meaningless gibberish to Qarakh as he lost the ability to comprehend speech. Qarakh bared his fangs and slammed his forehead into Arnulf's as hard as he could. The Goth grunted in pain and staggered back a few steps, but he didn't fall. Qarakh didn't give Arnulf time to recover; he drew his saber and dashed forward.

Qarakh swung his blade in a sweeping sideways arc designed to sever Arnulf's head from his neck, but the Goth brought his ax up in time to block the strike. Qarakh's sword clanged off the ax, and he used the momentum to bring the blade around and attack from the other side. Arnulf managed to block this blow as well, and the Goth retaliated by lashing out with a bone-shattering kick to Qarakh's left knee. Qarakh grimaced in pain and leaned to the side, momentarily off balance. Arnulf took this opportunity to move his ax into position for an underhand swing, clearly intending to open Qarakh up from crotch to chin. Sensing the blow coming, Qarakh used his imbalance and pushed off with his right foot. Arnulf's ax sliced through the air where Qarakh had been standing an instant before, the blade just missing the Mongol's right foot as he leaped to the side. As he fell, Qarakh drew his saber close to his body so he wouldn't risk it striking the ground and breaking when he landed. He hit the ground right shoulder first, rolled and came up on his feet, sword ready, kneecap fully healed.

Out of the corner of his eye, Qarakh noticed that the others had risen from the logs and moved back to give the two combatants room to fight. Other members of the tribe—Cainite, ghoul and mortal—had abandoned their duties and were rising to witness the fight. He paid them no notice. He needed his full attention to deal with Arnulf.

The Goth bellowed a war cry, and Qarakh saw that his teeth had grown longer and sharper. His face bristled with black fur. If Arnulf was in the midst of all-out frenzy, he might well be unstoppable.

The Goth charged and Qarakh waited—ignoring the screams of his Beast to run forward and meet their foe's attack head on. Instead he drew a second weapon from his belt, a sharpened length of oak. At the last moment, Qarakh dodged to the side and brought the blade of his saber down on Arnulf's wrist with all his strength. The blow severed the tendon. Though the Goth felt no pain, he couldn't maintain its grip on the ax, and the weapon fell to the ground with a dull metallic thud. Arnulf continued stumbling forward, and Qarakh jumped up, spun around in midair, and slammed his sword hilt into the back of Arnulf's head. The Goth warrior pitched forward and hit the ground face first. Before Arnulf could rise, Qarakh dropped his saber and leaped onto the Cainite's back. There, he shifted his stake to a two-handed grip and jammed it between the Goth's shoulder blades with all his strength—and through his heart. Arnulf stiffened and was still.

It was over.

No, it's not! His beast insisted. *Tear him to pieces with your teeth! Swallow his flesh, drink his blood! It's no less than he deserves for challenging the khan!*

Qarakh let go of the oaken stake and looked at his hands. The nails were long and black, and the backs and palms were covered with gray fur. He rode his Beast like a wild mare, but he could feel it bucking under him about to send him straight into a wild and frenzied killing spree. He could no longer resist—

But then he felt a hand on his shoulder once more, the grip strong, reassuring and—though he didn't allow himself to believe it—loving.

He looked up into Deverra's eyes, and though he felt his canines jutting forth from an upper jaw that was partially distended like a wolf's snout, he saw no disgust in her gaze. Only understanding and again, love.

"It's finished, Qarakh. You've won."

Kill the bitch, too! Kill them all!

Qarakh closed his eyes and concentrated on the feeling of Deverra's hand on his shoulder. He felt an urge to reach up and cover it with his own hand—now hairless and short-nailed—but he didn't. He was a Cainite and also a khan. Such a display of emotion would have been inappropriate. He felt his teeth recede into his gums as they returned to their normal size. He then opened his eyes, gave Deverra a grateful look, and stood up.

The stake protruded from Arnulf's back. Vitae soaked his leather jerkin and pooled on the ground around him. The Goth wasn't dead, though. At least, no more so than Qarakh or any other night creature. Wood through the heart caused paralysis until it was withdrawn.

Fully aware that everyone, mortal and no, was watching him, Qarakh crouched down next to Arnulf's head.

"I know you can still hear me. Normally I would slay anyone who challenged me as you did, but you are a mighty warrior, Arnulf, and your strong right arm would be missed if we should go to war with Alexander. In a moment, I will withdraw my weapon. What occurs afterward is up to you."

Qarakh paused to give Arnulf—whose body might be paralyzed but whose mind was still functioning—a chance to think about what he had just said. He took up his saber in his right hand. He then gripped the oaken stake with his left and yanked it free of Arnulf's body. The Mongol stepped back, blade held ready and waited for Arnulf's wound to heal. The Goth lay still for a moment, but his fingers eventually twitched. He moaned deep in his throat. With obvious effort, he pushed himself into a kneeling position then stood on wobbly legs. Though his wounds were healing, the front of his jerkin was smeared with vitae, and his skin was bleached white as a result of the blood loss he'd suffered. Arnulf would have to feed soon.

Though the Goth was in no condition to fight, still Qarakh did not lower his weapons. Even if Arnulf had met the Final

Death, Qarakh wouldn't have relaxed his guard—the warrior was that dangerous.

"Have you decided?" Qarakh asked.

Arnulf looked at him for a moment, jaw and throat muscles working as if he had forgotten how to speak during his temporary paralysis.

"Yes," he croaked. Then he turned, nearly falling over in the process, and began walking away from Qarakh, his stride becoming surer and stronger with every step he took. The entire tribe watched as the Goth continued walking away from the campsite and toward the line of trees not far distant. The message was clear. He hadn't chosen to continue their fight, nor had he chosen to remain with the tribe. Arnulf had chosen exile.

Wilhelmina was at Qarakh's side then. "He shall return. He merely needs some time for the fire within him die down." But the Viking maid's tone suggested she didn't quite believe it herself.

Alessandro, Deverra and Grandfather joined them.

"There was nothing else you could have done," the Iberian said.

"Except slay him," Grandfather added. "It might have been better if you had. He isn't the kind of man who forgives and forgets."

Qarakh knew the elder spoke truth, and he feared that all he had done was postpone their battle for another time and place.

Deverra said nothing. She merely stood by him and watched as Arnulf reached the forest, passed between two large oak trees and was gone.

Alexander sat in a small wooden boat in the midst of a vast slate gray sea. The sky was overcast, the clouds purple-black, as if the heavens had been bruised by the fist of some great merciless god. The wind was cold and strong, lashing the dark water into choppy waves and causing the small boat to rock and pitch. Alexander gripped the sides of the boat to steady himself. The turbulent waters did not alarm him. During his long existence, he'd had more than one occasion to take to the sea. While he was far from being a master mariner, he was comfortable enough on the ocean.

"Hello."

Alexander had been alone in the boat, but now he had company. Seated facing him was a youth of no more than sixteen or seventeen summers, handsome, with close-cropped curly black hair. He was dressed in a robe of royal purple, and there was something about the way he sat—a tilt to his head, a mocking hint of a smile—that gave off an air of patrician haughtiness.

Alexander was looking at himself.

The newcomer smiled, revealing Cainite teeth. "It's Narcissus's dream come true, eh? I'm far more solid than a mere reflection in a stream."

Alexander was disturbed by this—vision? apparition?—but he maintained his calm. He'd encountered all manner of strange beings and enchantments in the last two thousand years, and he'd managed to defeat, bargain with or evade them all. This time would be no different.

"Who are you and what is this place?" Alexander had to shout to be heard over the wind and waves, but the newcomer that wore his face had no such problem. He spoke normally and Alexander could hear him without difficulty.

"You tell me."

Alexander felt anger rise. He didn't like being toyed with; the role of tormentor was usually his. But he forced himself to ignore his feelings and think upon his doppelganger's challenge.

"This is… a dream?"

The newcomer's smile widened into a grin, but there was no mirth in his eyes.

Alexander was surprised by this revelation. While it wasn't unheard of for Cainites to dream as they slumbered, it was something of a rarity. A few dreamed quite regularly from what he understood, but he wasn't one of them. He'd had only a handful of dreams over the course of two millennia, none of which he could clearly recall. This was something of a novelty to him, and he found himself becoming intrigued. After two thousand years of unlife, novelties were very few and far between for Alexander of Paris.

"I can't say I think much of the setting I've chosen," he said aloud. "It demonstrates a regrettable lack of imagination."

The other chuckled. "You do Narcissus one better. Even he wasn't vain enough to imagine himself creator of the universe. This is a dream, yes, but it's not *your* dream." The other gestured toward the water. "It's theirs."

Alexander looked where the newcomer indicated and saw, just beneath the waves, the silhouettes of dark forms gliding through the water. They were roughly man-shaped and swam around the boat in slow circles. He extended his gaze farther and saw that the ocean was filled with the dark shapes. Hundreds, thousands, perhaps millions of them, as far as the eye could see in all directions, and all of them were swimming around his tiny, fragile wooden craft.

He turned his attention back to his mirror image. "You didn't answer my other question. Who are you? And don't tell me 'I'm you.' I can see for myself that you have assumed my guise, but that alone doesn't make you Alexander of Paris."

"You say your name as if it means something. But it's merely a collection of syllables, sound that is produced, then echoes for a instant or two before dying away. Hardly worth perceiving in the first place, let alone remembering."

Alexander refused to rise to his double's bait. "You still haven't answered my question. Or are you just another aspect of this dream, no more real than this sky, this sea and this boat?" Something kept him from including the gliding dim figures in his list, as if by mentioning them he risked making them more real than they already were.

"If you truly believed I was illusory, you wouldn't inquire so persistently about my identity. That should tell you that—on some level—you recognize I am real. At least, as your kind so imperfectly defines the term."

Alexander sensed the truth of the doppelganger's words. While everything else here might be no more substantial than night fog, he—or it—was a separate entity. "Let us say for the moment that I acknowledge your reality. That still doesn't tell me who you are and why I am here."

"If I had a name, I would tell it to you. I have been present in the land you call Livonia since before the sire of all your race slew his brother, and I shall be here long after the sun is nothing but a dead black cinder in the heavens. As for what you are doing here, you are here to receive a message."

"From you?" Alexander was a master at playing games of all sorts, but right now he was rapidly tiring of his double's game of semantics.

Once again the other gestured toward the surging waves. "From them."

One of the dark forms swimming near the boat lifted its head above the surface. It was human—a woman—with smooth grayish-blue skin and round black fish eyes. Still, Alexander recognized her despite these changes. It was the laundress he had fed upon—the one he had drained and discarded before speaking to the traitor Rikard. She was looking right at him, and he forced himself to meet her gaze, though he was unable to read any expression or even acknowledgment of his existence in her piscine eyes. She held his gaze a moment longer before slipping back beneath the waves and resuming her circuit around the boat.

Other heads broke the surface now, all with the same slick gray skin and dead black eyes. Alexander recognized them all—Lorraine, Olivier, Margery, Lucien, Renaud... Then more of the dark figures stopped swimming, and dozens, hundreds, thousands upon thousands of heads rose out of the water—no, not water; he could see that now. It was an ocean of dark red blood... Some of the beings were Cainites, but most were mortal women that had once been in love. But no matter what they had been, they all now possessed the same fishy skin and lifeless eyes. All of them—those close up and those so far away that their heads were nothing more than tiny dots on the horizon—glared at him and opened their mouths to reveal row after row of serrated shark's teeth.

"Do you understand what you're looking at?" the double asked.

Alexander, as is the way of dreams, knew precisely what he was looking at, though how he had come by that knowledge, he couldn't have said. "They are all my..." He couldn't bring himself to say *victims*. The word was overly dramatic, and it didn't come close to communicating the enormity of the sheer number of beings that surrounded him. Everyone he had ever killed to feed upon or slain in the thick of battle, for revenge, for amusement, or simply out of boredom, was here. Men, women (mostly women), children, Cainites, Lupines, demons—the intensity of their collective hatred pounded into him like a tidal wave of emotion. But mixed in with the hate were feelings of excitement and anticipation. He realized the blood-swimmers were waiting impatiently and with great eagerness for something to happen.

"They're waiting for you to join them," the other said. "The first has been waiting for two thousand years, and the last only a handful of hours. But no matter how long they've been waiting, they all sense the same thing: The time is nigh."

Alexander turned to his double. "What are you saying?"

The doppelganger frowned. "Don't be dense. Must I explain it to you as if you were a child? The Final Death will soon be upon you, Alexander of Paris—and for all your years of existence purchased with the blood you stole from others, for all you experience and power, there is nothing you can do to stop it. Nothing at all."

Alexander told himself that this was only a dream—well, a nightmare now—and that he shouldn't take the other's words seriously, but he couldn't help it. He had been born as a mortal into a culture that believed in signs, omens and portents, and no matter how much he wished to, his couldn't dismiss his double's words. In fact, they shook him to the very core of his being.

Still, he was Alexander of Paris, and he wouldn't permit himself to show his fear, no matter what. "If I cannot change my fate, if—as you hint—I am to be defeated by the Mongol Qarakh, then why bother telling me? It will happen soon enough on its own.

As I said before, I'm delivering a message for them."

Alexander heard a grinding, clacking sound over the waves and wind, and he realized the blood-swimmers were opening and closing their tooth-filled maws, as if in anticipation of a meal to come.

"When you meet your Final Death, they will be waiting for you." The other grinned, and now his mouth was also full of shark's teeth. "As will I."

Alexander woke with a muffled cry. He threw off his silk sheets, jumped out of bed and assumed a defensive stance, ready to fight. But he was alone in his tent. He waited for a moment to see if any of the ghouls who guarded his quarters during the daylight hours would call out to see if he was all right. They wouldn't open the tent flap and check; they knew better than to risk exposing their prince to sunlight. He chose his ghouls carefully for just the right combination of intelligence and tractability. And any ghoul idiotic enough to let a single ray of light into his master's tent wouldn't live very long afterward. But no one called out, so he must not have made too much noise upon awakening.

The Cainites' tents were made from black fabric so that even diffuse sunlight couldn't penetrate the cloth, and though Alexander sensed there was yet an hour remaining until sunset, he was safe as long as he remained inside. Normally the leaden sluggishness that came over him during the daylight hours would have pulled him back into (hopefully dreamless) sleep, but just as a mortal awakening after an especially disturbing nightmare finds it difficult to return to sleep, so too did Alexander find himself wide awake.

With nothing else to do, Alexander sat down at his desk and rolled out his favorite map of Europe. But this time when he looked at it, his gaze was drawn to the blue sections indicating bodies of water. He reached out to touch one—the channel between England and Normandy—but he hesitated and lowered his hand.

In his mind he heard the *shush-shush-shush* of waves, the wail of sea winds and the *clack-clack-clack* of hungry teeth.

Chapter Fifteen

When Qarakh rose that evening, he fed from a short, stocky peasant woman who reminded him somewhat of a Mongol female. He then found Alessandro and told him to select two of the tribe's best people—men who were not only skilled warriors, but stealthy, cunning and swift—and assign them to spy on Alexander's camp.

"Make sure to choose men who have demonstrated some measure of self-control," Qarakh said. "This is a duty that calls for patience and restraint, not battle fever." He thought of Arnulf and scowled. He wanted to ask Alessandro if the Goth had returned to the camp, but he didn't wish to demonstrate such personal concern before a subordinate, even his second-in-command.

"Right away, my khan." The Iberian started off, but Qarakh stopped him with a gesture.

"A moment more, Alessandro. Where are my other advisors?" What he really meant was *Where is Deverra?*

"Wilhelmina is with Eirik Longtooth and Karl the Blue, listening to tales of their battles with the Teutonic Knights, as is Grandfather. Deverra…" He frowned. "I am not certain where she is. The last time I saw her, she was headed in the direction of the woods." Alessandro didn't have to say they were the same woods that Arnulf had gone into last night.

"Go select your men."

Alessandro inclined his head and went off to do as his khan commanded.

Qarakh wanted to go in search of Deverra then, but as khan he had other duties. He needed to acknowledge those who had returned in their tribe's time of need, as well as greet those allies who had likewise answered the call. He spent the next several hours walking through the camp, speaking with both tribesmen and allies—even the ghouls and mortals. Some were old friends, but most were little more than strangers. Still, he made sure to spend a little time with each and make them feel welcome and appreciated. It was an important task, for he might soon be asking these people—Cainites, ghouls and mortals alike—to follow him into battle, and he needed to strengthen, renew or create bonds with each one of them. Just as a tribe was only as strong as its khan, an army was only as strong as its general.

Midnight came and went without Qarakh seeing or hearing anything of Deverra. Ordinarily, he might have thought nothing of her absence; he would have assumed she was off conducting one Telyavic rite or another. But these were hardly ordinary times. If Alexander's offer of an alliance was only a ruse—or if the Ventrue had simply changed his mind—he might even now be preparing an attack against the tribe, might have dispatched his own spies or assassins. Deverra was a strong woman in more ways than one, and he had no doubt she could handle herself in any situation. But even so...

With a muttered apology, he broke off his conversation with a Saxon Gangrel chieftain and started walking in the direction of the woods.

"Milord! A word, if you please!"

Qarakh almost didn't stop—almost, in fact, drew his saber and lopped off the fool's chattering head—but then he recognized the voice as belonging to Malachite. He was tempted to keep on going, but he stopped and allowed the Nosferatu to catch up to him.

"My apologies if I am detaining you from an important errand," Malachite said.

Qarakh tried not to let his impatience show. "What do you want?"

"To ask if you have come to a decision whether to reveal the details of this monastery."

Despite his growing concern over Deverra, Qarakh couldn't

help smiling. "You are a most determined man, Malachite."

The Nosferatu's answering smile was a sad one. "So it has been said."

Qarakh was reluctant to tell Malachite of his experience with the mysterious Cainite in the north. It was all he had to barter with when it came to dealing with the scholar, and he didn't want to sell the information too cheaply.

"I believe I saw you speaking with Alessandro earlier," Qarakh said.

"Yes. He was asking me questions about Alexander and the army he commands."

"And did you answer his questions?"

"I did. And before you ask, I did so truthfully."

"I find it difficult to understand why you would provide such vital information so readily."

Malachite's smile was broader this time. "You mean, why would I betray the man I accompanied to Livonia?"

"You must admit it is a pertinent question."

"Especially from one who wishes to determine whether or not I—and in turn, the information I have given your second-in-command—can be trusted." Malachite considered the issue for a moment before continuing. "I suppose that ultimately there is no way I can fully convince you of my sincerity—not by words, at any rate. Oh, I could tell you that I hold no love for Alexander, and that I despise the way he poses as a Christian merely to further his own ends. I could also tell you that I believe the world will be a better place when he goes at last to his final reward. But these are precisely the words you would expect to hear from me if I were trying to deceive you. I could ask you to judge me by my bearing and the tone of voice as I spoke, but these can be controlled easily enough—especially after several centuries of experience.

"Therefore, if words will not serve, perhaps actions shall." Malachite paused, as if wrestling with a difficult decision. "To prove my sincerity to you, Qarakh of Mongolia, Khan of the Livonian tribe, I shall swear a blood oath to you—if you will accept it from me."

Qarakh was stunned by the Nosferatu's offer. Oaths of blood

were no light matter among the undead, for they involved literally drinking the blood of the lord sworn to, and Cainite blood could bend the will. Three drinks was said to create an almost permanent bond, but even a single sip was critical. There was nothing else Malachite could have said or done to convince Qarakh so quickly and completely of how serious he truly was about finding the Dracon.

"Why would you do such a thing?" Qarakh asked.

"For you. For myself. For all Cainites." A pause. "But most of all, for the Dream."

Qarakh nodded. "Very well. I shall consider your offer. If I accept it, I will tell you all I know about these Obertus monks."

Malachite stiffened suddenly, but didn't say anything. He then bowed from the waist. "I thank you, great khan." The Nosferatu straightened, turned and silently moved off, his robed body seeming to blend into the night itself. Qarakh had a difficult time keeping his eyes focused on the scholar's retreating form. If Malachite was this difficult to track when he was merely walking, how much harder would it be if he were *trying* to move without being seen or heard? With the blood gifts of his clan, Malachite might have easily chosen to slip away from Alexander's camp and follow Qarakh and Deverra back to their tribe without being detected. Once there, he could have spied on anyone, gathering intelligence for Alexander or simply picking up hints to the location of this Archbishop Nikita.

But he hadn't. He had openly asked to accompany Deverra and him, and he had made his request for information clearly and directly, and he had now offered to swear a binding oath. It was possible of course that all of this was part of some greater deception, but Qarakh's instincts told him that the Nosferatu was a man of honor and could be trusted. Qarakh would have to think hard upon Malachite's offer, but right now he wanted— no, *needed*—to find Deverra.

He continued walking away from the camp and within moments had reached the edge of the woods. He paused and sniffed the air. Once more he caught the scent of rain coming: a lot of it, within the next few days, perhaps sooner. But beneath that smell he picked up Deverra's scent and—much fainter—Arnulf's. Deverra had come this way, probably to engage in one of her clan's rituals, just as he had guessed. Ultimately, he found her in one of the groves she tended. She was easy to trace by the intoxicating scent of her blood, which she was spilling on the soil.

"Why do you weaken yourself?" he asked in way of greeting.

She looked up, unsurprised. "Because I am still your shaman, and more. If the alliance with Alexander doesn't come to pass, we will need all the help we can get to defeat him. This rite and others will help, but my hope is that he is sincere in his intention to ally with us."

"So you trust the Ventrue, then?"

"No, but I do believe that he may well be my people's best chance for long-term survival—if he what he told us is true."

"If. You are willing to risk much on such a small word."

"The Telyavs are my people. They either followed me here or have accepted my blood in their veins. I am their leader, and I would risk anything for them."

"You are also a member of the tribe, and my shaman. Would you risk the tribe's existence in order to ensure your clan's?"

If she were upset by the implied accusation in his question, she gave no sign. "Of course not, but when you have two strong and equal loyalties, *yostoi* isn't always easy to achieve."

Qarakh smiled grimly. "No matter the circumstances, balance is never easy to achieve. That is what makes it worth fighting so hard for."

Deverra took a step closer to him, and Qarakh had to resist the urge to pull away. It wasn't that he didn't want to be physically close to her but that Deverra wanted it so much. They were Cainites, what mortals called vampires. Undead creatures that could not love in the ways of human men and women, no matter how much they might wish to. Still, he didn't step back.

"Have you made a decision yet? About an alliance with Alexander?"

Qarakh had not, but he wondered what she would do if he decided against it. Would she, as a member of the tribe, accept the ruling of her khan, or would she, as high priestess of the Telyavs, decide to oppose him for the good of her faith? It was a question he did not want to ask because he did not want an answer.

"I am still considering the matter," he said. "I shall decide by the next sunset."

"Then I shall wait as patiently as I can."

Sensing the issue was settled for now, Qarakh knelt and wiped his saber on the grass before standing and sheathing it. "I should return to the camp."

Deverra grinned. "Afraid people will notice we're both missing and start to gossip?"

Qarakh frowned in mock irritation. "No, but given the current uncertainty, it would be better if neither of us were gone too long. If nothing else, Alessandro would begin to get nervous."

She laughed. "He would at that! But you go on ahead. I must finish this rite and then I will be back. It's a simple ritual that should take less than an hour."

"Very well. But stay alert. There's no telling who or what else might be roaming the woods this night."

"Surely nothing as dangerous as you or I," she replied, a twinkle in her eye.

"Even so..."

She nodded. "I'll be careful."

"Good." He turned to go, then paused. "You said you were my shaman and more. What does that mean?"

Deverra cast her gaze downward, suddenly uncomfortable. "There is a bond between us, Qarakh. Like two wolves in a pack that are united by deep understanding, by... love."

Not knowing how to react, Qarakh nodded once, turned and started walking back to the campsite, trying to hurry without looking like he was trying to hurry.

Deverra watched Qarakh leave. Curse him for asking that! And curse her for answering him like that! What did the undead know of love?

You could have used another word, she told herself. *But you didn't.*

Aloud, she said, "It's just a word."

Is it?

"What if—"

What if what? He didn't want to know? He was unhappy you used the word? That he thinks you foolish for claiming a relationship with him that can't exist?

"Yes."

Do not attempt to fool yourself. You chose that word for one reason: Not because it is true, but because you hope it will become *true.*

Deverra had no rebuttal to that thought. How could she argue with the truth?

She looked down at the pool of her blood rapidly coagulating on the ground. There was somewhere she had to go, someone else she had to speak with, and she would prefer that Qarakh not know about it. Not until he needed to—if he ever did. But if the alliance with Alexander failed to come to fruition, and the tribe went to war with the Ventrue's army, they would need help if they were to have any hope of emerging victorious. And Deverra could think of only one other place to go.

The Grove of Shadows.

Chapter Sixteen

Despite what Qarakh had told Deverra, he returned to the campsite only long enough to feed—being careful to take only a small portion of blood from several different mortals. When he had drunk enough to restore his strength, he once again left camp.

He rode his mare this time, not wishing to take the wolf shape again so soon. Besides, it felt good to be in the stirrups again. Comfortable, reassuring. When he rode, he wasn't khan, wasn't Gangrel or Cainite. Wasn't anything but a man named Qarakh, a Mongol astride his mount.

He held the reins loosely, letting the mare have her head. She knew where they were going; he'd ridden her this way often enough. Though he rode standing in the stirrups in the manner of his people—his *mortal* people—he felt calm and relaxed. He closed his eyes and gave himself over to the sensations of riding: the rhythm of the horse's hooves; the jingle of her tack; the deep in and out of her breathing; the wind blowing lightly on his face and tousling his hair; the warmth of the horse's living body; the scents of lush green grass, crisp cold night air; and good honest horse sweat.

Far too soon, the mare slowed. Qarakh knew they had arrived. He opened his eyes to behold Aajav's mound and the two gray wolves that guarded it. The horse whickered nervously and shifted her weight from hoof to hoof. Though the wolves were his ghouls just as she was, she'd never been comfortable around them.

He dismounted, spent several moments stroking the horse's neck while speaking soothing nonsense to her and then

commanded her to stay put. Thought she hadn't been completely calmed by her master's actions, they were enough to
keep her from bolting.

Qarakh walked up to the male and female wolves and
allowed them to approach.

"The night grows old, and I would speak to my brother
alone. I give you leave to go off and hunt until dawn."

The wolves didn't understand his words, of course, but
Qarakh communicated with them on a level much deeper than
mere language. The guardians wagged their tails and yipped
like eager pups before bounding off across the plain. Qarakh
watched them go, for a moment wishing he could shift form and
accompany them, but then he climbed to the top of the mound
and settled into a cross-legged position. He bit his fingers and
thrust them into the earth.

At first he felt nothing, and he feared that Aajav had at last
retreated so far into slumber that he couldn't be reached even
by Telyavic magic. But then he felt the first faint stirrings of his
blood brother's consciousness, and he was relieved. One night,
Aajav might very well be lost to him, but that night was not yet
here.

"Greetings, Aajav. Much has happened since last we spoke.
So much that I hardly know where to begin."

Though he did not experience Aajav's reaction as words,
Qarakh had the impression that his brother was saying, *So pick
a place and just begin. You'll get around to everything eventually.*

Qarakh smiled. Even in torpor, Aajav gave good advice.

"Very well." And he began. He spoke of the parley with
Alexander, Malachite accompanying them back to the campsite,
the *kuriltai*, the fight with Arnulf and the Goth's leaving, the
return of tribesmen and the coming of allies. The only thing he
did not tell his blood brother about was his increasing... closeness with Deverra. He wasn't sure why. Perhaps because he
didn't quite know how to put it in words, or perhaps because he
feared that Aajav might be jealous. Maybe a little of both.

When he was finished, Qarakh waited for Aajav's response,
but there was only silence. He began to fear that Aajav's attention had wandered—even with the enchantment Deverra had

worked upon the soil of the mound, maintaining a connection between his mind and Aajav's wasn't always easy—and so he thrust his entire hand into the earth and redoubled his concentration. There! He sensed a tendril of Aajav's awareness. Ethereal, elusive… He reached out for it with his thoughts—

"Are you certain that I will be welcome?"

Aajav shook his head with mock disgust. "How many times must I repeat it to you, brother? The Anda told me to bring you to their next *kuriltai*—which, as you can see by the fullness of the moon, is tonight."

Qarakh and Aajav rode side by side, their hardy steppe ponies made even hardier by periodic sips of their masters' blood. The animals could run at a full gallop all night without tiring appreciably. There were many benefits to this new state of being, and Qarakh was grateful once again that his blood brother had possessed the courage to Embrace him despite the objection of the Anda vampires. They rode across the moon-splashed plain toward the sacred Onan River. It was there on the riverbank, within a circle of huge stones no mortal man could lift, that the Anda held council.

"Forgive me for doubting, my brother, but I find it difficult to believe that the Anda have changed their minds about my being remade." As Qarakh understood it, the Anda controlled who upon the steppe was Embraced and who wasn't. Aajav they accepted, after a fashion, because he had been Embraced by a wandering Gangrel who had not sought the Anda's permission before turning the Mongol warrior. But Aajav *had* asked permission to Embrace Qarakh, and the Anda had denied it. Aajav had given the dark gift to his blood brother anyway, arousing the Anda's ire. The Anda dealt harshly—and permanently—with anyone who broke their laws. But now, nearly two years after Qarakh's Embrace, it seemed that all was forgiven. The operative word being *seemed*, as far as Qarakh was concerned.

"The Anda who delivered the news unto me said that their change of heart was primarily a matter of practicality," Aajav explained. "The demons from the south have been growing bolder in recent months, attacking the Anda more often, more savagely and in greater numbers than ever before. If they are to defeat the demons, they need the sword of every warrior they can get."

Qarakh had heard this explanation before, of course, but it still didn't ring true to him. While the Ten Thousand Demons were a continual threat on the steppe, he hadn't noticed any appreciable change in the frequency or intensity of their attacks.

"Even if they do accept us for the time being, what is to prevent them from turning on us after the demons have been repelled?' Qarakh asked.

"It is true that they have summoned us out of their own need," Aajav admitted. "And I grant that there is a chance they will attempt to slay us once our usefulness has ended. But there also is a chance that if we distinguish ourselves in battle, we will gain the Anda's respect, and perhaps even their admiration. If so, we shall be able to earn a place within their clan."

Even if it occurred just as Aajav said, Qarakh wasn't certain that he wanted to be a part of the Anda's clan. He liked the way his new existence had been during the last two years— just Aajav and he, riding and hunting upon the steppe together. Still, he had to admit that it would be a relief not to have to avoid the Anda anymore, let alone fight them. Perhaps Aajav was right. Going to the *kuriltai* might be a risk, but it was a risk worth taking.

They rode in silence for the next several hours, but it was a comfortable silence. Mongols were used to riding great distances and saw no need to make irrelevant conversation, and so they let time pass in whatever manner it saw fit. The night was more than half over, but dawn was still hours away when they drew near the Onan. Qarakh heard the whisper-rush of water and smelled strong, clean river scent.

As the stone circle came into view, Aajav turned and gave Qarakh an eager grin. It was at this moment that Qarakh understood how much the Anda's acceptance meant to Aajav, though he would never have admitted it. In mortal life, Aajav had always enjoyed the camaraderie of other hunters and warriors, took pleasure in sitting around a fire, eating meat he had helped kill, drinking *qumis* and swapping lies. Qarakh had liked those things as well, but he'd never needed them the same way Aajav had. To Aajav, solitude was something to be stoically endured—like the bite of winter wind, or a season when game was scarce—but Qarakh preferred it. In solitude, in the quiet and the open spaces of the steppe, he came as close to *yostoi* as he ever had. Qarakh didn't need to be completely alone, not all the time. He loved Aajav and felt incomplete when they weren't together. There was no man, living or undead, that he'd rather ride with or share a tent with.

But the rest of it—the fire, the *qumis*, the tall tales, the laughter of an incredulous and appreciative audience for his stories—none of these things were truly necessary for Qarakh's happiness. And so he had made the transition from mortal to Cainite without a great deal of difficulty.

Qarakh understood now that the crossing from life to undeath had been much harder for Aajav. A vampire was forever a creature apart from both the worlds of men and of nature. Denied the light of day, denied mortal food and drink and all the other pleasures that a living body was capable of. For a man like Aajav, his new life in darkness would be a sentence in hell. Aajav had once informed Qarakh that some Cainites—especially those to the West—referred to themselves as the Damned. Now he knew why Aajav had told him this. But a true Mongol warrior would never speak directly of such feelings. It was a warrior's lot to be strong, to endure, to be a true stoic in every sense of the word.

So if Aajav desired the companionship of the Anda—poor substitute that it might be for what he had enjoyed as a mortal—Qarakh would do whatever he could to help his blood brother obtain it. Even if it meant—

He'd been about to complete his thought with the phrase *risking Final Death*, but they were within a dozen yards of the stone circle now and the hair on the back of Qarakh's neck stood up. He realized that his uncompleted thought might end up being not only prophetic, but also one of his last.

"Aajav, something is wrong...." The word died in his throat as Anda warriors began to rise forth from the ground around them. Heads, shoulders, chests, the heads of their mounts...

With a stab of fear, Qarakh realized the Anda had interred themselves with their steeds. Aajav could do this as well, when the need arose. He'd attempted to teach the skill to Qarakh, but he had yet to master it. But as swiftly as the Anda rose from the earth, there was no doubt as to their mastery.

The Anda had set a trap for them, using Aajav's need to be part of a tribe as bait. He and Qarakh had ridden right into it.

The Anda and their mounts were halfway out of the ground now, and their hands—which no doubt held bows with arrows nocked and ready—were almost free. The Anda had interred themselves in a circle, and they'd waited for their prey to ride into the middle of it before springing their trap. Qarakh and Aajav were surrounded.

Qarakh knew they had only seconds before the Anda attacked. He reached over, grabbed the bridle of Aajav's pony and turned both of their mounts around. Aajav stood in his saddle, staring blankly at the rising Anda, unable to comprehend what he was seeing.

"Tchoo! Tchoo!" Qarakh said, and both steppe ponies took off at a gallop, running through gaps in the circle made by the bodies of the rising Anda and their mounts.

They should've interred themselves shoulder to shoulder, Qarakh thought. *They must not have had enough warriors to do so.* Good. The fewer Anda that pursued them, the better.

Their ponies' hooves pounded on the plain, and wind lashed their faces. Qarakh turned to Aajav only to see that his blood brother was now sitting in his saddle like a westerner, his hands hanging limply at his sides, the reins of his mount dangling loose.

"But they invited us," Aajav said, so softly that even with his inhuman hearing Qarakh could barely make it out over the pounding of the steeds' hooves. *"They* invited *us."* He sounded like a heartbroken child.

"Aajav! Take the reins! If you do not, we shall both die!"

Aajav turned to look at his blood brother, his face a mask of confusion and disappointment. "But they *invited* us!"

That's when the Anda, who now rode full out in pursuit, loosed the first of their arrows coated in demon blood.

Qarakh opened his eyes. He withdrew his fingers from the earth and pondered the memory Aajav had stirred within him. That it was intended as a message from his blood brother, Qarakh had no doubt. But as to the meaning of the message...

Then all at once, understanding came to him. Aajav had wanted so desperately to be accepted by the Anda that he had trusted them when he shouldn't have, and it had almost meant both of their Final Deaths. As it was, Aajav had never fully recovered from the poison the Anda had wounded him with. Or perhaps it hadn't been the poison so much as the realization that he was doomed to live an unlife forever apart from all the things he had loved as a mortal.

Whichever the case, the memory-vision's meaning was clear: Aajav had made a mistake in trusting the Anda. It was a mistake he did not wish to see his brother repeat.

Qarakh had promised Deverra that he would come to a decision about allying with Alexander by the next sunset, but he'd come to one now. Like the Anda so many years ago, Alexander of Paris could not be trusted. There would be no alliance—and if that meant war, so be it.

"Thank you, my brother."

Qarakh stood and walked back toward his horse. He needed to return to the camp. There were still a few hours left until sunrise, and there was much to be done.

In the darkness, Rikard lay upon a wooden table—at least, it felt like a table. He wasn't sure. It was so hard to think. At first he thought he must be somewhere deep underground, in a cavern perhaps, although the air didn't feel cool or damp enough, and the sound didn't echo the way it should have, though since he had never been inside a cave, he was only guessing at this. Besides, why would someone place a table in a cavern? It didn't make sense. But it was the only explanation he could come up with for why he couldn't see *something*. After all, he was a Cainite, and his eyes were capable of—

And then he remembered. He no longer had any eyes.

"Still conscious? You have a stronger constitution that I

would've given you credit for. At first, I feared you would succumb to the pain too quickly and retreat into torpor. Cainites are less used to enduring pain than are mortals, you know. We forget how intense, how immediate and all-consuming true pain—especially pain inflicted by a master—can be."

The voice was familiar to Rikard. In fact, it was the only voice he could ever remember hearing, although he had to have known others in his life, hadn't he? But though he recognized the voice, he could not put a name or a face to it. Perhaps the voice had neither name nor face. Perhaps what he was hearing was the voice of God Himself. In the beginning was the Word, and the Word was the Voice, and the Voice was Pain and Blood and Darkness eternal, forever and ever, without mercy, amen.

"I wonder if you are still capable of controlling your body... or perhaps I should say what is left of your body."

Rikard couldn't see God's face—if indeed God had one—but he could hear the grin in His voice.

"Why don't you try moving a little? Not too much, though. I undid the leather straps that bound you to the table some time ago, right after I removed your last limb. But we wouldn't want you rolling off and falling onto the floor, now would we? After all, you might hurt yourself." God let out a girlish giggle.

Rikard didn't want to try to move. He was in so much pain... All he wanted to do was lie on the table—the warm, wet, sticky table—and listen to the voice and stare at the darkness inside his own skull. But the voice was God, and it would be disrespectful to disobey Him.

Rikard concentrated for several moments, building up his strength. And then, with a Herculean effort, he did as his God commanded. He moved.

"Excellent! You managed to purse your lips and turn your head an inch or so toward me. Bravo!"

Pride swelled within Rikard upon hearing his God's praise. He wanted to ask God to give him another task to perform so that he might please Him again, but he could not, for he no longer possessed a tongue.

"Do you want to know a secret, Rikard?" God's voice came then as a whisper in Rikard's left ear. "No matter what other amusements I indulge in, I always take care not to damage the ears. Functioning ears can continue to cause pain long after the rest of a man's nerves have gone dead. All I have to do is *shout!*"

Rikard grimaced—demonstrating that he could still work at least a few facial muscles. It felt like God had driven a white-hot spike into his ear.

"But the best part is that hearing allows one to exercise the imagination. For instance—"

Rikard heard the *whisk-whisk* of steel sliding against a sharpening stone.

"What does this sound make you think of?"

An image flashed through Rikard's mind then: the sharp point of a dagger coming toward his eyes. He remembered struggling against the restraints (this was before God had removed them) as the blade introduced him to a night darker than any he'd ever known before.

"Now that you no longer have any eyes to get in the way, let us see just how far the dagger will penetrate, eh? I like to keep on going until the tip of the blade scrapes against the back of the skull. Try to hold still now. Without the restraints, there's a good chance you'll thrash around a bit."

Anything for his God. Rikard tried to smile to show how willing he was, but the best he could manage was a lopsided grimace. The cold metal tip of the dagger touched the ragged-edged hollow ruin where his right eye had been.

"Looks like your eye has regrown a bit, but you don't have much vitae left in your body to fuel any significant healing. That's all right, a little push and a twist or two—there! All gone. Now let's see how much of the dagger's length you can take."

Rikard felt the blade slide slowly into his eye socket and keep going. He tried to scream, but not only didn't he have a tongue any longer, it appeared he had no vocal cords either. The dagger kept sliding in, deeper and deeper, until bright flashes of light exploded against the darkness in his mind. He knew the metal had somehow pierced the very core of him.

"Milord István!" Another voice, one Rikard did not recognize.

"What is it?" God snarled. "I told you never to interrupt me when I'm playing."

"Begging your pardon, milord, but his highness wishes to see you." The voice grew eager. "The rumor around camp is that we're going to march against the Tartar's tribe at last!"

This last sentence stirred some fragments of memory in Rikard but he was finding it so hard to think....

István (that must be God's name, Rikard decided) sighed. "I suppose his highness wants to see me this very instant?"

The owner of the other voice sounded amused. "Naturally."

"And just when it was getting good, too." Once again the voice came from next to Rikard's ear. "I'm afraid I'm going to have to leave you, my friend. I thoroughly enjoyed myself, and I will think back upon our hours together with much fondness in the centuries to come."

The blade slid out of his socket then, and Rikard wasn't sure what was going to happen next, but then he heard a soft movement of air, and he realized that God was bringing the dagger back down swift and hard—and then Rikard found himself falling, falling, falling toward an endless sea of blood.

Chapter Seventeen

Why do you come before me again?

"To speak for the Cainite called Qarakh."

And why does he not speak for himself?

"He knows nothing of the Grove of Shadows. And even if he did, he would not come here on his own."

He is too proud?

"He is a prideful man, yes, but he is also a sensible one. He will accept aid for the benefit of his tribe."

Then tell me: Why do you speak in his place?

"While he would accept your help, he would not accept its price. As a priestess in your service, half of the debt would be mine. And that is why he would not accept it—if he knew."

I understand. He will be angry with you for deceiving him.

"It doesn't matter. Should the tribe be faced with war—"

The tribe will indeed go to war. I have foreseen it.

"Foreseen it? Or helped cause it?"

You forget your place, priestess.

"Forgive me. I spoke before I thought. War is inevitable then?"

Yes.

"How soon?"

Soon.

"Weeks? Days?"

What is the difference? Soon.

"What must I do?"

When the time is right, you must bring Qarakh to me. I shall aid him—if he ultimately accepts the cost of my help.

"Tell me—if we do this, will Qarakh prevail over his enemy?"

That all depends on which enemy you mean.

"While I am glad to hear that you have decided to abandon your plan to form an alliance with the pagans, I would be remiss in my duties if I failed to point out that this might not be the most advantageous time to attack the Mongol's camp."

Alexander was seated at his desk while Brother Rudiger stood at attention. Alexander looked at the knight as he contemplated the best way to slay him. Beheading would be swift and efficient, but given the man's fear of fire—which was intense even for a Cainite—burning at the stake might be more appropriate... not to mention more amusing.

"Your highness?"

Alexander sighed. "And what, Rudiger, makes you say this?" He hadn't had a headache in two thousand years, but he felt as if he were going to get one now.

"Qarakh and the pagan priestess have both seen our camp. And you can be assured the Mongol kept his eyes and ears open the entire time he was here. Worse yet, Malachite left with them when they departed. Go d only knows how much more the Nosferatu has told them about our military strength."

Alexander felt like shouting. *There is no God—there is only us, you simpleminded idiot!* "Go on."

"We have lost the element of surprise. The pagans now expect us to attack."

"Qarakh and his people are likely still debating the merits of entering into an alliance with us." *With me,* he meant.

"Perhaps," Rudiger allowed. "But even if they are, they would be complete fools not to consider the possibility of our attacking. They may be beasts, but they still possess animalistic cunning."

"What are you telling me? That we should *not* attack the Mongol's tribe?"

"I am saying that we should wait for a more propitious moment. If the Mongol does choose to accept your offer of alliance—not realizing that it's been rescinded—you can allow him to believe that you will indeed join forces with him, and then, when his guard is down, we shall seize the opportunity to attack."

Alexander felt something very nearly like admiration for the knight. "Why Rudiger! I didn't know you had such a streak of deviousness in you!"

The Black Cross commander's mouth twitched, and Alexander knew he was fighting to keep from grimacing in disdain.

"It is merely a matter of practicality," he said stiffly. "Recent events"—he didn't say *your decisions, highness*, though Alexander was certain he thought it—"leave us with few remaining options."

"Practicality, eh? I suppose next you'll tell me that God helps those who help themselves. Never mind, don't answer. Though I understand your concerns, I do not share them. I have reached the conclusion that Qarakh's tribe and the Telyavs are not suitable allies." Meaning they were of no use to him. "Thus, as pagans, they must be destroyed for the greater glory of God, and the sooner, the better. The people of the land have worshipped false gods long enough." He paused. "Unless you think God is in no particular hurry to see the people of Livonia brought into his fold...."

Rudiger replied through clenched teeth. "Of course not, your highness."

"Then go inform your knights that we shall begin our march on Qarakh's campsite come the next sunset and begin making preparations."

Rudiger inclined his head. "As you will."

Which is precisely what you should have said in the first place. "You may take your leave of me."

A small puff of breath passed through Rudiger's lips. Even with his sensitive Cainite hearing, Alexander couldn't make it out, but it sounded as if the commander had whispered, "With pleasure."

Before Alexander could demand Rudiger repeat himself more loudly, the knight turned and departed the tent.

The audacity of the man! Not only did he question his orders—albeit in a less than direct manner—but he had the gall to whisper a comment like that before scampering off. He was a child who had worked up the courage to say a naughty word in

front of his father, said it, then fled, his meager supply of bravery spent. Many men—Cainite, ghoul and mortal—had died
for delivering lesser insults to Alexander of Paris.

The prince nearly stood and followed after the knight,
intending to tear off the German bastard's head with his bare
hands and drink deep from the fountain of vitae that gushed
forth from the ragged stump. But he remained seated.

Like it or not (and he most definitely did *not*), Alexander
had need of Brother Rudiger. The other knights would turn
on him en masse if he slew their commander. Alexander was
almost unimaginably strong for a Cainite, but even he didn't
relish the though of facing dozens of enraged and self-righ-
teous Teutonic Knights all at once. Their wills would break, of
course, but then he would be left with doe-eyed automatons
with which to wage his wars.

So let Rudiger have his trifling moment of rebellion.
Alexander would do the same with him as he did with everyone else. He would continue to use the knight for as long as
necessary, and then when he was no longer needed, Alexander
would dispose of him. All he had to do was, as Rudiger had
phrased it, wait for a more propitious moment.

Somewhat cheered by that thought, Alexander looked
down at the map on his desk. He turned his attention to its
eastern section, to the lands beyond Christendom. All maps
were nothing but rough approximations of actual lands, of
course, but this section was extremely speculative, drawn
from secondhand stories from Saracens, Persians and Slavs.
Still, at the edge was a marked *Land of the Tartars*. Tartarus
itself, perhaps. Whatever the nature of this semi-mythical
land, it had produced a Gangrel named Qarakh.

Alexander was mildly surprised to realize he was looking
forward to testing his strength, his cunning and his two millennia of experience against Qarakh.

He opened his mouth and put his thumb against his right
incisor and pushed. The sharp tooth pierced the finger's
flesh and blood welled forth. Alexander pressed his bleeding
thumb onto the edge of the vellum map, right on the word
Tartars, and began rubbing it around in slow, ever-widening

circles. He did not stop until the word was entirely covered in wet crimson.

One night passed...
    Two...
    And the sun set for a third time.

"Tonight we shall dispatch a messenger to inform Alexander that there will be no alliance."

Qarakh paused to gauge the reactions of those attending this *kuriltai*. The tribe's inner circle stood—Deverra, Alessandro, Wilhelmina and Grandfather—leaving the logs for their guests as was only proper hospitality. As khan, Qarakh was seated, but sitting alongside and opposite him were those allied leaders he had invited to the *kuriltai*: Eirik Longtooth, Karl the Blue, Borovich the Grim, Tengael, Werter, and Lacplesis the Beastslayer. On the other side of Deverra stood a half-dozen Telyavs—two male, four female—all wearing the simple brown robes favored by their coven. So far, they were the only ones that had answered their high priestess's call for aid.

Malachite was present as well, standing off to the side and ignoring the glances of mistrust the others gave him from time to time. Qarakh, however, had come to trust the Nosferatu enough to permit him to attend tonight's council, though not yet enough to let him out of sight for very long.

There were no objections to his pronouncement, at least none that were spoken. Qarakh was gratified, if somewhat surprised. He had expected some of his allies to object to sending a messenger and instead demand that they mount an all-out attack on Alexander at once. But after two nights of discussion and debate, even Wilhelmina must have finally realized that when their tribe went to war with the Ventrue's army, they weren't going to win by sheer strength or martial skill. Many of the allies had fought their own battles with knights and had learned the hard way that stealth and deception were among the greatest weapons they possessed.

"Has there been any word from your spies?" Eirik asked. Like most of the Cainites from the north—Finland, Sweden,

Norway and Denmark—he wore his blonde hair and beard long
and wild, and was garbed in a tunic stitched together from animal fur.

"Not yet," Qarakh said, "but it is almost two night's ride to
Alexander's campsite. Perhaps just under a full night for one
who can travel in animal form. Two nights past, we dispatched
three spies. Even the swiftest has not yet had enough time to
reach the camp, survey it and return."

"Have there been any signs that the Ventrue has sent spies of
his own?" Werter asked. The Gangrel leader of Uppsala looked
much the same as Eirik, though he was somewhat shorter and
his eyes were more bestial.

Many of the allies, as well as Deverra's fellow Telyavs and
Wilhelmina, turned to look at Malachite. To his credit, the
Nosferatu displayed no reaction to their stares.

"We have had warriors patrolling the camp's boundaries since Deverra and I first returned from our parley with
Alexander. No spies have been sighted."

"That doesn't mean that there are not any. Merely that they
have not been seen," Borovich the Grim said. The Prussian
Gangrel's childe Tengael nodded agreement with his sire.

Deverra addressed this concern. "My people have employed
their magic to set up wards around the campsite. We shall know
if anyone, friend or foe, approaches."

"Sorcery!" Borovich spat a gob of crimson-tinged saliva into
the grass, but said no more.

Qarakh felt a drop of rain strike the back of his hand, and
he knew the storm that he'd been smelling for the last several
nights was nearly upon them.

Grandfather looked up at the sky. Dark clouds covered the
stars and hid the moon.

"A bad omen," the elder said, and a number of the allies
nodded their agreement.

"It is only a bit of rain," one of the male Telyavs said. His
name was Sturla, and he was a tall, thin humorless man with a
shaven head and a thatch of black beard. "The mortals will be
grateful; their crops can certainly use it."

Deverra gave the man a stern look, and he fell silent, though he didn't look too happy at having been quieted.

He most likely resents having to humor a pack of superstitious strangers, Qarakh thought. If their situation hadn't been so serious, he might've found this amusing—a sorcerer unable to accept the mystical beliefs of others.

The rain began to pick up then, but it was still hardly more than a light patter. Besides, they were all of the Damned—what was a little rain to them?

It was Malachite's turn to ask a question. "Have you decided who will carry your message to Alexander? If you send a Cainite of low station—or worse yet, a ghoul—the prince will be most insulted."

"Let him be!" Wilhelmina said, setting several of the allies as well as a few Telyavs to laughing.

Malachite, however, did not seem bothered by the others' laughter. "You must understand: Alexander values matters of personal pride above all else. For all his calculating and scheming, in the end he bases every decision on it. It is the one true weakness that he possesses."

"Then we must find a way to exploit it," Alessandro said.

"Easier said than done," Sturla said.

Qarakh frowned. It was one thing to think such thoughts, but it was another to speak them aloud—especially at a *kuriltai* at which one was a guest. He might have rebuked the Telyav for wasting the others' time with his irrelevant comments, but since Sturla was one of Deverra's clan, he chose to keep silent rather than embarrass her. He looked at the priestess and saw she was scowling at Sturla. Qarakh almost wished the Telyav hadn't responded to his high priestess's summons, but as khan, he knew the tribe needed all the allies it could get right now.

Deverra herself had been something of a puzzle to Qarakh for the last few nights, though he supposed that should've come as no great surprise to him since he'd never understood her completely. She had said no more about hoping an alliance with Alexander would come to fruition. In fact, she'd begun to act as if she believed war was inevitable, helping him and the other warriors plan strategy and directing the other Telyavs in the creation of wards. He had attempted to speak to her once or twice about this seeming change of attitude, but she had merely evaded the subject. She seemed grimmer for some reason, her usual spark of humor gone. Perhaps she was simply responding to the overall mood of the tribe as it prepared for the battle to come. But he couldn't help feeling there was more to it than that.

"So how do we fight this Ventrue?' Lacplesis asked. The Beastslayer wore a hooded black cloak that concealed his features, but his hands sported patches of thick fur, and his ebon nails were long and sharp.

Grandfather spoke. "There is an old saying: 'Cut off the head and the body will die.' If we can find a way to destroy Alexander, his army will be as good as defeated."

Now it was Qarakh who felt like saying, *Easier said than done.* But he held his tongue; he would never speak disrespectfully to his tribe's lore-keeper—especially not in front of guests. "Alexander is what the westerners call a Methuselah. He is too powerful to be fought directly. He must be tricked."

"What of the Telyavs' magic?" Karl the Blue asked. "Perhaps it would prove a potent weapon against the Ventrue."

All eyes turned toward Deverra.

"As Qarakh said, Alexander is extremely old and strong. When I was in his presence, I could feel his power. I believe he would detect any enchantment directed at him in time to evade it, if not nullify it altogether."

Malachite spoke. "As you might well imagine, Alexander never said anything to me about his knowledge—of lack thereof—of sorcery. But I have heard rumors over the years, and I have seen some of the books and scrolls he carries with him. My impression is that while he is no sorcerer himself, he possesses enough knowledge of the mystic arts to make using magic against him a risky proposition."

"After two thousand years, he likely possesses knowledge of just about everything," Alessandro said. There was some mumbling and downcast looks, and while the statement Alessandro had made was no doubt true enough, Qarakh wished the Iberian hadn't spoken it. An army that allowed itself to become demoralized was an army that was already beaten before ever setting foot upon the field of battle.

"We have discussed many plans—both of attack and defense—over the last few nights," Qarakh said, "and while all have had their merits, none has emerged as the best route to take against Alexander. I suggest that we do as Malachite says and turn the Ventrue's pride against him." He continued on before anyone—especially Sturla—could comment. "Alexander is a deposed prince seeking a return to power. If we refuse his offer of alliance, then he will surely attack us in order to gain a military victory that he might use in his quest to regain his throne. He is an ancient vampire of refined and high blood." This brought mutters and snarls from the assembled Gangrel. "And thus he believes we are little more than animals, and he will expect us to fight as such, riding forth to engage his knights in full force. The one thing he will not expect from us is subterfuge, for he does not believe our kind is capable of it."

"You speak as if you have a plan in mind," Karl the Blue said.

"If he does, I wish he'd get around to it," Borovich murmured.

Qarakh's sword hand itched to go for his saber, but he restrained himself. If they began quarreling among themselves, Alexander would have already won. "My plan is a simple one, yet I believe it will prove effective." *Just as it did for the Anda many years ago*, he thought. He wondered if Aajav had stirred that memory not only to warn him against allying with Alexander, but also to give him the means of defeating the Ventrue. Even in torpor, Aajav still took care of his brother.

"Here is what we will do."

But before Qarakh could go on, Deverra stiffened and her eyes grew wide. One by one, the other Telyavs reacted the same way.

"Someone has activated a ward." Deverra closed her eyes and cocked her head to the side, as if listening to a sound only she could hear. Seconds later, her eyes flew open, a look of alarm on her face.

Qarakh knew what her words would be before she spoke them.

"It has begun," she said.

Alexander was coming.

Chapter Eighteen

Those sitting jumped to their feet, and everyone drew their weapons. Qarakh left his saber in its scabbard, though, despite the urgings of his Beast. He turned to Deverra.

"How far are these wards from the camp?"

"A little less than four miles. We would've placed them farther out, but in order for the spells to be fully effective—"

Qarakh held up a hand, cutting her off. This was no time for lengthy explanations. "If Alexander sensed the wards, he is aware that our tribe wields magic, though he cannot know to what extent. He will assume that the wards provided us with an early warning, and therefore he will not waste time sending an advance force, nor will he attack on multiple fronts. He will come as swiftly as he can, bringing the full power of his army to bear in the hope that such an overwhelming display of strength will either cow us or break our discipline. That way, instead of facing a united tribe, his knights will be fighting dozens of individual battles."

"What of it?" Eirik Longtooth said, stabbing his sword at the night sky. "However he comes, we shall crush him!"

Qarakh scowled at Longtooth's gesture—it was an insult to Father Tengri—but he said nothing.

Many of the others shouted their agreement, and Qarakh knew he had only seconds before they broke away and raced off to the attack, all pretense of military order forgotten.

"If we do not stand together as a tribe, Alexander and his knights will surely defeat us. Not all of us shall meet the Final Death, but the tribe will fall, and then Livonia will belong to Alexander and the Christians. Before long their numbers will increase, and mortals will follow. They will establish more villages that will in time become cities. They will cut down the trees and slay the wildlife for food. Alexander brings worse than the Final Death with him. He brings civilization."

Qarakh looked around at the faces of the assembled Cainites—a number of whom now looked more bestial than they had a few moments ago. In their eyes he could see the struggle taking place as cold intelligence warred with ravening Beast. But they remained standing where they were, and they still listened.

"How can you be sure of these things?" Tengael demanded.

Qarakh didn't know how to respond to that, but Deverra answered for him.

"Because he is Qarakh, and he is khan."

The struggle between thought and appetite continued a moment longer, and though the Beast didn't recede completely (did it ever?), Qarakh could see in his allies' gazes that intelligence had won—for now.

Karl the Blue got down on one knee and bowed his head. One by one all the other Cainites—including the Telyavs—did likewise.

"What are your orders, my khan?" Karl asked.

Qarakh took no pleasure in the others' submission. He was simply glad that they could now attend to the work that lay before them.

"Rise and listen well, for we have little time to prepare."

Alexander rode next to Rudiger in the middle of the formation. In front of the central group (called the battle) rode the vanguard, to the right and left sides were the wings, and riding behind came the rearguard. The vast majority of the ranks was made up of mortals and ghouls, with the Cainites riding primarily in the battle, though a half-dozen rode in the other formations, commanding the ghouls and mortals. The Cainites rode ghoul horses—Alexander was particularly fond of the midnight black stallion that served as his steed—while the human ghouls and mortals sat astride ordinary mounts. Everyone was equipped with the same complement of arms and armor: lance, sword, helmet and mail hauberk. None had bows, however. The knightly classes emphasized personal combat, and thus disdained their use—an attitude Alexander found ridiculous but knew he couldn't change. Four separate standards were emblazoned on flags carried by heralds that rode with each formation: those of Alexander, Jürgen, the Teutonic Knights and the Black Cross knights. Alexander would have preferred to ride beneath a single standard—his, of course—but sometimes one had to make sacrifices to keep one's soldiers happy.

All together, the army numbered thirty-one Cainites, fifty-four ghouls and thirty-nine mortals, making for a total fighting force of one hundred and twenty-four. The remainder of their people—the servants, blacksmiths, stable masters, cooks, laundresses and simple feeding stock—now camped two miles behind the army, well out of the range of battle, but close enough for the soldiers to return to them once the fighting was finished.

The army rode across a grassy plain, a small thatch of forest off to the right. An *empty* thatch... at least, according to Rudiger's scouts. The man might be an officious, humorless bore, but Alexander had to admit that he was an effective field commander.

If all goes well, Alexander thought, feeling in a generous mood, *perhaps I won't kill him after all.*

"It's a lovely night for conquest, is it not, Commander?" It had started to rain a short while ago, and Alexander had feared that Rudiger would insist on calling off the attack, for muddy ground and armored knights on horseback were not an effective combination. Though Alexander would have insisted they continue on, regardless of the weather, he doubted he could have convinced Rudiger to order the knights to do so, save by backing his request with the crushing force of his will. Rudiger was not some weak-minded simpleton that could be easily swayed by another's will, but he would bow to Alexander of Paris—eventually.

But the rain had dissipated without becoming a major storm, and the ground, while damp, had not turned to muddy soup. The sky was clearing and patches of stars were visible, along with occasional glimpses of a nearly full moon.

"It's the sort of night that inspires bards to song, eh, Rudiger?"

"There'll be time enough to contemplate such things after the fight is won."

"I value a man who believes in keeping his mind on his work, but when you're as old as I am—assuming that you're fortunate enough to survive that long—you'll understand that taking the time to appreciate the small details is often what keeps you focused."

Alexander found himself wishing that István was here. He'd have no more understanding of Alexander's insights than Rudiger, but at least he would pretend to. But István, along with several handpicked men, was off on a separate mission, one just as vital—if not more so—than that of the army as a whole.

"I *am* thinking of the small details. For example, the Mongol sent spies to watch over our camp—all of whom we found and killed. Yet our scouts have discovered no sign of any sentries here, so close to his own camp. Why?"

Alexander wondered if he should tell the knight that the army had ridden across a subtle line of sorcerously charged pebbles a half mile back. While Alexander hadn't been able to determine the exact nature of the enchantment, he was certain that it meant Qarakh knew they were coming. He had considered keeping this knowledge from Rudiger, knowing that it would make little difference in their strategy at this point. Besides, he wanted to see the look on Rudiger's face when he realized the pagans had somehow known about their attack ahead of time.

But as pleasurable as that would be, Alexander decided it would be a petty indulgence, and while he was not above petty indulgences in the least—in fact, they were one of the main things that kept him going after two millennia of unlife—he'd rather see this campaign completed swiftly and successfully. And despite Qarakh's relative youth, Alexander sensed that he was not a man to be taken lightly. So he told Rudiger, and when he was finished, the knight cursed.

"*Scheisse!* No wonder there are no sentries—the Mongol doesn't need them!"

"He doesn't need them here, but he *does* need them elsewhere, or he would have allowed some to remain in order not to arouse our suspicions. This tells us that he does not have the number of warriors to match our own."

Rudiger looked at Alexander. "I'm impressed, your highness."

Alexander did not fail to note that the knight had added an honorific this time. "I've fought in and survived so many battles, both large and small, over the centuries that I quite literally cannot remember them all."

A shout came from someone riding in the vanguard, interrupting Alexander. He turned his attention forward, but because the land was flat here—and because even seated upon a stallion he still was shorter than the average knight who rode before him—he couldn't see what was happening. But he could well guess: The Mongol was making his move.

Alexander smiled. *So the alliance dies without ever being truly born.*

"Stay here!" Rudiger said, and before Alexander could tell him that he didn't take kindly to being ordered by one who was supposed to be serving him, the knight snapped his horse's reins, kicked his heels into the animal's side, and the mount surged forward. Rudiger guided his steed through the ranks with an ease born of long practice.

Alexander understood why Rudiger had "requested" he remain in the battle formation. Here, he was surrounded by the highest-ranking and most skilled Black Cross knights—Cainites all. Alexander would be protected here, as much as any soldier could be when the enemy had been engaged. He was a prince, a Methuselah and supreme commander of this force. As such, he could hardly ride into combat like a common frontline soldier, as much as he might have preferred to. So he remained where he was, in the exact center of his army, surrounded by one hundred and twenty-three warriors. He told himself that he tolerated staying here because it was the most logical course of action (or *in*action), at least for the moment. His acceptance of Rudiger's advice had nothing to do with a dream of floating upon a crimson sea as a mirror image of himself spoke prophecies of doom.

Nothing at all.

Alessandro rode at the forefront of the tribe's assault force, which was comprised of four *arbans*, or squadrons of ten, making for forty riders altogether. The warriors rode side by side in the Mongol fashion. They would be able to fire arrows more easily and—if the need arose—turn and retreat. The tactical withdrawal, shunned as it was by Europeans, was considered an honorable and useful maneuver by Mongols. Alessandro rode standing in the stirrups, as Mongolian horsemen did, another technique that permitted a mounted warrior to fire arrows more efficiently. Only a third of the assault force's riders employed this technique, though. Some were too new to the tribe to have mastered it, while some had never been able to do it, no matter how much training they had received.

Hooves pounded across the plain like rolling thunder as the four *arbans* rode toward Alexander's army, but the warriors themselves remained silent. It was not the Mongol way to shout battle cries in an attempt to bolster one's courage or rattle one's foe. The Mongol warrior preferred to let his strength and skill do the talking for him.

The Iberian judged the distance to the vanguard of Alexander's army to be approximately two thousand yards. Cainites were able to draw bows and loose arrows with greater speed, distance and accuracy than either ghouls or mortals. But three-quarters of this attack force—by design—was made up of ghouls, so Alessandro knew they would have to get closer before firing.

Closer…

"Nock arrows!" he ordered.

Closer…

"Get ready!"

The tribesmen pointed their bows skyward.

Closer… "First volley, fire!"

Bowstrings twanged in almost perfect unison. Arrows shot into the air, howling as they arced into the night sky.

The knight on Rudiger's left said, "What is that sound?' And then, with a howling like a thousand ravening demons, a rain of arrows fell upon the vanguard.

Helmets and hauberks protected most of the knights, but many of those who were foolish enough to look skyward, curious to see what was making such an eerie noise, received arrow wounds to their faces and necks. If they were particularly unlucky, a wooden shaft now protruded from the socket where one of their eyes had been. The knight riding next to Rudiger was one of the unlucky ones. The idiot looked up, lost his right eye to a falling arrow, and shrieked in pain as he slipped off his mount and fell to the ground. Throughout the vanguard knights were crying out in agony or terror, the wounded often falling out of their saddles and the fearful pulling back on their reins, cursing horses that were too frightened or in too much pain from their own arrow wounds to obey.

It was a cowardly attack, but Rudiger had to admit it was damned effective. One volley of arrows, and already the army was on the verge of breaking ranks. The wounds the men had suffered weren't all that serious, at least not for the Cainites, but the fear and confusion brought on by the swift and unexpected attack were far worse. Rudiger knew from experience that once an army's discipline was broken on the battlefield, it was nearly impossible to rally the soldiers back to the fight. He had to act fast or this war would be over before it had begun.

"Ignore the howling!" he bellowed. "It is merely a pagan trick!"

He heard someone say, "Sorcery!" and he knew he was losing them. The sound the arrows made as they'd flown had nothing to do with sorcery and everything to do with how they had been carved, but there was no time to explain this, not that the knight would believe him even if there were. There was only one thing to do when a soldier's mind and heart had been captured by the enemy: use the body.

Rudiger drew his sword and raised it high over his head, even as a second volley of arrows howled down from the sky. One struck his wrist and lodged there, but he ignored the pain and held his sword steady.

"For the glory of Christ and for our Lord Jürgen—*Charge!*"

He slammed his heels into his mount and the horse leaped forward, trampling a fallen knight as it galloped. Rudiger recognized the man and knew him to be a Cainite. Whatever injuries he had sustained were temporary, but even if the knight had been a ghoul or a mortal, Rudiger wouldn't have spared the time to ride around him. After all, this was war.

He broke free of the vanguard and rode toward the pagans. He didn't look back to see if anyone was following his lead. Either they were or they weren't, and Rudiger, commander of the Black Cross knights, gave the matter no further thought as he rode forth to meet his enemy.

The tribal warriors had nocked a third volley of arrows, but Alessandro raised a hand and shouted, "Hold!"

The first two volleys had done their work well, wounding a number of knights and mounts in the Christian vanguard and creating chaos in the ranks. But now a lone rider came charging across the field, sword held high. A few knights followed after him, but that was all.

Alessandro smiled. Perfect.

"Retreat!"

As one, the line of riders turned their mounts around, shouted *"Tchoo! Tchoo!"* and rode off at a furious gallop. The course of their retreat was set to take them past the small wood which, Alessandro was certain, the Christian knights had searched and determined to be empty.

He grinned. They should have searched with greater diligence.

He cracked his reins. *"Tchoo! Tchoo!"*

Rudiger heard a chorus of shouts erupt behind him, and he allowed himself a quick smile. It sounded as if he had managed to seize the reins of the army after all.

Before coming to Livonia, Rudiger had studied every account he could find about Tartar battle tactics. They were very few. The Tartars had apparently been harassing the easternmost cities in Rus and other Slavic lands, but very little detail was contained in any letter Rudiger had been able to get ahold of. Still, these pagans seemed to be a more savage version of the Turkish horsemen who had done such damage to crusaders in the holy land.

It seemed that Qarakh favored a strategy of attack and withdraw. It was a tactic that had served the Turks well throughout the centuries, for the larger, less agile horses of Europeans couldn't match the swiftness of their smaller steeds, and thus a pursuing army could never hope to catch its foe. But the heathens could stop, turn, loose another flight of arrows and ride off again, always remaining maddeningly just out of touch as they whittled down their enemy bit by bit.

But Qarakh had made a serious mistake. His tribesmen weren't Turks or Tartars who were born to the saddle and learned to ride before they could walk. And these weren't the open plains of Anatolia or the far steppe. The pagans didn't stand a chance of escaping.

The tribesmen angled toward the stand of woods, and at first Rudiger thought they were going to ride into it—which would have been an extremely stupid move, as the knights would have trapped them there. But the pagans continued riding past the trees, and Rudiger put their change in direction down to a frantic, undisciplined retreat and nothing more.

By now the others knights from the vanguard had caught up to him, and Rudiger rode at the head of a triangular formation of Christian warriors, all hungry to spill—and if possible, partake of—pagan blood.

A fierce bellow cut through the night air, sounding more animal than human.

Rudiger turned to look. At the edge of the woods, Qarakh himself rose out of the ground on the back of a gray horse, saber in hand, battle lust twisting his features into the face of a mad demon. And the Mongol wasn't alone—all around him other Cainites emerged from the earth. Wild-haired, wild-eyed, some wielding swords, some axes, others armed with nothing more than dagger-sharp fangs and curved talons. Aside from Qarakh, none was on horseback, but it mattered little.

Rudiger swore. Damn those Gangrel tricks! Rudiger had

heard that the animalistic Cainites often slept through the day within the earth, but it had never occurred to him that they might be able to use this ability for concealment.

Rudiger yanked on his mount's reins, trying to stop the horse so that he could turn the dumb beast to meet this new attack, but the horse only spun around in a circle, chuffing air and raising and lowering its head. Some knights were trying to get their steeds to halt as well, while others—evidently unaware of the Gangrel's deception—continued riding past.

Rudiger then saw something that made him doubt his senses: six brown-robed figures stepping out from six oak trees. He wasn't certain, for his horse still refused to settle down, but it looked as if the newcomers' hands were bleeding. As the Gangrel raced forward with Qarakh in the lead, the robed ones—could they be Telyavs?—knelt and pressed their bleeding palms to the grass. There was a rustling whispering sound, and the grass surrounding the knights began to sway back and forth as if stirred by a restless wind, though the air remained still. Then the blades stretched forth from the ground, growing longer and thicker as they came and—Rudiger was certain he must be hallucinating this—each blade of grass now possessed a small gaping mouth ringed by rows of hard toothlike thorns. The grass (or whatever it had become) struck serpent-swift, tiny mouths affixing to horses' flanks, bellies, withers, barrels or necks—and they began to drink.

The horses shrieked in agony, bucking and jumping as they tried to tear free of the horrible mouths that had clamped onto their flesh and were now sucking their blood with loud moist sounds. But no matter how hard the equines fought, they couldn't dislodge the parasites.

And then, just as swiftly as it had come upon them, the enchantment faded, and the mouths fell away from the horses, like leeches that had finally had their fill. Though the mounts bled from dozens of wounds apiece, none had been killed and no knight had been unseated. Had the spell somehow failed?

Rudiger looked up to see Qarakh bearing down upon him, the other Gangrel running alongside, some still in human form, some changed into bestial things that ran on two legs, and others that had forsaken all pretense of humanity and ran on all fours. Rudiger understood: The purpose of the grass creatures hadn't been to slay the knights' horses, but rather to hold them in place long enough for the Gangrel to attack in force.

Rudiger didn't have any more time to think. Qarakh the Untamed was upon him.

Chapter Nineteen

Qarakh recognized the German knight from his visit to Alexander's camp. He wasn't certain what the man's rank was, but it was clear he was leading the Christians' charge, so Qarakh rode toward him. Around him ran his fellow Gangrel—Wilhelmina, Karl the Blue, Eirik Longtooth and all the rest.

All save Arnulf, his Beast reminded him.

Many of the Gangrel were in the midst of transformation, either by choice or as a result of succumbing to frenzy. Wilhelmina concerned him the most. Given her deep hatred of Christians, she was especially vulnerable.

Qarakh risked a quick glance at her. The Viking maid's eyes were wild and bulging. Her tongue had become long and gray, and it lolled against her cheek. Her skin was covered with patches of amber fur, and her nose and mouth protruded from her face—almost but not quite merged into a snout. Her mouth was filled with wolf's teeth, and white froth flecked her lips.

Forget her and concentrate on the German—unless you intend to become a martyr for your tribe this day.

Qarakh didn't know if the voice was his or the Beast's, and he supposed right now it didn't matter. He gave forth a war cry that was more monster than Mongol. With subtle changes in the pressure of his legs against the mare's sides, he directed her toward the German.

The knight was having trouble controlling his own horse. Frightened and weakened by the Telyavs' spell, the animal struggled against its rider's commands and was attempting to flee the battlefield. And regardless of how he worked the reins or how much he swore at the animal in German, the knight couldn't make his mount obey.

Qarakh grinned, revealing teeth that didn't look much different than Wilhelmina's. Qarakh galloped toward the German, and the Mongol warrior raised his saber, preparing to slash at the Cainite's neck as he rode past. He hoped to lay open the knight's throat, perhaps even decapitate him. But given the erratic movements of the man's horse, Qarakh would have to time his strike just—

A wordless, soundless cry echoed through Qarakh's mind. A cry of anger, of fear, of helplessness…

He knew at once that the cry came from Aajav.

Qarakh forgot all about the German knight and the army of Christian warriors. He forgot about the Gangrel loping alongside him, and about the Telyavs back in the woods, resting after the exertion of casing their spell. He even forgot about Deverra. Only one thing existed for him now: his brother.

He yanked his steed's reins hard to the right, shouted, *"Tchoo! Tchoo!"* and urged the mare away from the battlefield at the fastest pace the horse could manage.

Rudiger watched in stunned surprise as the Mongol broke off his attack and rode away at a full gallop. At first he thought that it must be another trick of some kind, for he could not imagine Qarakh purposely refusing to fight, but then he realized what had happened. Somehow the Mongol had sensed what István and his men were up to, and he was riding to his blood brother's aid. The tactic hadn't quite worked the way Alexander had hoped, but it had at least removed Qarakh from the fight— though Rudiger didn't envy István when the Gangrel chieftain caught up with him.

Rudiger stopped thinking then as a bestial female Cainite with amber-hued fur ran toward him and leaped into the air. He tried to bring his sword around in time to meet her attack, but the she-wolf was too swift and slammed into him before he could defend himself. The two Cainites tumbled toward the ground, and Rudiger's mount—free of its rider at last—took off at a feeble trot.

The savage bitch tried to sink her fangs into his throat, and he brought up his forearm just in time to protect himself. The she-wolf bit into his arm instead, and vitae gushed forth, hot and red. Then Rudiger's own Beast rose to the fore, and he began to fight for his unlife.

The air was filled with screams and growls as Cainites, ghouls and mortals fought, rending each other's flesh with swords, daggers, claws and teeth.

Deverra knelt on the ground beside the other Telyavs. The enchantment they had just worked had never been tried in this way before. It had been designed only to spur crops to lush growth, but it had succeeded. The horse blood drained by the surrogate tendrils (which in her mind Deverra referred to as snakes in the grass) had needed to go somewhere, though, and that somewhere was into the bodies of the Telyavs themselves. They were now suffused with blood, swollen and bloated with it, their purplish skin stretched tight and shiny. Deverra could feel equine blood pooled at the back of her throat, as if she was a well nearly full to overflowing after a long, hard rain. The sensations were strange—a warm, pleasant drowsiness combined with an uncomfortable feeling of pressure and a slight tinge of nausea from ingesting so much animal blood. It would take some time for the Telyavs' bodies to completely absorb what they had taken in, hours for certain, perhaps even a night or two, but in the end—

"Hurts... so much..."

The voice was distorted, wet and gurgling, but Deverra could tell it belonged to Sturla. Weak as she was, the high priestess crawled on fleshy knees and sausage-thick fingers toward the acolyte. He lay on his back, staring up at the dark sky. Clouds now hid the stars, and Deverra knew it would soon rain again. The fabric of Sturla's robe was stretched tight across a body swollen to grotesque proportions—easily twice that of the other Telyavs, Deverra's included. Blood trickled from both nostrils, bubbled over his lips, dripped from his ears and ran from the corners of his eyes like viscous red tears. Worse, tiny beads of crimson welled up from the pores in his skin, as if his body was unable to retain the vast amount of blood he'd absorbed.

"Couldn't stop... knew... I should, but... couldn't." Sturla coughed, and a gout of brackish blood poured out of his mouth.

Deverra understood what had happened. It was precisely what she had feared might occur. Sturla hadn't been able to maintain control over his Beast while linked to the surrogate tendrils, and he had drained far more equine blood than he should have. His body was struggling to absorb it all, or failing that, to expel it, but it appeared Sturla wasn't succeeding in doing either.

A fissure opened on his right cheek, and a stream of blood spewed forth. A second fissure opened on his forehead, then another just beneath his chin.

"Sorry." His mouth and throat were so clogged with blood that the word was barely understandable. "I'm so..."

Deverra knew there was nothing she could do for the man. She took hold of the edges of Sturla's hood and brought them together, obscuring his face. The man's bloated arms and leg wobbled, as if he were trying to get up, and then there was a loud ripping sound, and torrents of blood ran from his sleeves and from under his robe, splashing over Deverra's sandaled feet and soaking into the earth.

An offering for you, Telyavel, she thought. *Perhaps not one freely given, but hopefully one freely taken.*

Sturla's robe began to collapse as his body released what it had stolen, until the fabric—soaked in equine blood—lay in a crumpled wet heap. Nothing remained of Sturla, not even dust.

Deverra let go of the hood, whispered a quick prayer in Livonian, and then hastened to check on the other Telyavs. Though all were barely conscious—thankfully, they hadn't witnessed Sturla's death—none were in danger of going the way of their companion, and for that she was both relieved and grateful.

A form emerged from the murk of a nearby shadow. Deverra was startled at first, until she realized it was Malachite. The Nosferatu came silently toward her, moving with a liquid grace that seemed unlikely for one as misshapen as he. Then she remembered what she now looked like; she was hardly one to judge another's appearance at the moment.

"I am truly sorry for your loss," he said.

She acknowledged his words with a nod. "It is war," she said, as if that explained everything. "How goes the battle?"

"Your deception worked well. The vanguard was taken completely by surprise, and the Gangrel are fighting the knights even as we speak. Once the vanguard was engaged, Alessandro brought his cavalry around and returned to harry the remainder of Alexander's army with flights of arrows. While the battle and rearguard formations appear to be holding, the right and left wings are in disarray, all pretense of military discipline forgotten."

Deverra smiled in grim satisfaction. The tribe was a long way from winning this war, but it had accomplished an effective first strike.

The other Telyavs were sitting up now, fully conscious but still very weak. She felt a drop of rain strike the back of her swollen left hand—the slight impact surprisingly painful upon her tight skin—and she knew the rain had returned. All to the better, for rain would not hamper the Gangrel's efforts, nor would it affect Alessandro's archers unless it came with strong winds. But the change in weather might well prove an impediment for a mounted force as large as Alexander's. If Qarakh was here, she knew he would thank Father Tengri for his gift.

"And what of Qarakh?" she asked Malachite.

"Your khan led the charge against the vanguard as planned, but for some reason he broke off at the last moment and rode northwest. I assume there was some purpose underlying his actions, yet I confess to being unable to determine it."

Deverra frowned. It was inconceivable that Qarakh would abandon his people in the midst of a battle, yet she could think of no reason why he would... and then something Malachite had said finally sank in. Northwest. That was where Aajav's mound lay.

She realized then that the tribe wasn't alone in knowing how to practice deception. Alexander did too, and he'd had century upon century to become a master of it. Was the entire attack by his army ultimately nothing more than a distraction so that the

Ventrue prince could abduct—or perhaps slay—Aajav? To strike at Qarakh where he was most vulnerable? She wouldn't put it past Alexander to use his knights as little more than sacrificial pieces in a deadly chess match.

She wished there was some way that she could go to Qarakh's aid, but she had no horse, and even if she did, she was in no physical condition to ride. All she could do was see to the recovery of the surviving Telyavs and pray to their dark god to grant her khan strength and keep him safe.

She then tried to put all thoughts of Qarakh out of her mind as she knelt next to the Telyav closest to her and got to work.

By the time Qarakh reached Aajav's mound, the rain had returned. It fell heavier now, and Qarakh was soaked to the skin. He barely noticed, let alone cared. Though she was a ghoul and stronger than a normal horse, his mare was breathing heavily, and heat radiated off her lather-coated body in waves.

Qarakh saw the wolves first—or rather, what was left of them. The raiders' swords had done their work all too well. The mound itself also had been violated; soil lay scattered, cast aside as the raiders had dug. Qarakh sniffed the air. The only blood he smelled belonged to the wolves. The raiders hadn't slain his brother. They had abducted him--for Alexander to use as a bargaining chip? Or perhaps merely to enrage Qarakh to such a degree that he was incapable of leading his tribe. Knowing Alexander, Qarakh bet on both possibilities.

He dismounted then, but he did not immediately rush up to the mound to confirm with his eyes what his nose had already told him. Doing so would be a waste of time, and he had already taken too long to get here as it was. The blood within him was burning with the exertions of interring himself and his steed in the woods and with the boiling need for battle. His muscles were swollen and straining and it had been all he could do to resist taking the wolf form on the way here. The extra speed might well have driven him into a feeding frenzy, and he still would not have arrived. Now he was here, and there was no longer any need to resist. But before he hunted, he needed to feed.

He stroked the mare's muzzle. "I'll take only what I need," he promised. Then he bent his head to the horse's neck, bit into her flesh, and began to drink.

Drain her dry! the Beast shouted. *She's your ghoul, and you've fed her much vitae. It's time she gave it back!*

Qarakh was still drinking when the mare collapsed to the ground. He didn't waste time to check if she would survive; either she would or she wouldn't. He turned away from the horse and ran toward the mound, exchanging his human shape for his wolfish one as he went. Once atop the excavated mound, he lowered his nose and inhaled, trying to pick up the raiders' trail. The rain didn't help, but it hadn't washed away the scent completely. He found it with little trouble and leaped from the mound and bounded across the plain.

The hunt had begun.

Istvan congratulated himself. The task had gone far more smoothly then he'd imagined. Only the two guards had been present—the Tartar's ghouls, most likely—and while the wolves had fought ferociously enough, they were no match for three knights of the Black Cross. Istvan didn't count himself, as he'd not done any of the actual fighting, nor any of the subsequent digging. Rank had its privileges.

Now the four of them—five, he supposed, if one counted the insensate Gangrel—rode at a fast trot across the Livonian plain in the direction of their new campsite, Istvan and the three knights on horses, the Gangrel lying across the back of a fifth mount, lashed to the saddle with strips of leather. A rope was tied to the horse's bridle, the other end knotted around the pommel of Istvan's saddle. After all the trouble he'd gone through to get the Gangrel (well, that the knights had gone through) Istvan wasn't about to lose him.

A bolt of lightning lanced across the sky, followed a moment later by the rumble of thunder. Istvan hoped the rest of the army had already conquered the pagans, even though that would render his mission irrelevant. If the storm grew much worse, the knights might well have to break off their attack and wait for better weather to resume the battle.

But that wasn't his concern. Alexander had tasked him with a mission, and he'd carried it out. His role in this fight was done, at least for the time being. He considered ordering the knights to slow their horses to a walk—he wasn't in any hurry to see Alexander again and perhaps be given another mission to carry out—but he doubted the knights would agree. They were too full of their idiotic chivalrous code to take advantage of an opportunity to seize a bit of rest while their fellow knights fought a war. Morons.

The rain picked up. Though he felt no cold, István shuddered and drew his cloak tighter against his body. Then again, the sooner they reached camp, the sooner they could get dry.

His thoughts drifted to a mortal woman he'd had his eye on for a while. She was the wife of one of the blacksmiths, and she'd been growing increasingly frail over the last few weeks as the wasting sickness spread through her. She was in constant pain—István was adept at sensing such things—and he thought her agony had ripened quite nicely. Once they returned to camp and made sure this torpid animal was secured, István thought he would send for the woman and enjoy her pain even as he delivered her from it.

Lost in thoughts of his meal to come, István was unaware that anything was wrong until one of the knights shouted. István turned just in time to see a large gray wolf slam into the warrior and knock him out of the saddle. The other two knights turned their horses about, drew their swords, and converged on the wolf, which was now savaging their screaming companion.

István didn't know if the wolf was another guardian ghoul, one of the Gangrel, or even Qarakh himself, and he didn't much care. All he cared about was surviving long enough to deliver his captive to Alexander, so that he might continue to survive in the nights ahead. He cracked the reins and kicked his horse into a gallop, pulling the other mount along with him.

Rain poured down upon the battlefield, and Grandfather walked among the carnage as Cainites, ghouls and mortals struggled to deliver the Final Death rather than receive it. He walked calmly, dodging arrows, ducking swords and evading the claws of his own people who had allowed the Beast too great a hold upon what remained of their souls. He carried no weapons, but he didn't need any. As he walked, his hand would dart out faster than any eye—human or Cainite—could see, talons sprouting from his fingertips, and another Christian knight would suddenly be missing a significant portion of his throat. Grandfather never stopped. He tossed each grisly handful of flesh to the wet ground and continued walking, leaving the wounded knights to bleed to death or, if they were Cainites, to be finished off by other Gangrel.

To an observer, the ancient vampire would have appeared serene, at peace with himself despite the violence that surged around him. But the truth was far different: inside his Beast screamed a song of blood and death, thrashing against the reins Grandfather had lashed to it so long ago. But Grandfather knew how to give the Beast what it needed, not what it wanted. And so he walked, and from time to time he killed, and when the Beast was almost to the point of breaking its leash, Grandfather would feed. The Beast would be satiated, at least for a time.

The number of Gangrel that had succumbed to all-out mindless frenzy disturbed him. They could not ride the Beast as Grandfather did. Now they attacked one and all, even one another. Most were new members to the tribe that he had only begun to instruct in his ways. Several were caught in terrible cycles of transformation, warping between wolf and man in a mad flow that burned away their blood and drove their hunger and mindless fury to new heights. These Gangrel were in the most danger of being left with permanent aftereffects of frenzy. Features that remained bestial were among the most common. He thought of the fur covering his arms, a legacy from a night many centuries past when his own control had slipped. But if a Gangrel spent too long a time in the grip of the Beast, he or she might well be marked in mind as well as body, becoming an animal in both spirit and flesh.

This thought was still lingering in his mind when he saw Wilhelmina. The Viking maid crouched before a Christian knight, more wolf than Cainite now. Her body was covered with amber fur, her nose and mouth merged into a wolf's snout.

Her fingers had lengthened into curved talons. She bled from dozens of wounds—so many that she should have been too weak to fight—but she showed no signs of relenting. The frenzy had too strong a hold on her. The knight was also wounded. An arrow protruded from the wrist of his sword arm, and his face and neck were crisscrossed with deep gashes. His tabard was soaked in crimson. But he too displayed no sign of giving up the fight. He held his sword before him in a steady grip, and his gaze remained focused on his adversary.

Grandfather wasn't overly concerned with Wilhelmina's wounds. A good feeding or two and she would be fully healed. But he was worried about the effects frenzy might have on her. Wilhelmina hated Christians with a passion greater than any he'd ever seen in his long unlife. Now here she was, with an entire army of Christian warriors to slay. He had no doubt that she would keep on fighting until every knight in Alexander's army lay mutilated and dismembered on the field of battle. That is, if the Final Death didn't claim her first.

Grandfather decided it might be best if he remained close to her until the fighting was done. That way, should she slip too far into the bestial side of her nature, he could remove her from the battle and stay with her until she (hopefully) returned to normal. But first he had to deal with that knight.

Grandfather walked toward the two combatants, his fingers itching to bury themselves in the Christian's throat.

Wilhelmina's world consisted of two equally strong visions, one overlapping the other. In the first, she crouched in front of a sword-wielding knight, looking for an opening so that she might finish off the bastard. But in the second she stood before the smoldering ruins of a burnt longhouse, the greasy stench of seared flesh still heavy in the air.

Bjorn was gone, as were the others—slain by those who professed to follow a god of peace. She was one of Bjorn's shield-maidens. She should have been here to add her sword to theirs—to fight and, if necessary, to die at the side of her lord and the rest of her war band. But perhaps the gods of the north had spared her for a reason: so she could seek vengeance upon the Christians for what they had done. If so, she would accept the gods' will. She would hunt down and slay every follower of Christ she could find, and she would not stop until all were dead and gone, and Jesus Christ was just another man who had lived and died, only to be forgotten by history.

She snarled and coiled her muscles, preparing to leap at the knight, but out of the corner of her eye she saw a figure approaching: an old man in a gray robe. There was something familiar about him, but it was so hard to think... there were so many distractions... the sounds of battle and falling rain, the stink of burnt wood and Cainite flesh, the flash of lightning and rumble of thunder... and above it all the blood-fury roaring in her ears.

The robe—old man—a monk—must kill, kill, kill!

Wilhelmina spun around and lashed out with her claws. Blood sprayed the air and the monk stiffened, eyes wide with surprise. His head teetered and fell backward, prevented from falling to the ground by a single strip of flesh that kept it connected to the body. The old man collapsed to the grass, the impact causing the strip of flesh to tear, and the monk's head— no, *Grandfather's* head—rolled across the wet grass and came to rest with its right cheek in a rain puddle.

Wilhelmina stared at Grandfather's head, unable to believe what she had done. She let forth a howl of despair and then bounded off, sometimes running on two feet, sometimes four. She had no idea where she was going. All she wanted to do was run as fast and as far as she could. Perhaps if she ran far enough, she might even outrun the memory of the look in Grandfather's eyes as awareness faded and they grew dim. A look of understanding, of pity and above all love.

Rudiger lowered his sword as he watched the she-wolf dash away. He wasn' t sure what had just happened—why she had slain the old Gangrel and then fled—but war was chaos and ultimately beyond anyone's understanding, save that of almighty God.

He could afford to spare no more thought for the matter. The rain was coming down harder now, and the pagans' ambush had proven most effective. The vanguard was in complete disarray, and he had no sense of how many casualties they had suffered, let alone how the rest of the army fared. There was no hope for it; they needed to fall back (he didn't think of it as a retreat, for a true knight would never do something so dishonorable).

He yanked the arrow from his wrist and threw it to the ground. He turned and began jogging toward the main body of the army, keeping his eye out for a horse he could commandeer.

Alessandro's horsemen were almost out of arrows when he heard the sound of trumpets echo over the battlefield. He ordered the archers to hold their positions. Moments later, the Christian knights began to retreat. A cheer went up from Alessandro's men, but the Iberian didn't join in the exultation. They had fought and won but a single battle.

The war was by no means over.

Chapter Twenty

Qarakh ripped out the knight's throat and spat the bloody hunk of flesh in the man's face. He then leaped to the side to avoid a sword blow from one of the other abductors, then leaped again as yet another knight took a swing at him. In less time than it takes an eye to blink, Qarakh shed his wolf form and once again became the Mongol warrior known as the Untamed. He intended to show these two Christians exactly how he had come by that name.

As one of the remaining knights rode toward him, Qarakh ducked the man's sword and sliced opened the horse's throat with one stroke of his saber. The animal tried to whinny, but the best it could manage was a chuffing and gurgling sound as it went down. The knight flew over the horse's head, arms and legs flailing.

Qarakh turn to meet the charge of the second knight. He drew a dagger from his belt and hurled it with all his strength at the man's chest. The blade pierced the undead knight's mail hauberk with an audible *chunk*. The impact ruined both his balance and his charge. As the knight struggled to retain control of his destrier, Qarakh leaped and drew a heavy wooden stake. Before the knight could regain control, the Mongol drove it into his undead heart. The Christian stiffened, suddenly paralyzed, and slid sideways off his horse and crashed to the ground.

Qarakh turned back to the first knight, who was staggering to his feet after a less than gentle landing. After four quick strides and a slash of Qarakh's saber, the knight no longer had a head. Six more steps in the other direction and the paralyzed knight suffered the same fate as his companion. Qarakh bent down, yanked his stake from the dead knight's chest, wiped it clean on the man's tabard, then straightened and tucked it back into his belt. The Mongol warrior felt no elation at his victory. He felt nothing beyond the determination to rescue Aajav.

He once again donned wolf-shape—though it was more difficult this time and he knew he would soon have to feed once more—and resumed the hunt.

Lightning flashed and thunder roared. The rain sliced down from the heavens like a hail of miniature knives. István couldn't see a foot in front of his face. His mount, and the one the unconscious Mongol lay astride, were both so spooked that he was having trouble controlling the animals. He had no idea if he was heading in the right direction anymore. All he knew was that he couldn't afford to slow down, not if he hoped to—

Out of the darkness and the rain, blazing eyes and wide-open jaws came leaping at him, and István had time to think, *At least it's not Alexander,* before Qarakh was upon him.

Qarakh, in man-shape once again, led the knight's horse by the bridle toward a stand of pine trees. The steed upon which Aajav lay came along obediently. The horses were skittish, but he spoke to them in a soothing voice as they walked, and though they didn't calm down completely, they were docile enough.

The taste of the last knight's blood lingered bitter in his mouth. He leaned his head back, opened his mouth to catch some rain, swished the water around and then spat into the grass.

Once beneath the shelter of a large pine, Qarakh tied the horses to one of the branches before seeing to Aajav. He knew he should have examined his torpid blood brother right away, but he had been too afraid of what he might find. Now a quick once-over convinced him that while Aajav remained in torpor, he had suffered no injuries at the hands of his abductors. Relieved, Qarakh untied Aajav and carried him over to the trunk of the pine tree. Qarakh sat with his back against the pine's rough bark and cradled Aajav in his lap as if he were but a child.

"Alexander will pay for this insult, my brother. I swear it."

Aajav didn't react. Qarakh hadn't expected him to.

"That invading prince abandoned all thought of alliance and attacked us. If it hadn't been for the Telyavs' wards, we might not have known he was coming at all." Qarakh continued speaking, telling Aajav of all that had happened since Deverra had announced that Alexander's army was upon them.

When he was finished, Qarakh leaned his cheek against the smooth skin of his brother's head. "We are a great distance away from those two Mongolian boys who used to complete at archery and wrestling and anything else they could think of, eh, my brother? A very great distance in far too many ways."

He felt motion then, and with a start he realized that Aajav had moved. Not much, just a slight turn of the head, but it was the most he had moved in five years. Qarakh shifted Aajav around to look at his face. His brother's eyes remained closed, but his lips quivered as if trying to form words. Qarakh leaned down close to Aajav's face so he could better hear whatever words his brother might say after so long a silence.

"Take... me..." The words were little more than exhaled breath, and Qarakh wasn't sure he hadn't imagined them.

"What, my brother?"

Aajav repeated the words, louder this time but still barely more than a whisper.

"Take me."

Qarakh frowned. "Take you where? Back to your mound? I shall do so as soon as the rain stops."

"No. Need... strength to fight... Alexander. Take... mine."

Qarakh understood then what his brother was telling him. He was asking Qarakh to drink his vitae—all of it—and add Aajav's strength to his own. Deverra called it diablerie and said it was the consumption not only of blood, but of the very soul.

"I cannot! Do not ask me again!"

Silence for a moment, and then, "You... must."

Qarakh remembered then what the ancient Cainite he'd encountered outside the Obertus monastery had told him: *Victory is in the blood.* Qarakh shook his head. "Defeating this Christian is not worth that."

"To protect... tribe."

"No!"

"Alexander... too strong. You... must let me fight... with you."

"I will not! And nothing you can say will change my mind!"

Another silence, longer this time. Then Aajav spoke a single word.

"Please."

In that one word, Qarakh heard a desperate longing for the lost pleasures of a mortal life on the steppe—riding the plain, hunting, being a mortal man among other mortal men... Qarakh understood then that Aajav would never come out of torpor, even if he should continue to exist beyond the end of the world. Drinking his heart's blood would be a mercy—if only Qarakh could bring himself to do it.

He looked down upon the face of the man who was both his brother and his sire in darkness. Did he love this man enough to slay him?

Of course he did.

He kissed Aajav's forehead and then, red-tinged tears brimming in his eyes, he fastened his mouth to Aajav's neck and began to drink. For once, his Beast was blessedly silent.

Only an hour remained until sunrise by the time Qarakh returned to the battlefield, riding the gelding that Aajav had been lashed to. His own mare hadn't survived his feeding.

The storm had passed, though its energy lingered in the cool, still air, making it feel as if the world had been born anew. The sensation clashed with the reality of the battle's aftermath. Bodies lay scattered across the ground—knights and tribesmen, Cainites, ghouls and mortals, as well as quite a few horses. The dead had met various ends--some pierced by steel, others mutilated by claws. Arrows protruded from many of the corpses, especially the horses. A quick survey of the battlefield revealed that the bodies of more knights littered the ground than tribesmen, and Qarakh knew that his people had been the victors this night. He should have felt triumph and pride, but while his body was on fire from adding Aajav's essence to his own, his heart felt dead and cold.

Members of the tribe were gathering the bodies of their dead and laying them across the backs of horses or stacking them like firewood in wagons. The Christians were left where they had fallen, the Cainites to be greeted by the morning sun, the ghouls and mortals left for whatever scavengers might find them.

"Qarakh!"

He turned to see Deverra hurrying across the battlefield toward him, Alessandro following behind. Qarakh didn't feel like talking to anyone right now—especially Deverra—and he was tempted to ride off before they could reach him. But he remained where he was. Alessandro looked none the worse for wear, but Deverra's flesh was puffy and discolored, as if she had been bruised all over. Had she been involved in the actual fighting or was her condition an aftereffect of her sorcery? Most likely the latter, he decided. Deverra was many things, but a swordswoman wasn't one of them.

When she reached his side, she looked up at him with eyes full of sadness. "Aajav?"

"My brother is no more."

For an instant, it appeared that Deverra might question him further, but all she said was, "I'm sorry."

"As am I, my khan," Alessandro said as he took a place at Deverra's side. "Should I send one of our people to retrieve his body so he may be properly laid to rest?"

Qarakh thought of how Aajav's body had begun to decay after the diablerie was finished. Qarakh had waited until his brother was nothing more than a pile of ashes, and then he had carefully gathered the remains and placed them in one of the gelding's saddlebags. One day he would return to Mongolia and scatter the ashes on the shore of the Onan River, the Anda be damned. He almost patted the saddlebag to reassure himself that Aajav's ashes were still there, but he resisted. Though he thought it likely Deverra might suspect what had occurred— he seemed unable to hide anything from her—he didn't want Alessandro to know. Perhaps because he was ashamed, but also because what had transpired between Aajav and himself had been an intimate, private thing.

"That has already been dealt with," Qarakh said in a tone that indicated he wished to speak no more about it.

Alessandro looked at his khan for a moment before nodding his acceptance.

Qarakh took another look around the battlefield. The stench of blood and voided mortal waste hung in the air like the residue of agony and fury. *Delicious,* his Beast said, and Qarakh had to fight to keep from salivating. *Too bad we missed all the fun. Then again, Aajav was delicious, too.*

"How did the tribe fare?" Qarakh asked.

"Well, my khan," Alessandro said. "By my count, we've slain sixty-seven of the enemy: seventeen Cainites, thirty-one ghouls and nineteen mortals. I estimate the number to be roughly half of their fighting force."

Despite his sorrow at Aajav's loss, Qarakh was pleased with this result. It was better than he had hoped for—especially since he hadn't fought alongside his tribesmen.

"And Alexander?" Qarakh asked.

The Iberian shook his head. "His body has not been found."

It was possible that the prince had been killed and his body removed by the surviving knights, or even that his body had eroded to ash like Aajav's, but Qarakh doubted it. Alexander still survived.

"How many warriors did we lose?"

"Only twelve, and that number includes the Telyav Sturla."

Qarakh sniffed. He wasn't sorry to hear of that sorcerer's demise.

"Among the fallen are Eirik Longtooth and Tengael—and Wilhelmina is missing, though there is no reason to presume she has met the Final Death. Knowing her, she pursued the Christians as they retreated."

"Most likely," Qarakh agreed. He sensed that Alessandro had something more to tell him and was stalling, reluctant to get to it. Qarakh felt like yelling at the man to spit it out, but he forced himself to wait patiently.

"We also lost Grandfather," Alessandro said, clearly struggling to keep the sadness out of his voice. The news struck Qarakh like a physical blow.

Grandfather had not only been the tribe's lorekeeper, he had been its greatest teacher. The elder had instructed countless Gangrel and other vampires on how to find *yostoi* with the Beast. His teachings had set the landmarks for many travelers on the most primal philosophical road a vampire could follow through the night. Alessandro had made it something of a personal mission to learn all he could of the ways of the Beast, and Grandfather had served as both mentor and role model to him. The death of the ancient Gangrel had no doubt hit the Iberian especially hard.

"It is a great loss," Qarakh said. "We shall add his name to the list of those to be avenged."

Alessandro didn't appear especially comforted, but he nodded anyway. "What are your orders, my khan?"

"Continue to gather our fallen, but make sure that all Cainites return to the camp well before dawn. As much as we might like to honor the dead with a proper funeral pyre, we don't want to lose anyone else. If that means leaving some of our casualties to be devoured by the sun's rays, then so be it. Also, post sentries—both ghouls who can keep watch during the day and Gangrel who can inter themselves until the next sunset. Alexander will be stung by this defeat, and he will surely attack again, sooner rather than later. We must be prepared."

"Yes, my khan." Alessandro departed to carry out Qarakh's commands.

After the Iberian had gone, Deverra laid a swollen reddish purple hand on Qarakh's leg. "I'm so sorry about Aajav," she said.

Emotions warred in Qarakh: gratitude for Deverra's sympathy, revulsion at the sight of what she had become, guilt at the knowledge that it was his command that had led to her transformation, and a fury whose source was unclear to him.

"I am weary and must return to my tent and rest. I suggest you do the same."

A hurt look came into Deverra's eyes, and she withdrew her hand from his leg. Before she could say anything else, Qarakh turned the gelding around and headed away from the battlefield at a brisk trot.

Deverra watched Qarakh ride off. She knew how Aajav had died—not all the specifics, but she knew enough—and she understood how hard diablerizing his blood brother had been for him. It was just like the stoic Mongol not to want to talk about it.

I'm weary and must return to my tent to rest. I suggest you do the same.

What a splendid idea. Deverra started walking in the direction of the camp.

Alexander sat at his desk, his great map of Christendom and the lands still unconverted spread out on the surface before him. He looked first at the Christian kingdoms, than at the pagan lands, before placing one hand on each section. Then slowly he curled his fingers and began crumpling the map. Within moments he had wadded it into a ball slightly larger than his fists. He then began to squeeze the wad, compacting it even further with his great strength. Then, when he had squeezed the map down as far as he could, he raised his fists up over his head and brought them crashing down onto his desk, reducing it to kindling. He then stood, opened his hands, and dropped the wad of vellum on top of the pile of splintered wood. Afterward, he stood motionless for a time, staring at the debris that had been his desk, not blinking as cold dark thoughts slithered through his mind.

"Milord?" A voice from outside his tent. It was Rudiger. "May I enter?"

It took Alexander a moment to remember how to make his body speak. "Yes."

He turned as the German knight entered. Rudiger's eyes widened when he saw the ruin of broken wood where Alexander's desk had been, but he wisely didn't remark upon it. "The camp is secure and sentries have been posted. A full complement of ghoul and mortal knights shall stand guard during the daylight hours."

"And just how full is that complement after tonight's grand campaign?"

"Forty-three: twenty-three ghouls, twenty mortals."

"If I am not mistaken, we began the battle with seventy-three ghoul and mortal knights."

"We did, milord."

Alexander noted the commander wasn't omitting honorifics this time. "And we lost nearly half that many Cainites, did we not?"

"Seventeen, my prince." Tiny beads of blood-sweat welled forth on Rudiger's forehead.

"And how many pagans did we send to hell this fine night?"

"I... There was no way to make a clear estimate given all the confusion. But I'd wager that we slew two dozen at most."

Alexander walked over to Rudiger until he stood toe to toe with the knight. To Rudiger's credit, he didn't back away. "Not precisely a glorious victory for the vaunted Teutonic Knights."

Rudiger's jaw muscles tensed. "I believe we first went wrong when—" Alexander's hand shot out and clamped around his throat, choking off his words. The unliving knight was in no danger of fainting, but there were still many other ways Alexander could harm him if he wished. From the look in Rudiger's eyes, the knight knew it.

"Not 'we.' *You* were in command of the knights on the field. *You* rode off of your own accord to join the vanguard, and it was *you* who ordered a retreat without consulting me. We still might have carried the night if it hadn't been for your inept leadership and cowardice."

The fear in Rudiger's eyes changed to anger. He reached up and gripped Alexander's wrist and tried to pry the prince's hand from his throat, without success.

Alexander laughed. "You can't possibly hope to match my power, childe, so don't bother trying. I should grab one of the sharper pieces of my desk, shove it through your heart and then leave you out in the open to be consumed by the sun. Unfortunately, I have little time to deal with those of your brother-knights who would surely become foolhardy after such a public display. So, as much as I would like to, I will not slay you—"

Relief showed in Rudiger's eyes.

"—that way. Instead, your knights will learn tomorrow evening that you incurred wounds during the battle—wounds you gallantly hid from them—and that you finally succumbed to your injuries in your slumber."

Rudiger's eyes were wide with terror. He tried to shake his head, but with Alexander gripping his throat so tightly, he had very little range of movement.

"I suppose you're thinking that your men will not be taken in by my deception."

Rudiger attempted a nod.

"Fear not, sir knight. I will *make* them believe. Now that they have fought one battle against a foe they thought they could defeat easily and suffered significant losses—including that of their beloved commander—they shall be eager to go up against the pagans again. I should have little trouble getting them to believe whatever I want, just so long as I promise them another chance to fight Qarakh's tribe. And if that is the case, then I no longer have any need for you, do I?"

Before Rudiger could so much as blink, Alexander jerked his wrist. The knight's neck snapped like a twig caught in a gale. Alexander then reached up with his other hand and in a single smooth motion tore Rudiger's head from his shoulders. The knight's body slipped to the ground, vitae gushing up from the neck stump.

Alexander gripped the head by the hair and brought it close to his face. He watched the light slowly fade from Rudiger's eyes as the Final Death settled upon him. When his gaze was glassy and staring, Alexander dropped the head to the ground beside the body that was already fading into a pile of ash.

He had little time before sunrise. He needed to get digging. He selected a large chunk of wood from the remains of his desk to use as a digging tool and picked a suitable spot. He was surprised to find himself almost cheerful.

As he dug, Alexander hummed a tune that he'd first heard played upon a lyre as a youth in ancient Athens. He couldn't recall the name of it now, if he'd ever known it, but it was a sprightly, bouncy tune that spoke of high spirits and good times. It was well worth Rudiger's destruction, as well as those of all the other knights who had fallen in battle this night, to be reminded of that song after so very, very long. He continued humming to himself as he dug

Rudiger's grave.

Chapter Twenty-One

When Qarakh rose from the ground inside his tent that night, he found Deverra waiting for him. The priestess lay upon the bed that had once been shared by his two human ghouls, Sasha and Pavla. Her robe lay folded next to the bed, and she slept beneath a fur blanket, her red hair spread out around her like the halo of a Christian angel. Her skin was less swollen than the previous night, the color almost normal again. Another night or two and she should be completely recovered.

He gazed down upon her sleeping face, torn between two equally strong urges. He wanted to leave the tent as quietly as he could before she woke. He knew that she had slept here because she had sensed something was wrong and wanted to talk to him about it when he rose. But Qarakh didn't want to talk to her—or to anyone else—about what had happened last night.

But he also felt an impulse to remove clothing and climb beneath the fur blanket and wrap his arms around her. Their cold Cainite bodies would not warm one another, regardless of how much time they spent in each other's embrace, nor would they respond to the physical closeness in the same manner as the bodies of mortal men and women. But they would still be together, and that was all that mattered.

Qarakh was still trying to decide what he wanted to do when Deverra opened her eyes. They retained a pinkish tinge from all the equine blood she had ingested the previous night.

"I'm surprised you're up," she said. "Usually you sleep later than I do."

"You were weary after last night." Due to the infusion of

Aajav's vitae, he felt stronger and more full of energy than ever before. It was obscene that the murder of his brother should leave him feeling so good.

Deverra sat up, not bothering to keep herself covered with the blanket. "I know what happened last night. I've worked so many spells on both you and Aajav over the years that I've become linked to you both. You've taken your brother's essence into yourself, and it has left you with great sorrow."

Qarakh did not know what to say to this, so he said nothing.

"I also know that whatever his reasons, Aajav chose to end his life, and he asked you, his brother, to grant him the mercy of oblivion. What you did was an act of love, Qarakh. You must believe that."

"Do you want to know what I believe? I had time to think as I rode back to the battlefield last night, and more time again as I returned to the camp. I came to understand where Aajav's error lay. He was unable to give up his mortal life on the steppe, and because of this, he could never accept his existence as a Cainite."

"He tried to live in *yostoi*," Deverra said.

"He did not truly understand *yostoi*, and neither did I, until last night. Like Aajav, I too believed that the only way to live with what I had become was to attempt to take the best elements of both worlds—mortal and Cainite—and combine them. But all I managed to do was make myself into a walking contradiction: a creature neither fully human nor fully Cainite."

"You speak from your sorrow. You do not truly mean these words."

"I do. I am a Mongolian wanderer who pretends to be khan of a tribe bound to the grasslands of Livonia. I am a hunter, yet I keep mortals, watch over and protect them, as if they were sheep and I their shepherd. I pretend to fight the Christians and their civilization, but I keep my own Beast on so tight a leash that it haunts my dreams. And last night both Alexander and I fought as mortal men do—with strategy and carefully planned battle tactics. But such is not the way of the Beast. The way of the Beast is to attack swiftly, matching your strength to your enemy's, to fight as savagely as you can until one of you is the victor and the other is no more. It is that simple, that pure."

"You are wrong, Qarakh." Crimson tears brimmed at the corners of her pink-hued eyes. "True *yostoi* means carefully keeping all the aspects of one's nature in balance: nobility and savagery, hunger and gluttony, necessity and excess. One in *yostoi* kills out of need and want both. You have successfully balanced these elements, Qarakh, and you have created a place where others can learn to do the same."

Qarakh shook his head. "All I have created is a mockery—a tribe of predators who play at being herders. I have long been referred to as the Untamed, but that name was not accurate. I *was* tamed—by myself and by my foolish, childish dream."

Red tears flowed freely down Deverra's cheeks. "It is a beautiful dream, and one that I share."

"It was only a delusion, and one I am well rid of. Starting this night I shall truly live up to the title of the Untamed. I shall embrace my bestial nature, and no one—Cainite, mortal or sorcerer—shall be able to stand against me."

"You cannot mean this!"

Part of him wanted to agree with her, to tell her that he was speaking out of pain over Aajav's loss, that perhaps his dream was still worth fighting for. But another part—a darker, hungrier part—said otherwise.

"Make yourself ready," he said. "Tonight we shall meet Alexander's army in battle once more. And this time there will be no plans or formations. We shall line up at opposite ends of the battlefield, and then we shall ride at one another and fight until one side is victorious—exactly as we should have done in the first place."

Qarakh thought that Deverra would argue further with him, but the priestess wiped the tears from her cheeks, making bloody streaks on her flesh, and then nodded.

"As you will, my khan."

Qarakh nodded once, then left the tent. He needed to speak to Malachite.

After Qarakh had gone, Deverra threw aside the fur blanket and quickly donned her robe. She left the tent and hurried to the nearby stand of trees where the other Telyavs had spent the day.

She knew something about diablerie. After all, she had once belonged to the Tremere, a clan whose very existence was due to the practice. It was more than simply consuming another Cainite's blood. Diablerie entailed the consumption of the very heart's blood, the last nugget of essence. Diablerie was to eat the very soul of another. This conveyed power, yes, but it could also overwhelm the diablerist's own personality. The initial period of time immediately after diablerie—a few days to a few weeks—was marked by irrationality and impulsiveness as the Cainite struggled to adjust to his newfound strength and to integrate the elements of his victim's personality into his own. It was an extremely dangerous time, and many did not survive it.

She knew that there was no way she would be able to talk Qarakh out of confronting Alexander one more time, but she was far from helpless. First she would speak with the surviving members of her coven, and then she would make one more journey to the place where she had known all along that she would end up: the Grove of Shadows.

Alexander finished with the red-haired girl and lay her body gently upon his bed. She had been a sweet, gentle creature that had pined for a minstrel that had visited her village when she was but a child. He desired to keep her around for a bit longer so that he might look upon her beautiful face from time to time as he made his plans.

He sat in his chair. The remains of his desk had been cleared away by a ghoul servant. The trunk where Alexander kept his books and scrolls now sat several feet to the left of where it had been—right over the place where Alexander had buried Rudiger.

Breaking the news of the commander's death to the other knights hadn't gone quite as well as Alexander had hoped. While they had accepted his lie about how Rudiger had met his end easily enough—thanks to his superior will—they demanded his ashes be handed over to them so Rudiger might be given a proper Christian burial. Alexander had cursed himself for not anticipating this development, and it had taken quite a bit of

talking—and even more application of willpower—to convince
the knights to allow him to keep Rudiger's remains "in state"
until after they achieved victory over the pagans. Alexander
had been ravenous by the time he'd returned to his tent and
called out for István to bring him someone suitable—and then
he remembered that István was gone.

He couldn't escape the feeling that he was losing control
somehow. Not just of the current situation, but of his own existence. He thought once more of facing his grinning doppelganger upon undulating waves of blood, and he couldn't keep
from shuddering. He reached out to the empty space beside
him, hoping to somehow summon up those who had abandoned him despite all his love. Lorraine. Saviarre. Rosamund.
All gone.

He would send the ghoul and mortal knights to make a
daytime raid on the pagan camp, he decided. They would view
such an attack as unchivalrous, of course, so he would need a
plausible rationale for why they ought to do such a dishonorable thing. No, he decided. Mortal wills were fragile things and
he would simply bend them. If some broke in the process, such
was the cost of war.

Without warning, the shadows in one corner of this tent
thickened and a black-robed form stepped out of the darkness.

Malachite.

Alexander surprised himself by not immediately attacking
the traitorous wretch. "Good evening, Malachite. Should I welcome you as a returning prodigal?"

The Nosferatu glanced at the body of the dead girl lying
on Alexander's bed, and a look of sorrow briefly passed over
his leprous features. Alexander smirked. Malachite always had
been too soft-hearted. It was a fatal flaw in a Cainite, one that
Alexander was grateful that he did not possess.

"I have come to bring you a message," Malachite said.

Alexander sneered. "From your new master?"

"From Qarakh."

"How much did you tell him?"

"About your army? All that I knew."

Cold rage filled Alexander, and he had to fight to keep from springing to his feet and launching himself at Malachite. "From one deceiver to another. I'm impressed. I knew you accompanied me to Livonia for your own reasons, but I did not expect you to switch allegiances so quickly, or so thoroughly."

"Qarakh has dealt with me fairly. But even beyond that, having seen your rule in Paris and your actions here, I can say without hesitation that Qarakh is the better prince."

"But they are pagans, or do you forget? I admit that means little to me, but I should think that you would desire their destruction even more than I."

Malachite smiled sadly. "You understand no motivations beyond the satisfaction of your own desires. Despite your great age, Alexander, in the end you are nothing more than a spoiled child that never had the chance to grow up."

Fury so overwhelmed Alexander that he could barely see. He forced words out between gritted teeth. "You have a message to deliver. Deliver it."

"Qarakh wishes to meet you once more in battle at midnight. He is already in the process of assembling his army near the field where you clashed before."

Alexander frowned. "What trick is this?"

"No trick at all. Qarakh has grown weary of deception and subterfuge, and he wishes to fight directly and openly—army against army, strength against strength—to determine once and for all who shall be victorious."

Alexander was intrigued despite himself. "I assume you gave the Tartar an opinion of what my reaction would be?"

"Of course. I told him you would be skeptical at first, believing the offer to be a deception because that's what you would do in his place. But ultimately your curiosity and your pride would lead you to accept."

Alexander's fury had dissipated for the most part, to be replaced now by irritation. "I should decline the challenge just to spite you both."

"Perhaps. But you will not because you cannot."

Alexander hated to admit it, but Malachite was right. He was tired of thinking, planning, plotting and scheming. He wanted to act.

"Very well. Midnight, at the same place we fought last night. Now go—I have an army to prepare."

Malachite inclined his head. "Yes, milord." Then the Nosferatu hobbled out of the tent to go relay Alexander's response to Qarakh.

The prince knew there was no need to order his people to give Malachite safe passage out of the camp. The Nosferatu would be able to sneak out as easily as he had sneaked in.

Alexander stood and walked over to the dead girl. He stroked her hair lovingly for a few moments, marveling anew at how much it felt like silk, then he bent down and kissed her forehead.

"My thanks for your blood, sentimental one. I shall put it to good use this night."

Qarakh sat upon the gelding he'd taken from Aajav's abductors. The horse had been fed on one of the slain knights' blood, so it was stronger, swifter and hardier than a normal mount. But Qarakh had no special bond with it. This steed would not anticipate his commands and respond to his moods the way one of his mares would have. He would have to remember that during the battle to come.

His force was arranged in a single line—mounted warriors in the middle, flanked on either side by those who by choice or necessity planned to fight afoot. There were no divisions, no commanders save Qarakh, and no elaborate battle plan. When the Christian force arrived, as Qarakh was certain it would, he would give the signal and the battle would begin, and the fighting would continue until one side or the other emerged victorious.

What if the other side wins? his Beast asked. *What if all that is achieved here this night is mutual destruction?*

"Then so be it," Qarakh mouthed silently. His Beast practically purred at the response.

Alessandro was to Qarakh's right. The Iberian sat upon his brown mare with an ease that the Mongol knew he didn't feel. To his left was Karl the Blue. He kept his gaze fixed on the horizon, watching for sign of the enemy's approach. He growled softly, perhaps without even being aware of doing so.

It felt strange to be here without the rest of his inner circle: Arnulf, Wilhelmina, Grandfather and especially Deverra. He had not seen her since the conversation in his tent. The other Telyavs were missing, too. Qarakh feared that Deverra, disapproving of the way he intended to conduct this battle, had left and taken her sorcerers with her. If so, so be it. The tribe would win this battle without the aid of witchcraft.

Still, without her here, it felt as if a part of himself was missing. The better part.

Forget her and concentrate on the fight to come, his Beast urged. Qarakh was determined to do as it said, but it wouldn't be easy.

There was no hint of rain tonight. The sky was clear of clouds, allowing the full moon to paint the battlefield in a soft blue-white glow. For Qarakh and the other Cainites, it would be like fighting in broad daylight. Qarakh took this as a sign that Father Tengri approved of his battle plan for this night. A good omen, indeed.

"My khan, are you certain he will come?" Alessandro spoke in a whisper so as not to be overhead by the others.

Qarakh replied in a whisper as well. "He will be unable to resist."

"I fear we are not taking the wisest course by engaging the Christian knights in a direct confrontation."

Qarakh nearly laughed. "You might have brought this up before our army left the camp."

"I confess that at the time I believed that there was more to your plan which you had chosen to keep hidden for your own reasons."

"And now?"

"Now I do not. I cannot see how we can hope to defeat Alexander and his knights in head-to-head combat."

"After last night, our numbers are more evenly matched," Qarakh said. "We may well outnumber them now."

"If he doesn't bring reinforcements."

"If Alexander could have fielded more soldiers last night, he would have. Restraint is not one of his strongest virtues."

"It used to be one of yours," the Iberian said, so softly that

Qarakh could barely hear him above the sound of the night breeze wafting across the field.

Qarakh chose to let the comment pass without remark.

From nearby came the plaintive howl of a wolf. Karl the Blue smiled.

"The Christians draw near." The Finnish warrior had commanded one of his men to take wolf form and act as sentry. Even now the Gangrel was no doubt speeding back on his four strong legs to rejoin Qarakh's army.

Up and down the line, warriors made ready, drawing swords, nocking arrows or entering into the first stages of transformation to animal shape. They knew the enemy would be upon them soon. Even now Qarakh could hear the faint sounds of hundreds of horse hooves pressing down on grass, like the whisper of an incoming tide.

But when the first figures came onto the battlefield, there were only two of them, and they came from the north, and not the west as Alexander's army would. At first, Qarakh allowed himself to hope that Deverra had changed her mind and returned. But one of the figures was too large to be her, and the other walked hunched over, occasionally dropping to all fours. It wasn't long before the two were close enough for Qarakh to recognize—especially in this moonlight. But even if it hadn't been so bright out, Qarakh would have been able to identify them by their scents: Arnulf and Wilhelmina.

The Goth warrior walked up to Qarakh, the Viking maid keeping up with him as best she could. Arnulf looked precisely the same as he had when he'd left the camp, but Wilhelmina bore the unmistakable signs of terrible frenzy. One of her ears was human, while the other was that of a wolf. Both eyes shone yellow with bestial cunning, but with little indication of intelligence. Her teeth were all sharp, though of varying lengths, and some had grown crookedly, jammed together or jutting out from her mouth at odd angles. Her fingers and toes ended in curved dagger-length talons so long that she had trouble walking upright. Somewhere along the way she had divested herself of armor and clothing, and she stood before her khan naked, her body half covered with patches of amber fur. Her breasts were smaller than they had been, the nipples erect in the cool night air, and she had six now instead of two, just as a she-wolf would.

"I found her like this in the forest," Arnulf said, his voice thick with pity. "Or perhaps she found me, I don't know. She can still talk after a fashion, and she told me of last night's battle. She urged me to return to the tribe and fight the Christian army, and… well, here I am. I swore an oath to you, Tartar, and I will live up to it one last time."

Qarakh knew the Goth warrior would never apologize for leaving. It wouldn't even occur to him to do so. Still, he had returned, which could not have been an easy thing for a creature of his pride.

Qarakh was still considering how to respond when Wilhelmina opened her mouth, and with an animal's tongue and throat said, "'eeeeeaaaaase?"

She was almost impossible to understand, but Qarakh nevertheless knew what she'd meant: *please.*

She's an abomination. Put her down and be done with it!

Qarakh ignored his Beast. He remembered something he had told Rikard:

Like any good father, I would miss my children, should they stray from the camp. Miss them so much, in fact, that I would hunt them across all the lands of the earth until I had found them again. And do you know what I would do once we were reunited? I would clasp them in my arms and say, "The tribe misses you… I miss you. Come home."

"It is good to see you both," Qarakh said. "Take your places alongside Alessandro."

"And my oath?"

"When this battle is over, you are released, free once more to run alone."

Arnulf nodded and Wilhelmina's mouth twisted in what Qarakh assumed was intended to be a smile. The two then walked to the other side of Alessandro, and the line of tribesmen adjusted to make room for them.

It was then that Qarakh caught sight of Alexander's army.

Chapter Twenty-Two

The Christian knights rode in a single line, one next to the other, standards flying. All were on horseback, and Alexander rode upon a large black stallion in the exact middle of the line.

Many of the tribesmen and women growled at the sight—Wilhelmina one of the loudest—but Alessandro said, "Steady now," and they held their places.

Alexander led his knights to within fifty feet of Qarakh's force, then softly commanded them to halt. The knights brought their mounts to an immediate stop, and Qarakh knew the knights were tightly under the prince's thrall. So much the better; the expenditure of power would leave him all the weaker.

"Good evening, Qarakh. It's a splendid night for crushing one's enemy, is it not?"

"Yes." Qarakh noted that the German knight did not ride next to Alexander as expected. Had the Cainite been slain in last night's battle, or was he elsewhere, perhaps leading a separate group of knights intent on executing a surprise attack, despite the Ventrue's agreement to fight a straightforward battle?

What if Alexander is planning to break his word? Would that truly be a surprise?

"No," Qarakh answered his Beast in a whisper.

"Not to insult your honor," Alexander said, "but I find it difficult to believe that you intend to forgo the aid of your sorcerous allies. If I possessed such an advantage, I would not willingly give it up."

"That is because you are not one of us."

The tribe cheered, snarled and howled in approval of its khan's reply.

Alexander smiled. "And praise be to Enoch's first childe for that. But enough of this banter. We have all come here to fight, not talk. Shall we begin?"

Qarakh nodded. "When you are ready."

Alexander cracked his reins, and his ebon stallion leaped forward. The knights let forth a battle cry, drew their swords and urged their mounts to follow their leader.

"Archers, fire!" Alessandro ordered, and a hail of arrows flew at the advancing enemy, striking knights and horses alike. A number of ghoul and mortal knights went down, arrows protruding from the throats and eye sockets. Many Cainites were similarly wounded, but they remained in the saddle, swords held tight, ignoring the pain of their injuries.

As planned, Alessandro himself targeted the Ventrue prince. His first arrow was aimed at Alexander's right eye, but the ancient Cainite dodged it easily. The first arrow had only been meant as a distraction, though. As soon as he'd let it fly, Alessandro drew, nocked and released another with blinding speed. This one struck Alexander's mount in the chest, piercing the stallion's heart. The horse whinnied in pain and went down on its front legs, causing Alexander to tumble out of the saddle and fly over the steed's head.

"*Tchoo! Tchoo!*" Qarakh urged, though his new mount had not been trained to respond to the Mongolian signal. He snapped the reins and dug his heels into the animal's sides, and the gelding bounded forward. Qarakh drew his saber and rode hard toward the Ventrue ancient, who was only just getting to his feet. He intended to lop off the prince's head with a single stroke and end this battle before it had truly gotten started.

Qarakh heard Alessandro call out behind him. "Archers, with me!" The Iberian would lead the bowmen away from the main fighting so they could fire from a safer distance and have more time to choose their targets. The remaining tribesmen charged, swords, axes and claws held high, all of them wild to spill the blood of their enemies.

As Qarakh rode toward Alexander, he felt a sense of rightness. *This* was the way it was supposed to be. *This* was true harmony with the Beast.

Alexander rolled onto his feet, sword in hand, ready to meet Qarakh's charge. Qarakh swung his saber as fast and as hard as he could, but Alexander spun to the side, and the saber only managed to nick his shoulder, tearing the Ventrue's tabard and taking a small chink out of his mail vest.

As Alexander came back around, he chopped at the gelding's front legs, shearing them cleanly in two. The horse went down at once, but Qarakh launched himself from the saddle and landed nimbly on his feet in front of Alexander. His Beast crooned a song of sweet slaughter, and the Mongol warrior stepped forward and swung his saber at Alexander of Paris. Grinning, eyes flashing with a mixture of fury, bloodlust and delight, the boy prince brought his sword up to block the blow. The battle began in earnest.

Malachite watched the fighting from within the shadows of the nearby woods. He'd returned to Qarakh's camp, informed the chieftain that Alexander had accepted his challenge, and then the Tartar, satisfied, kept his word and told Malachite the story (and location) of the Obertus monastery. The Nosferatu's mind still boggled at the news. The Obertus order had been founded by the Dracon's progeny in Constantinople but had no known holdings here. And it certainly had no love for the Cainite Heresy or Archbishop Nikita. But the coincidence was too much—it was another sign and Malachite would follow it.

But not yet. First, he would watch what was likely to be the final encounter between the knights and the tribesmen. Malachite wasn't certain why he felt he must. Perhaps it was a need to sate his scholar's curiosity, or perhaps he wished to witness what might very well prove to be Cainite history in the making. Or perhaps he had come to sympathize with the tribe and wanted to stay and help them, if only by watching and wishing them success.

He heard a rustling of underbrush behind him, and he instinctively melted into the shadows to conceal himself. A moment later, he saw a group of Telyavs. They approached the edge and stood close to the trees, their brown robes seeming to change color and texture to match that of the bark. Malachite noted that Deverra was not among them. He wondered at the absence of the high priestess. He knew that Qarakh wished to conduct this battle without the aid of witchery, but that hardly explained her absence from her followers' sides.

The Telyavs watched the fighting for several moments before turning their backs on the battle and walking over to the spot where they had sat the previous night when casting their spell. They settled into a small circle, crossed their legs, and then withdrew waterskins from the folds of their robes. The Telyavs bit their lips and vitae welled forth. They leaned forward and allowed the blood to drip upon the ground while they chanted words in a language Malachite didn't recognize. The Telyavs then uncorked their waterskins and raised them to their gore-slick lips, but they did not swallow. They swished the water around in their mouths for a moment and then spat the liquid—now mixed with their blood—onto the ground before them. They linked hands, closed their eyes and resumed chanting.

Moments later, shouts of surprise and anger drifted from the battlefield as whatever enchantment the Telyavs had worked took effect.

Qarakh raised his saber barely in time to parry a sword thrust aimed directly at his heart. Alexander moved with a speed and grace beyond anything the Mongol warrior had ever seen. He was hard-pressed to counter the Ventrue's moves, let alone make any attacks of his own. Worst of all, he had the sense that Alexander was merely toying with him, and that he could move even more swiftly if he wished.

Kill him! his Beast shrieked. *Kill him now!*

For once, Qarakh would have loved to give in completely to his Beast's wishes, but even with the additional strength and speed he had gained from Aajav's sacrifice, he knew he was still no match for his ancient opponent. He could continue fighting as savagely as he could, but he knew it was only a matter of time before Alexander defeated him. Qarakh would survive only as long as Alexander was amused by their sparring match. The moment the Ventrue grew bored, he would deliver Qarakh unto the Final Death.

Qarakh was not dismayed by this knowledge. Part of him thought he deserved to die for his foolish belief in a dream of creating a tribal nation of Cainites in Livonia, and more, for taking the life of his beloved brother and sire. Even so, he was determined to fight on to the last, if for no other reason than to honor Aajav's memory. But before he could swing his saber at Alexander again, shouts erupted from the combatants around them, both pagans and Christians.

The ground they stood upon—which had already been damp and muddy from last night's rain—had suddenly grown more so. It continued to liquefy until horses and foot soldiers sank. Mounts whinnied in frustration and fear as they slid into muck up to their bellies. Their riders yanked on the reins and shouted commands for their steeds to pull free from the mire, but the horses were unable to escape.

Those warriors afoot fared just as poorly. The bog swallowed them up to their knees, and the more they struggled, the deeper they sank. Some were in up to their waists, some up to their chests. Of all of the assembled warriors, only Alexander and Qarakh still stood upon solid ground.

The Ventrue glared at Qarakh. "I knew you would never give up witchcraft!"

Qarakh fought to contain his fury. Not at Alexander, but at Deverra and her fellow Telyavs, for surely this was an enchantment of their making.

"I have nothing to do with this," Qarakh said. "I commanded the Telyavs to stay out of this battle."

Alexander sneered. "Of course you did."

"Upon my honor, Ventrue. Besides, this spell is working as much against my people as it is yours."

Alexander considered this for a moment. "In that case, then, either your sorcerers lost control of their enchantment, or they have turned against you and your entire tribe."

Qarakh glanced down at the ground beneath their feet. It was difficult to tell, but it looked as if the solid earth extended in a rough circle around them for a radius of fifteen feet or so.

"So what do we do now?" Alexander asked. "Declare a draw and resume our conflict on another night? Or should we combine forces long enough to slay the Telyavs? That way they wouldn't be able to interfere with us when next we fight."

Qarakh bared his teeth. "Nothing could ever convince me to ally with you for any reason, Ventrue. I have come to know you too well."

"Pity, but then I can't say as I blame you." Alexander looked around at the knights and pagans trapped in the grayish-brown soup, many of whom continued to try to kill one another, despite the fact that they could barely move.

Qarakh recalled something Grandfather had said during a *kuriltai: Cut off the head and the body will die.*

"I have a proposition," Qarakh said.

Alexander turned to him and raised an eyebrow.

"We continue this fight, just the two of us. And whichever one survives shall be declared the victor of this battle."

"An intriguing notion, as well as an amusing one. But regardless of the outcome, how can we be sure our respective armies will abide by the result?"

"I do not think they will have a choice," Qarakh said. "For whatever reason, it seems that the two of us are destined to decide the outcome of this battle. Why else would we still be standing on dry ground?"

"Far be it from me to defy destiny." So saying, Alexander lunged forward and swung his sword in a vicious arc, the blow clearly aimed at Qarakh's neck.

The Mongol moved to block the strike and then—

—found himself elsewhere.

He stood in a grove of trees draped in shadow, and he no longer held his saber. The sky above was a dull, featureless gray, and the air was still and stagnant. He sniffed and smelled the stink of decaying flesh mingled with the acrid odor of burning wood and the tang of hot metal.

"What sorcery is this?" His voice was muffled by the dead air, almost as if he had spoken the words underwater.

"Mine." A robed figured emerged from the shadows between two trees. Deverra.

Despite the strangeness of the situation, Qarakh was glad to

see her at first, until he remembered: the battlefield... the bog...
Alexander... "I do not care what this place is or why you have
brought me here. You must send me back at once! I was—"

"About to face Alexander in single combat," Deverra finished for him. She walked over to Qarakh, reached out and took
his hand. He surprised himself by letting her. She smiled. "Who
do you think arranged it?"

"Then the bog *was* created by Telyavic magic."

Deverra nodded. "It's a spell we use to help draw water to
a farmer's field in times of drought or famine. We don't usually
try to concentrate so much water in one place, though."

"Why would you work such an enchantment on the
battlefield?"

"Because if I didn't, the tribe was going to be defeated by
Alexander, and you..." She squeezed his hand but didn't complete the thought, not that she needed to. "It was shown to me."

Qarakh wanted to ask by whom, but instead he asked, "Why
did you leave the camp?" *Why did you leave me?*

"If you were to defeat Alexander, there were certain preparations that needed to be made. That is why I have brought your
spirit here, to the Grove of Shadows."

Qarakh's eyes had adjusted to the dimness of the grove—
though if he was a spirit here, then he didn't have physical eyes
that needed to adjust, did he?—and he could more clearly make
out the trees around them. They were not trees of wood, but
instead formed of intertwining coils of intestines and other
organs, splintered lengths of bleached bone and sharp-edged
leaves that appeared to have been made from blue-gray steel.
He looked down at the ground and saw it was formed not of
earth, but rather taut skin inlaid with runes of metal that resembled intricate tattoos. Beneath his feet, he felt a slight rise and
fall, and he realized that the ground was breathing.

Despite his earlier assertion to himself that he would not, he
asked, "Where is this place?"

"As I said, the Grove of Shadows. I have brought you here to
talk to someone. Someone who can help you defeat Alexander."

This was disconcerting but not wholly unheard of. Deverra
was a shaman and part of the shaman's lot was to travel the

spirit realms. Still, this charnel grove felt wrong to Qarakh.

"But what is happening to my body while my spirit is here? Is it not defenseless against Alexander?"

"This is a place of the soul and the mind. No time shall pass in the physical world while you are here."

Qarakh didn't see how such a thing was possible, but if Deverra said it was so, then he believed her. "Take me to this person I am to meet, then."

There was a sadness in Deverra's eyes as she nodded. She led him by the hand deeper into the Grove.

They walked without stopping for what seemed at once a period of days and only a few moments, moving across the breathing ground and between the meat, bone and metal trees. Eventually Qarakh became aware of two separate and distinct sounds: a hammer clanging on an anvil and the susurration of waves breaking upon a shore. And then he saw a pinpoint of light in the distance, a yellowish orange glow that grew larger as they approached, until Qarakh could see that it was the light from a fire. He was mildly surprised to find that he felt no aversion to the flames. Evidently his spirit did not possess the same undead weaknesses as his body. He wondered if it also lacked his physical strengths.

He realized something then. Not only hadn't his Beast made itself known since Deverra had brought him here, he couldn't sense it at all. For the first time in years, he was free. It was an exhilarating sensation, and he nearly laughed out loud from the joy of it.

They drew close to the fire. A man stood next to it, bent over an iron anvil mounted upon an old tree stump. He held something steady with a pair of tongs, bringing his hammer down upon the object in a regular rhythm.

ka-KLANG! ka-KLANG! ka-KLANG!

This smith wore only a leather apron and thick cloth pants. No gloves to protect his hands, no shoes or boots upon his feet. As they reached the anvil, the smith looked up, and Qarakh found himself staring at his mirror image.

"Welcome, Qarakh of Mongolia, my good and faithful son."

Chapter Twenty-Three

The voice was Qarakh's as well, though the words and manner were not.

"Why do you wear my shape?"

"Because I do not have one of my own? Because I prefer to put my guests at ease by showing them a visage they find comforting? Or perhaps I wish instead to unsettle them. Choose whichever answer you like. All are equally valid."

"Valid, perhaps. But are they all correct?"

The smith smiled but did not answer. He returned to pounding a lump of metal he held with a pair of iron tongs. The lump was beginning to take form, but Qarakh didn't recognize what it was in the process of becoming.

The smith frowned then. "This one is being stubborn."

He picked up the shapeless lump and thrust the tongs into the fire. A tiny shriek of agony came from within the flames, and the smith withdrew the metal, which now glowed orange-red, though it had been inside the fire for only a moment. The smith then placed the lump back on the anvil.

"He still has a little bit of life left inside him, I think." The smith lifted his hammer high and brought it down swiftly. This time the metal screamed when the hammer struck it, and a thin stream of crimson shot forth from one end, bringing the scent of blood to Qarakh's nostrils. The blood ran along almost imperceptible furrows in the surface of the anvil—furrows that either Qarakh hadn't noticed before or which had only just appeared. The blood trickled over the side and fell through the air like a small red waterfall, only to vanish down a hole dug into the earth (into the *skin*, and it wasn't a hole, but rather an *orifice*) next to the anvil.

"Where does the blood go?" Qarakh asked. The scent of blood didn't stir any appetite within him, but that was because here, if only in this place, he was not a Cainite, but only Qarakh.

"Out to the ocean, of course," the smith said, and then continued hammering the metal.

Qarakh heard the shush of waves, and for some reason, he envisioned a vast sea of blood.

The metal made no more sounds now, which seemed to please the smith. "Much better!" He worked the metal more easily, and soon a definite shape began to take form: a leaf.

The smith smiled and held it up for their inspection. "How does it look?"

"Like all the others," Qarakh said.

The smith grinned with Qarakh's mouth. "Excellent!" He relaxed his grip on the tongs and released the metal leaf, but instead of falling, it was taken by a sudden gust of wind and borne away, tumbling end over end into the darkness, presumably to end up on one of the trees here in the Grove of Shadows.

"I hope you don't mind if I continue to work as we speak," the smith said.

On top of the anvil—which had been empty a moment ago—now rested a small, naked man, no more than a foot long. He was alive, and he looked around in terror and confusion. The homunculus tried to sit up, but before he could, the smith grabbed him with the tongs, crushing the tiny man's rib cage, and plunged him into the fire. The man screamed and screamed and when the smith removed the tongs from the flames, they now held a hot piece of metal ready to be shaped. The smith put the metal on the anvil and began pounding on it, steaming blood squirting out with each hammer blow, running along the furrows and falling into the orifice below.

Qarakh turned to Deverra for guidance, but though she gave him a sympathetic look, she said nothing. He sensed that she was restraining herself from saying anything—perhaps because she was not permitted to.

Qarakh was on his own, so he asked the next logical question. "Who are you?"

The smith continued to work the once human metal as he

answered. "I have been known by many names in the past and will doubtless be known by many more in the future, but that hardly answers your question, does it? In Livonia, I am known as Telyavel, Protector of the Dead as well as the Maker of Things."

Qarakh was not certain that he believed he was truly speaking with a god, though whatever the smith was, he was obviously a being of great power. "I do not see how the two go together."

The smith finished the new leaf and released it to the air. Another homunculus appeared on the anvil, this one a naked obese woman, and he snatched her up with the tongs. She screamed as she went into the fire, and the process continued as before.

"Why not?" the smith said as he worked. "Life and death, creation and destruction have always been linked. Without Making, there can be no Unmaking, and therefore no *Re* making. You surely understand this."

Qarakh wasn't certain, but he thought he did. Mongols believed that the body contained three souls: the *suld* soul, which merged with nature after death, the *ami* soul and the *suns* soul, both of which reincarnated into a new human form. If Qarakh understood the smith correctly, he was reincarnating the souls of the dead, using them as raw material to create the metallic leaves, whatever they were.

"Why do you wish to help me defeat Alexander?"

The smith looked up from his work and smiled. "Because it is well past time to Unmake that one. Besides which, he threatens my children, and what father can stand by when his offspring are in danger?"

"What must I do?"

The smith finished his latest leaf and gave it to the wind to carry away. The anvil remained empty then, and he set both the tongs and the hammer down. "Not much." He reached into a pocket of his apron and brought forth a handful of soil. "All you have to do is swallow this."

"It is... dirt?"

"Livonian soil," the smith said. "If you eat it, you shall be bonded to the land, and as long as you remain in direct physical contact with it, you shall be able to draw upon my power for short periods of time."

Qarakh eyed the dirt skeptically. "Will this enchantment give me enough strength to defeat Alexander?"

"Even your body is only capable of containing a minute fraction of my power, but it should be enough to give you a fighting chance against the Ventrue."

Qarakh turned his hand palm up, and the smith gently deposited the soil into it, then shook off the last few remaining bits. Qarakh felt no special power contained within the earth; it felt like dirt and nothing more. He lifted it to his face and sniffed it. Smelled like dirt, too.

He then looked into the smith's eyes and was shocked to see they contained swirls of stars set against fields of utter darkness—just like the eyes of the strange Cainite Qarakh had encountered outside of the monastery.

"There must be a price," Qarakh said. "Such power does not come free."

"True." The smith glanced at Deverra before returning his gaze to Qarakh. "For you, the price is simple, though you may be unwilling to pay it. As I said, once you swallow that soil, you will be bound to the land. This means that you shall be unable to leave Livonia except for short lengths of time, and no matter how many centuries you live, you will always be forced to return in order to replenish your strength. If you do not, you will grow weaker and weaker until you eventually meet the Final Death. This will last so long as my bond with your priestess does."

Once again, Qarakh looked at the soil in his hand as he thought about what the smith had told him. To be bound to one place would mean giving up the freedom to roam whenever and wherever he wished. No longer would he be able to follow the path of the nomad. No longer would he truly be Qarakh.

"You must ask yourself one final question," the smith said. "How badly do you wish to defeat your enemy?"

"You mean, how badly do I wish to protect my tribe." Qarakh looked to Deverra. "As well as the Telyavs."

The smith shrugged. "Rephrase the question however you like; it remains essentially the same. You know the price—are you willing to pay it?"

Deverra's expression was unreadable, and Qarakh knew she was trying to keep from influencing his choice one way or another. But in the end, there really was no choice. He had already allowed Aajav to offer his life so that he could defeat Alexander, but the additional strength he had received from his brother had not been enough to counter the Ventrue's power. There was only one way Alexander was going to be stopped.

Qarakh brought the soil to his mouth and began eating.

Deverra watched as Qarakh became a phantom and then vanished. She knew his spirit had returned to its body upon the battlefield to resume the fight against Alexander.

"It is done," the smith said. Instead of Qarakh, the being now resembled a red-headed woman garbed in a brown robe. "And now, my daughter, it is time for you to pay your half of the price."

"Yes." She did not know precisely what that price might be, only that it would be high indeed.

The smith smiled and reached for Deverra with slender, feminine hands.

Qarakh got his saber up in time to meet Alexander's strike, but as disoriented as he was, he wasn't prepared to counter the strength of the blow. The saber went tumbling out of his hand. He jumped backward just as the Ventrue slashed at his midsection. The tip of the blade sliced through his leather vest and cut a line across the flesh beneath, but it was a minor wound and healed almost immediately.

Despite the smith's promise, Qarakh felt no stronger than he had before his vision of the Grove of Shadows.

… you shall be bonded to the land, and as long as you remain in direct physical contact with it, you shall be able to draw upon my power…

Qarakh understood then what he needed to do. Alexander rushed forward with inhuman speed, sword now held in a two-handed grip over his head, ready to bring the blade down like an ax upon his opponent. Qarakh fell into crouching position and pressed his bare hand to the earth. Power surged into his being, unlike anything he had ever known before. It was beyond the heady sensation of blood gushing down his throat, beyond the exhilaration of riding into battle upon the back of a hardy steed, beyond the wild abandon of being swept up in the hunt.

Is this what Alexander feels? Qarakh thought. *No wonder he believes he is unstoppable.*

Qarakh's perceptions altered, and suddenly Alexander was moving no more swiftly than an ordinary Cainite. As the Venture brought his sword down—clearly intending to cleave Qarakh in twain, the Mongol warrior reached up with his free hand and caught Alexander's wrists in an iron grip. Qarakh's Beast howled with delight while the prince's eyes widened in surprise, but before he had a chance to react, the Mongol warrior twisted the Ventrue's wrists as hard as he could. Alexander cried out in pain and dropped his sword. Qarakh then yanked Alexander in the other direction. Off balance and confused, the prince slammed into the ground and lay there, stunned.

Qarakh's first impulse was to grab the Ventrue's sword, rush over and cut off Alexander's head, but he knew that if he removed his hand from the ground, he would lose the strength and speed granted by the dark god who dwelled in the Grove of Shadows. Without that power, he would be no match for Alexander. What he needed to do was free his hands so he could fight while still maintaining physical contact with the earth. But how could he—

And then it came to him. As Alexander struggled to rise, Qarakh took his hand away from the ground. He felt a sudden loss as energy drained out of him and his perceptions returned to normal. Alexander seemed to leap to his feet; he came striding toward Qarakh with death in his eyes.

The Gangrel sat back and reached for his left boot. He didn't have time to be neat about this. He gripped the leather and tore it to pieces and then did the same to his right boot. Scraps of shredded leather clung to his feet, but for the most part they were now bare.

Alexander bent down and retrieved his sword so swiftly that it appeared the blade flew upward into his waiting hand. But before the Ventrue could strike, Qarakh planted his feet on the ground and stood up. Strength surged through him once more, and Alexander again moved at what appeared to Qarakh to be normal speed.

As the Ventrue drew back his sword for another blow, Qarakh stepped toward Alexander, moving in so close that the prince no longer had room to wield his weapon. Before Alexander could do anything, Qarakh grabbed him by the throat and squeezed as hard as he could, concentrating all the power granted him by the smith into his hands. At the very last, he hoped to snap Alexander's neck and render him helpless long enough to finish off the ancient Cainite. Though as strong as Qarakh felt, he wouldn't have been surprised if he severed Alexander's head with his bare hands, just like a child popping off the head of a flower with a flick of his thumb.

Yes! his Beast urged. *Do it now!*

Alexander dropped his sword once more and tried to pull Qarakh's hands away from his throat, but he was unable to. The Ventrue's face grew red, then purple, and his hate-filled eyes bulged forth from their sockets. He snarled and spat, a wild animal caught in a trap it could not escape. He then balled his hands into fists and slammed them into Qarakh's ears.

Bright bursts of light flashed behind the Mongol's eyes, and his ears roared with a sound not unlike the breaking waves he'd heard while in the Grove of Shadows. Alexander continued hitting him, but Qarakh ignored the pain and continued to squeeze. He thought he could feel the bones of Alexander's neck grind and begin to give way under the pressure. A few more moments and the battle would be finished.

As if realizing this as well, Alexander stopped striking Qarakh's head. He gripped the Mongol's sides and then lifted him off the ground as easily as a mortal might lift a small child. Qarakh's feet were no longer touching the earth.

He continued to choke Alexander, but his hands were far weaker than they had been a second ago, and the Ventrue no longer appeared to be in distress. His usual Cainite pallor returned to his face, and he smiled.

"You are as great a deceiver as I, Qarakh the Untamed." His voice was a raspy whisper at first, but as he spoke, it gradually returned to normal, the internal wounds Qarakh had inflicted healing with supernatural swiftness. "Only sorcery could allow you to stand against me as an equal. It seems your Telyav friends decided to borrow a page from Greek legend, eh, Antaeus?"

Qarakh had no idea to what legend the Ventrue referred, and he didn't care. He needed to break of free of Alexander and get his feet back on the ground once more. Qarakh hit, kicked and clawed, but no matter how much he struggled, he couldn't loosen the prince's grip. Alexander continued to hold him in the air, only inches above the ground. But inches or miles, it made no difference. If Qarakh couldn't touch the earth, he couldn't draw on the smith god's power.

"It appears we have reached an impasse," Alexander said. "Like a man who has caught hold of a poisonous snake just behind the head, I am safe as long as I maintain my grip, but if I put you down to reach for my sword, you will bite me."

Qarakh let go of Alexander's throat and clawed at his eyes, but the Ventrue turned his head back and forth with such speed that all Qarakh managed to do was scratch the prince's cheeks. Vitae welled forth from the gouges, the scent different from any Cainite blood Qarakh had ever smelled before. This was vitae aged like the finest of wines for two millennia, suffused with time and power. The Mongol began to salivate, and he heard once more the words of prophecy given to him by the ancient Cainite at the Obertus monastery.

Victory is in the blood.

Qarakh realized then that the Cainite with the stars in his eyes had not been speaking of diablerizing Aajav; he had been referring to the vitae of another.

Alexander's eyes grew wide with fear, and Qarakh knew the Ventrue sensed what he was thinking. But unless he could find a way to free himself from Alexander's grip, he could not—

Free me! the Beast roared inside him. *I will slay the Ventrue, but only if you release me from my chains!*

Giving in to the Beast would mean allowing himself to fall into unchecked frenzy. Qarakh thought of Wilhelmina and the awful transformation she had suffered. A similar fate might well await him if he were to give his Beast the freedom it desired.

Release me!

Qarakh inhaled the heady bouquet of Alexander's blood. He had come too far, fought too hard, sacrificed too much to turn back now. He freed his Beast.

At last!

Qarakh's body shimmered as it shifted into wolf form. The alteration in size and mass dislodged Alexander's grip, and the gray wolf fell, landing all four feet upon the ground. Power flooded the wolf's body, and it lunged forward and fastened its jaws around Alexander's leg before the Ventrue had a chance to move. The wolf bit through boot leather and sank its teeth into the flesh beneath until its teeth found bone. Vitae, hot and sweet beyond measure, gushed into his mouth, the taste and the power it contained driving the wolf to even greater frenzy. Alexander screamed in pain as the wolf—infused with the strength given to him by the god of the grove—bit clean through the bone, severing the leg at the calf.

Alexander tottered and fell over on his side, and the wolf was instantly upon him. The Beast—for that was truly what Qarakh had become—clamped down on the Ventrue's throat and began to draw forth the prince's life essence in great, gasping, ravenous gulps. The Beast sensed its prey attempting to resist, felt it grabbing fistfuls of fur in an attempt to dislodge the predator that was stealing its vitae, but it was no use. The Beast had already drained too much, and the prey had grown too weak to defend itself any longer. Alexander's hands released their grip on Qarakh's wolfish hide. The former Prince of Paris slumped to the ground as the Beast continued to fill its belly full to bursting.

When it was done, the Beast lifted its blood-soaked muzzle skyward and released a howl that shook the very stars in the heavens.

Alexander was floating, drifting, almost weightless... He

opened his eyes and saw a gray sky above him, and surrounding him in all directions, a sea of crimson.

"No..." he whispered as the first of the blood-swimmers came toward him. As it drew closer, he saw that the creature had Rudiger's face, and it was grinning. The bloody sea churned as thousands of sharp-toothed, fish-eyed monsters surged toward the man that had slain them in the world of the living. And as the monstrous apparitions tore into him, Alexander's last thought was a surprisingly tender one of a woman called Rosamund.

And then he thought no more.

Chapter Twenty-Four

Qarakh, in man-form once more, stood looking down at the corpse of Alexander. The body of the ancient Cainite was rapidly falling away to dust, and in moments it would be gone. He understood that he had somehow defeated the Ventrue, but he couldn't quite remember how. Then he looked at the backs of his hands and saw they were covered with wiry gray-black hair that was almost but not quite fur. He ran his tongue over his teeth and found them still sharper. He'd allowed his Beast to take control, slaying and—from the energized way he felt—diablerizing his foe.

He looked around at the knights and tribesmen still trapped by the Telyavs' spell. The earth that held them was no longer a wet mire but had become dry and cracked, the grass brown and dead. The Telyavs' enchantment had run its course.

The soldiers of both armies were looking at Qarakh in stunned silence, and then the tribe—led by Alessandro—let out a chorus of cheers. Realizing the battle was lost, the knights struggled to free themselves from the ground that encased them, tearing up chunks of soil with their bare hands. The Gangrel, however, had no such need to rely on brute strength to win free. The same blood gift that allowed them to inter themselves within the ground allowed them to slip out of the earth with ease.

"Slay the Christians!" Arnulf bellowed, waving his ax over his head. Wilhelmina—looking more bestial than ever—growled her assent, and the Gangrel fell upon the knights, most of whom were still stuck in the ground.

It was a slaughter.

Qarakh merely stood and watched as his people wallowed in an orgy of bloodletting. Even Alessandro, plucked from the ground by Arnulf, was soon covered with vitae as he chopped his sword into the neck of one knight after the other. Arnulf's ax was a blood-smeared blur as the Goth warrior reduced enemy Cainites to wet piles of ragged meat and splintered bone. Wilhelmina buried her snout deep within the bellies of her victims and thrashed her head about like a hound worrying a well-chewed and beloved bone as she sought the tender meat of their hearts.

Despite the savagery surrounding Qarakh, his Beast remained silent. Perhaps it was finally sated—at least for the time being.

Qarakh saw a few knights dig free of their earthen prisons and flee the battlefield on foot. His tribesmen chased after most of them, but one or two escaped without pursuit. *Let them go,* Qarakh thought. The war was over.

He sensed someone approaching and turned to see two robed figures—one in black, the other in brown—coming from the direction of the nearby woods. One was Malachite, but the other's face was hidden by a hood. Qarakh assumed the Nosferatu's companion to be one of the Telyavs, but which?

"My congratulations on your victory," Malachite said.

Qarakh felt a darkness stir somewhere deep within him, and he heard a whisper of an echo of a thought: *Traitor.* The voice was Alexander's. He told himself that it was only his imagination, that his mind had not yet settled after experiencing the vision of the grove, of being filled with the smith god's power and diablerizing Alexander. He almost believed it, too.

The Telyav reached up with age-gnarled hands and pulled back her hood. Her skin was wrinkled, eyes receded into the sockets, their bright emerald green now dull and cloudy. What hair remained was thin and white, no longer a thick, lustrous red. But when she smiled with her dry, cracked lips, a ghost of her wry humor was still there.

"You may have to start calling me Grandmother," Deverra said, her voice soft and quavering.

Qarakh wanted to ask her what had happened, but he couldn't find the words.

"You paid your price to Telyavel," she said. "And I had to pay mine. I still retain my immortality, but my appearance will forevermore reflect my true age."

Qarakh reached out to take her hand, and though she tried to pull away, he grabbed it and held it gently but firmly.

"The other Telyavs?" he asked, fighting to keep his voice steady.

"Recovering. The enchantment of the land cost some of them a great deal. Some may not survive much longer."

"I'm sorry."

Deverra nodded and squeezed his hand.

The three of them stood and watched as the tribal warriors finished their grisly work. It didn't take long, and when the last knight finally lay slain, Alessandro, Arnulf and Wilhelmina walked over to join their khan. The trio gave Deverra puzzled looks but didn't remark upon her transformation.

The battlefield was littered with severed limbs, detached heads, strewn viscera, abandoned weapons, spent arrows and dead horses. Tribesmen sat among the carnage, talking and laughing, already recounting exaggerated war stories. Those still in wolf form lapped at puddles of vitae or gnawed on bones.

"The tribe has won," Alessandro said, his voice full of pride. "Livonia shall remain a free land, thanks to you, my khan."

Arnulf looked on, then without a word turned away from Qarakh. He became a huge black wolf by his third step and was gone.

"Yes, it was." Qarakh couldn't keep the sarcasm out of his voice. Still holding Deverra's hand, he looked up at the stars that filled the night sky. He had seen similar lights in the eyes of the ancient Cainite outside the Obertus monastery, as well as in those of the dark god who had helped him achieve such a costly victory.

Great Father Tengri, he thought. *What has my tribe become? What have I become?*

But the stars did not answer, choosing instead to remain as they always had: silent, distant and cold.

About the Author

B ram Stoker Award-winning author Tim Waggoner has pub-
lished over forty novels and four short story collections in
the horror and urban fantasy genres. He teaches creative writing at Sinclair Community College.

Visit him on the web at www.timwaggoner.com..

Curious about other Crossroad Press books?
Stop by our site:
http://store.crossroadpress.com
We offer quality writing
in digital, audio, and print formats.

Made in the USA
Coppell, TX
11 September 2023

21498705R00149